TEETH AND TAROT

A LE FAY ROMANCE
BOOK 1

A. A. FAIRVIEW

CONTENTS

CONTENT WARNINGS

This novel contains the following content: violence, gang activity, references to emotional abuse and manipulation by a parent, references to ritual murder, MC involved in law enforcement (FBI agent), references to drug and alcohol use and addiction.

This novel features sexual content and is not suitable for readers under the age of 18: Knotting, oral/face fucking, choking, anal, cock warming, biting/marking, mating ritual, frontage, dubious consent, masturbation, verbal degradation.

CHAPTER ONE

LANCE

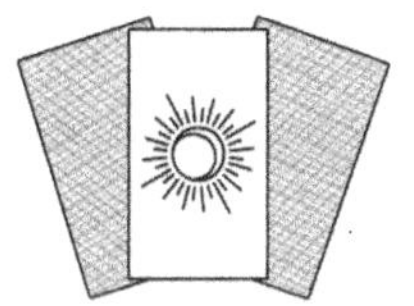

I'm so accustomed to waking from nightmares, I no longer recall waking any other way. Bits and pieces from my nightmare return from my unconscious to conscious memory as I sit up, clammy and out of breath. Looking at the clock grounds me: 4:30 AM. I fall back onto my pillows and groan. Most mornings I make it to 5:30. Early riser hours, when some gyms and cafes are open for business.

Getting out of my apartment grounds me: talking to people—to humans. I might have been born a witch, raised with the knowledge of ancestors reaching back centuries, but I let it all go. Which isn't that strange. Plenty of people stop going to church when they leave the nest. I just started denying my whole being.

Despite wishing I could sleep an hour more, I know I wouldn't fall back asleep. Honestly, I never attempt to fall back asleep. I know the nightmares are waiting for me, hiding under my eyelids.

So, a shower it is—a cold one to wash away the night sweat. As water pours down my face I try not to think about the nightmare. But as I feared, when I close my eyes, letting the water flow down my face, I see it again. That girl, that witch, from years ago, her face a mask of fear and pain. Her mouth tearing itself open to let out a piercing scream.

It's not my fault, I remind myself. Daily affirmation.

Unfortunately.

As I step out of the shower, I consider what I can do to pass the next hour. I'm not feeling a gym day, but there is a cute coffee shop across from my apartment. It's Friday, so Davey is opening. Sweet old white guy, gives off Dad energy. I like to flirt with him. He always tells me if he were twenty years younger, he'd go for it. I appreciate that he doesn't scoff or make some lame gay joke out of it like most guys his age.

I check the clock again: 4:50. Forty minutes till I can flirt with Davey and get my cinnamon cortado. I take extra time picking out my outfit, starting out simple and then ramping up to something fancy. It's 5:10 by the time I've finished dressing, opting for a dusty pink overcoat with matching pants and a white shirt. I've made it past the five o'clock mark. I could just go wait outside? Davey and his other opener will be in, getting things ready. And I'll look in like a Russian orphan about to light his last matchstick.

I find myself sitting on my couch. There is a TV in front of me and a coffee table covered with magazines I've written for, but I just stare at the door to the second bedroom of my apartment. The room that's been locked since I signed the lease. I remember lying to the landlord telling them it would be an office. *'Not a guest room?'* I must have made a face because they dropped the conversation and left soon after.

As much as I want to let go of magic I can't bear to part with my things. My chalks, cauldron, grimoire, my crystals... All locked away untouched since I shoved them into that would-be guest room. The only thing I let out of the cage is a tarot deck. I even still have my first wand packed up some-where. No one bothers to keep their first wand.

Hoarders: Witchcraft Edition.

When I check my phone it's 5:20. At this point I don't think I'll seem too sad waiting outside the shop.

I make my way to the elevator and push the button for the lobby. It's dead of course, no one wants to be up this early. Crossing the city street takes no effort and soon I'm standing next to the big windows of Marble Ax, the bougie coffee shop with a heavy emphasis on wood interior. I try to hide behind the wash-off-paint mural painted across the windows celebrating the return of fall, but Davey spots me and waves with a genuine smile. I wave back sheepishly. I know it's his job, but it's like he is actually glad to see me at this hour. Dad-energy for sure.

I can't say the same for the other opener. It's a teenager —or a freshly minted adult, who looks like they just rolled out of bed. I give them a wave. Even from far away I can see myself in their glassy gaze.

Davey walks up to the door and unlocks it, opening up with that smile of his that makes the world feel more awake. "Hey, Lance! Cold out here without the sun. Come on." He walks back into the store, clearly expecting me to follow.

I do but check my phone as I walk. "It's five minutes before you guys open."

"He's right," the teen groans. "It is five minutes before we open."

"Everything is ready to go, we might as well open for a regular." Davey gives me a wink and a smile like he's the cafe's mascot. Which he is. In my heart.

The teen rolls their eyes. "The machines are still warming up."

"Oh, that's not a big deal," Davey waves a hand. "I

know Lance's order. You want a pastry as well? The blueberry muffins are still warm."

I should probably eat. "Sure, you've sold me with that smile of yours Davey-dear." I grin wider than usual. The other barista looks at me like a frightened owl; wide eyed and head cocked.

Davey just laughs. "Such a charmer. Where were you in the 80s when I was young?"

"Not yet a concept I'm afraid," I tell him.

"It'll be ten smackaroos."

I give him a twenty and get ten back along with a blueberry muffin. I could take a seat on the one couch in the café, but it feels weird to have a couch all to myself. Even if there is no one around to judge. Except the teenager. But fuck them. If they can't understand the love between Davey and I, I don't care for their opinion. I decide to take a seat at one of the loner tables right by the counter where they place drinks.

The doors to the cafe open, catching my attention immediately. I'm not the only regular, so I'm expecting a few different people. None of whom actually enter the shop. Instead, I choke on my muffin as I lock eyes with an absolute stud. It should be illegal to be that hot in the morning while I'm still waking up. Though his direct eye contact with me does invigorate me more than my morning shower.

He's got blue eyes that make me feel like I'm staring out into the open ocean. He's got a large Greek nose that matches his other chiseled features. He's wearing a beat-up leather bomber jacket, underneath is a white tank top that hugs his build. How a guy like him isn't waiting outside a gym right now, I'm not sure. We break eye contact, and he walks over to the counter to place his order. Meanwhile I continue to gawk. His short brunette hair is almost the same warm shade as the leather of his jacket.

Davey's question breaks my concentration. "Can I get a name for that order?" I blink away my haze of lust. There's no one else in the shop. Why would he need this guy's name? It's only when Davey shoots a glance my way, I realize he's asking for my sake. I shove muffin in my mouth trying to act cool.

"Adam," he announces.

"Coming right up, Adam."

The hunk, apparently named Adam, leans against the counter, shifting his body to face me. We make eye contact again, and unfortunately this time I've got half a muffin in my mouth. He smiles at me. On top of everything he's got perfect dimples. I swallow hard. Real hard.

My teenage friend saves the day. "Cortado." I stand up like I've just sat on a tack, grab my cup, and go, abandoning half a blueberry muffin.

I speed across the street back to my apartment. I'm not a prude. On the prude-to-hoe scale I am definitely leaning towards the latter. But something about Adam doesn't feel right. No one chooses to be up at 5:30 in the morning. We're downtown, there is a coffee shop about every two blocks, so why is he at *mine*?

It pays to be paranoid when you have a past like mine.

Before I know it, I'm back at my apartment with my back pressed against my front door.

I feel like a coward. A rabbit who's just been chased into its burrow by hunting dogs—or maybe just spooked by my own shadow. It's not enough that my Father's insane antics haunt my dreams, now I'm worried he's got eyes on me. Beautiful blue eyes. *At least he knows my taste.* Creepy, but if Arthur le Fay is anything, he's thorough. If he's sent a goon after me, he would take the time to make sure I'm attracted to him.

With a huff I push myself off the door and walk deeper inside my apartment. I set my drink down on the counter and look at the locked door leading to my old magic collection. When I did practice, my strength was in divination, the ability to look past one's self. Sometimes it's astral projection, sometimes it's being able to find something, often it's attempting prophecy. Many threads determine the path of time, but a skilled witch with the right tools can follow those threads and, generally speaking, determine the future. Be those tools: a crystal ball, tea leaves, bones, or if you're me, tarot.

I walk back into my bedroom and pull out my tarot deck. Simple but striking, hand painted silver over a blue background outlining the major and minor arcana. The detailed etchings of cups and swords strangely comforting. Yet I keep the deck shoved in my bedside table as if it were a black hole. Holding the thick cards in my hands, I consider shoving it back into the drawer and pretending the deck doesn't exist.

Instead, I take it into the kitchen.

If I really wanted an accurate reading, I'd stop being a coward and go into my old magic boxes and find my Mother's old deck. Divination was her specialty too. We bonded over it, she even let me touch her cards. Which is a big deal. Unless you're giving a reading to someone you really shouldn't let people touch your divination tools. In hindsight, Mom never read my future. I guess she was worried about what she might see. The anxiety of the future must have been too much for her because she gifted me her deck when I turned fifteen. The sight is as much a gift as it is a curse.

I huff before shuffling the deck of cards, really getting a feel for the paper. The cardstock is stiff, stiffer than I remember. It doesn't make me super confident. To add insult to injury a few cards slip from my hands and onto the counter. I groan, rolling my head back. "Why am I doing this to myself?" I ask the universe, though maybe that should be the question guiding my reading.

Cards, why am I like this?

I pick up the loose cards and start shuffling again, this time focusing on what's plaguing my mind. My Father. This Adam hunk. My nightmares. The way Adam and I locked eyes. Are they all connected?

The question now clear in my mind, I set the deck down. I'm going to keep it simple, I decide, before drawing my first card: past.

I'm met with the Nine of Swords, a miserable looking figure sobbing in front of a wall of swords. It feels very deliberate, like the cards are mocking me. The card, like the art suggests, represents suffering and anxiety. Even being associated with nightmares. I'll admit I have woken up a few nights in the same manner as the figure on the card. So, I don't really gain anything from its appearance in the reading.

Next card represents the present. I blink as I pull the Two of Cups. The suit of cups is all about emotion, and this card is specifically about budding romantic relationships. Except I just fucked up a chance at romance. Unless I haven't royally fucked it up yet? Maybe running away from coffee-stud Adam will become a funny story we tell one day.

I draw the final card and almost groan out loud. It's The Moon, associated with the unconscious, a person's intuition. The Moon acts as a guiding light on a dark night. So basically, I should just trust my stupid gut and go for whatever it is I'm feeling. As if that's never ended poorly.

I push all the cards together and shuffle them again before abandoning them.

What a waste of time.

CHAPTER TWO

LANCE

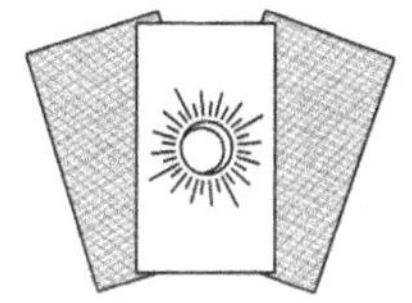

Fridays mean meetings at work, which I'm fine with. They give me the perfect opportunity to ruminate over coffee-stud Adam. I might have just run away from the hottest guy I'd ever seen like Cinderella at midnight, but it was just too convenient. Fairy godmothers don't exist, but my narcissistic, violent Father does. For some reason, he's let me live my life for the past decade separate from the family. No phone calls, no dipping into the generational wealth, and no being called to magic rituals that left me so worn out I either didn't leave my bed for days or tossed my cookies right in the middle of the magic circle.

This always got a wicked laugh out of my little sister. Psycho bitch. My phone buzzes in my pocket. I must not be doing a great job of pretending to pay attention because Jason's just texted me. He's sitting across the conference table, and I realize I've probably been zoned out looking right at him. Or looking right at my ghostly reflection in his thick glasses. He's giving me a look with a light pursed lip, clearly wanting to know what's on my mind, but we're professionals, so we both keep pretending to listen to our boss complain about how no one wants to work anymore despite the full conference room of people sitting in front of her.

As soon as we're all set free, Jason pounces on me, his wide eyes even bigger behind his glasses. "Spill. It's only eleven o'clock, so how have you managed to create drama for yourself? I'm dying to know. I need to see the artist at work."

I roll my eyes with a forced grin as I stand up from the chair and start walking back to my desk. I should say *our* desks since they're right next to each other. The office is open concept, so Jason and I didn't have much of a choice on becoming friends. When I got this job, I was desperate for friends, and Jason loves dragging people out on the town. He's seen me stick my tongue down so many stranger's throats that I don't blame him when he asks, "Is it a guy?"

I let out a heavy sigh and see Jason open his mouth to speak again but I interrupt. "Do you ever get sad about your family for no reason?"

Jason's face falls. "Yeah," he admits. "But it's never for no reason. There are reasons behind it. Maybe not relevant reasons—"

"Okay but when does childhood trauma stop becoming relevant?"

He shrugs. "If my therapist had the answer, I probably would stop paying him." That finally gets a laugh out of me.

The fact is that I ran from Adam because I don't know that he's not an agent of my Father's out to kill me, or worse, drag me back into the family mess.

The cards might have hinted otherwise, but I'm still not sure I could have trusted him. Not that there is any point in reflecting on it now. Jason and I sit down at our desks and when I look up from my computer, he's got a grin on his face. "Let's go out," he offers. "The Cathedral has a drag show tonight. Or we could go to Giovani's and get wasted."

"Is it bad that the wasted option sounds better?"

Jason shakes his head, still grinning, and I feel a smile tug at my own lips. Getting drunk might not be the healthiest way to deal with all of this but if I cared about my health I'd have my own therapist.

I FEEL safe at the bar. I know it's only humans here.

Alright, I don't know that for sure, but there are supernatural establishments and that tends to be where non-humans gather. They're pretty obvious if you know what to look for. A place with a few too many signs that say 'no dogs' is a vamp establishment. Werewolf establishments usually have 'no fangs' or 'no suckers' signs. Witches love to decorate the place with harmless runes. Little things that most people would shrug off, but if you know, you know.

Giovani's is definitely human. I sit at the neon-lit bar, looking at all the men in tanks and crop tops dancing and wonder how many degrees of separation there are between them and my previous hook-ups. Jason and I are still in our work clothes so needless to say, we're overdressed. "Hey, heartbreaker—" Jason snaps his fingers to get my attention.

I look over at him. "What?"

"*Please* don't abandon me for some hook-up tonight."

"Uh, rude. I wasn't scoping out the crowd, just watching people dance." Jason raises a brow. "I'm serious! God you can be so jealous sometimes."

"Jealous?" He snorts. "If I wanted to have a new hookup every night I could. I just don't want to." If he had long hair, I just know he'd flip it right now.

"*Every* night is a little presumptuous." As I fight for my life, I look past Jason and notice a guy hanging off on the side of the bar. Dark hair, a tight shirt, and somehow even tighter pants. I freeze up just as a light flashes on his face to reveal ocean blue eyes. "No way," I think aloud.

Jason looks over his shoulder and spots Adam. He rolls his eyes. "Guess I'm gonna have to UberPool my way home tonight."

"Shut up," I hiss, as if Adam can hear us over the booming music. I lean over so I can whisper to Jason. "I saw that guy this morning at the coffee shop across from my apartment."

Jason furrows his brows in confusion, but then it clicks. "So, you *were* moping about a guy this morning?"

"I think he knows my Dad."

"What?" Jason looks at me like I'm crazy, then shakes his head. "Okay I can *not* support that level of paranoia. Your Dad is not scouting men to honeypot you."

"That's exactly what he wants me to think." I look over Jason's shoulder again and Adam is walking towards us. "Shit." I face forward and pretend like I'm interested in the bottles of liquor on the back wall.

Adam slides in next to Jason and starts eyeing one of the laminated menus. Jason eyes us both, as if betting with himself to see who will make the first move. A few awkward moments pass before Jason plays referee. "I'm gonna powder my nose," he informs me before getting up to leave, effectively breaking down the wall between Adam and me.

We make eye contact. Even in the dark neon haze of the club I find myself lost in the depth of his eyes. He's fucking breathtaking. I see his lips pull into a smirk. "Hey stranger."

He looks back down at the menu. "It's funny. This morning I was gonna ask you what you recommend at that café before you ran off." There's a pause. "So, uh…"

"The espresso martini is good here," I offered as a little nod to this morning.

"Good to know. But what can I get you?"

I can't decide if I want Jason to come back or not. It is crazy to think this guy has anything to do with my psycho Father, but I recall The Moon card: *trust your gut.*

I was ready to write off that reading this morning, but that Two of Cups card is starting to feel promising. And is it so wrong for me to want this hunk in my bed? A fun romp to get my mind off my nightmares? I've earned a little fun— the cards even said so.

I let myself engage with Adam. "I like the paloma… and to sit in a booth." He raises a brow. "It's a little easier to talk there."

"I imagine a lot of things are easier in one of the booths," Adam teases, and my heart skips a beat like I'm a schoolgirl. He waves down the bartender. "A paloma and whatever dark beer you've got on tap."

My gut keeps wish-washing like ocean waves hitting the deck of a ship. For my own sanity I've got to decide if I trust this guy or not. The bartender sets down our drinks. I decide that if by the time I finish my paloma I haven't figured Adam out, I'll bail.

We find an empty booth and sit near each other, but not quite next to each other. "I don't know your name," Adam points out.

"Well, I know yours." I take my first sip of my drink and notice a confused look on his face. "It's Adam, right? Or did you give a fake name at the coffee shop?"

He chuckles and I can't explain it but there is an

awkwardness to it. "Adam, yeah. So, you did notice me at the coffee shop?"

"We made direct eye contact..." I point out, sheepish.

"We did, didn't we?" He smiles. "So, did you get my order or just my name?"

I think back to this morning. I actually didn't catch what he ordered. I was too busy thinking about his tight shirt. I eye his tall glass of beer. "Black coffee," I answer with way too much confidence.

But Adam chuckles, "That's right."

Predictable. Dark beer. Black coffee. Next, he's going to say he likes documentaries and missionary sex. "I was sort of surprised when you ordered the unicorn cookie though. I only ever hear kids order that."

Adam blinks then realizes I'm teasing. "Keep my secret, will you?" He winks.

Suddenly I'm okay with missionary sex.

"I still don't know your name," he points out.

"Lance," I tell him. "Lance le Fay."

"I get a last name too? My lucky night." He smiles and his teeth are so white they reflect the club lights. "So, Lance, why'd you run?"

I choke on my drink. *How does he know I ran away from home?* I look back at Adam and he's got a worried look on his face. "Uh... sorry, I was just joking. I didn't really mind that you ran off this morning."

I clear my throat feeling stupid. Of course he's talking about this morning. "Sorry I uh..." Adam still looks concerned. "I've run away from a lot of things... but hot guys usually aren't one of those things."

"Now you've got me confused. You find me attractive—thank you, by the way—but you left this morning without even giving me your name?"

I raise a brow. "Hurt your ego, champ?" He looks a little flustered. "You kinda..." I realize I'm going to have to lie to him. I can't exactly say, '*sorry I thought you worked for my Dad.*' Talk about a mood killer. "I kinda thought we'd hooked up before."

"So, I'm your type?" he asks without missing a beat.

"Um. Muscular guys with pretty eyes I think are everyone's type? But yeah, you're my type." I lean back in the booth. "And are short skinny guys your type?"

"Uh..." Adam mutters like he's taken aback by the question. "I'm... not sure I have a type? I just see things I like and... go for it."

"You're sparing some details." I look down at my drink. Halfway done. I've still got time to make my decision. "What do you see that you like?"

Adam is quiet. Maybe he just wants to hookup with *someone,* a companion to warm the bed. I've been there, more than once. Then, Adam slides closer to me in the booth so our knees are touching. He looks down at me, swinging his arm around the back of the booth so he's looming over me. "I like blonds," he tells me. "I like big doe eyes. You've got a nice jawline..." His voice tapers.

I sip my drink. "Go on."

Adam chuckles, hanging his head a moment before he looks back at me. "I like caterpillar brows."

"Rude—"

"I mean it!" I scoff but he continues. "It's distinctive. Expressive..." his other hand takes my chin and lifts it so I'm looking right at him. "You're very distinctive." I feel his thumb run along my bottom lip. "I never noticed, but you've got some gold in your eyes mixed with all that green." I don't know how he can see that in the dark of the club, but he's not the first person to make that compliment.

"You have nice lips." The words slip out of my mouth like silk out of a magician's hat.

His voice drops to almost a growl. "How long have you been thinking about them?"

I haven't for very long, but now it's all I can think about.

I stop myself by taking a drink, then roll my wrist, making the ice melt a little faster. I need to buy myself some more time to pin this guy down. Yeah, he's probably not one of my Father's men, but there is something there. Something he's not telling me.

"It's weird we've never ran into each other before." I point out.

"I'm new in town."

I can't stop myself from snorting. "That's such a boring answer."

Adam once again looks taken aback. "It's the truth," he says with a shrug and a grin. "My job transferred me here."

"What do you do for work?"

"Construction. You?"

"I'm a journalist," I tell him. "Nothing hard hitting. I work for this contracting company. People pay us to write articles and do graphics for magazines. I write articles, usually about the arts or fashion."

"You ever meet Hedi Stromme?"

It's my turn to be taken aback. Guys ask me all the time if I've met random famous people. The classy ones ask about 90s supermodels, the younger ones ask me about Instagram hotties I have to Google later, and the rest ask about the big names. Not that Hedi isn't a big name. Far from it. It's just that most people know her from being in *Sports Illustrated*. This club isn't exactly her target audience.

"So, you really do like blondes." I comment, sipping my

drink and giving him a knowing glance. I see him chew the inside of his cheek. It's starting to make sense. Dark beer, black coffee, construction job, Hedi fucking Stromme. "Have you ever been with a guy?"

"Of course," he says, just defensive enough I know I've finally figured it out.

I cut him off, "I'm honored you want me to be your first."

Adam slides back a little to grab his beer. We're now as far apart as we were when we sat down. "How'd you know?" He mumbles.

"You just... It all feels like you're trying too hard. I mean that shirt," I point to the tight white tank top. "Makes sense here, but you've had that on since this morning."

"Maybe this is my construction outfit. Gets hot working all day in the sun."

"Is that an OSHA regulated baby tank, or...?"

Adam shakes his head, but I can see the smile forming on his face. "You were wrong about my drink order by the way," he sips at his beer.

"What?" I furrow my brows. "Why did you say I was right?"

"Because you're cute." Something about him calling me cute gets my cheeks all flustered. "And I thought it would ruin the mood if I told you that you were wrong."

"Okay, then what did you order?" I ask, curious now.

"A cappuccino with cinnamon." I raise my brows. That's pretty far off from a black coffee. "And I got the ladybug cookie, not the unicorn one."

He's got me with that one, and I start laughing. "I like cinnamon in my coffee too," I tell him, moving closer. Feeling bold, I place my hand on his knee. Adam glances down at the gesture before placing his hand atop mine.

"Guess we're a match made in Heaven." He spreads my fingers apart with his own so our hands are intertwined.

I go to sip my drink only to find it empty, just a few chunks of ice left over. I set it down on the table and look him in his ocean eyes. "Look, I know you're new to this, but I really don't mind." Adam tilts his head. "Experimentation is good, right? You don't need to label it."

Adam blinks as he realizes what I'm talking about. "Uh... thanks." He looks away from me, but his hand squeezes mine tighter. "I haven't ever been with another man," he admits. "But I like the idea of it. So that's something, right?"

I shrug. "That's up to you to decide. But if you want to try some things..."

Adam squeezes my hand. It all feels so cheesy, so star-crossed lovers. I think about my Two of Cups card I pulled this morning: two men in robes exchanging cups, the ocean in the distance with two snakes intertwined above them.

"Lance." I blink as Adam says my name. He leans down, pressing his forehead against mine. "I'm glad we're officially meeting now. We have the whole night now."

He's right. I couldn't exactly have invited him back to my place this morning with work in a few hours. Plus, I wouldn't have had time to do that tarot reading. Not that I needed the cards to give me a go-ahead to invite this guy back to my apartment, but a little magic assurance doesn't hurt.

As it pains me, I pull away from Adam. "Could you... I just want to let my friend know where I am." Adam sits up and I realize just how close he'd gotten to me. We weren't on top of each other, but he was definitely going in for a kiss. "Yeah, of course, I'll be here." He grabs his beer and takes his first sip.

I slide out of the booth and head back to the bar to find Jason, who is sitting right where we were before. He rolls his eyes as I approach. "You could have at least left a note."

"Okay listen—"

"I'm surprised you're still here. I thought you'd already left with that guy. Or did you slip into the bathroom without me noticing?"

"Um, ew." My face scrunches. "I am too classy to hook up in the bathroom."

"Don't knock it till you try it. The acoustics are great," he grins and I smack him on the arm. "So, are you going to his place or yours?"

"We haven't decided yet."

"But you *have* decided to go home with him?" I must have a guilty expression on my face because Jason rolls his eyes again. "Ugh, look, just give me all the juicy details on Monday. Have fun, use a condom, and if he lives with his mom, run."

"That last one won't be a problem, I think. But I appreciate your concern." I give Jason a little kiss on the cheek and he in turn purses his lips and makes a smooching sound against my ear.

I go back over to Adam. He's already standing at the edge of the booth, waiting for me. "Someone is eager," I tease, but then he grabs me by the waist. Adam pulls me close, our hips pressed together. His hand finds my cheek and he looks at me for just a moment before kissing me.

He hums into my mouth, one hand caressing my cheek while I feel his other one touch the small of my back. His hand starts moving south as his tongue brushes my bottom lip. He coaxes his tongue into my mouth, meanwhile his hand grabs my ass. The thin fabric of my pants gives him ample opportunity to feel my curves, and I find myself moaning. Adam pulls away and my lips are still parted as I pant. He's literally taken my breath away.

He looks at me, a sparkle in his eyes, like he's proud of himself. I guess he should be. I'm not usually left gasping for air this early. He leans down again, and I close my eyes, expecting—wanting—another kiss. Instead, he presses his forehead against mine and whispers in a gravelly voice, "Let's go back to your place."

CHAPTER THREE

LANCE

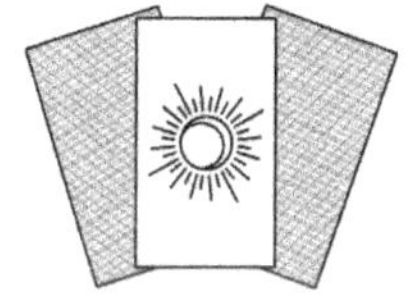

In the car heading to my place, Adam has his hand firm on my thigh, but he's not looking at me. He's looking out the window, and I'm looking at him. I must look pretty desperate to our cab driver. "Hey," I say softly, and Adam looks back at me. "You've been quiet."

The corner of his lip twitches into a smirk before he leans over and whispers in my ear. "I'm just saving my energy for your place." Then he nibbles at my earlobe, chuckling to himself as his hand strokes my thigh.

With his lips pressing against my ear and his hand groping my thigh, I can't really find it in me to complain. I remind myself that this is his first time with a guy. I don't recall being particularly chatty the first time I went home with a man—and I knew well and good I was gay. Adam doesn't let up, his lips falling to my neck where he wastes no time giving me a little love bite. I shiver and push my lips into a hard line to keep myself from moaning or making any other noises that might tip off the cab driver. Not that we're doing anything scandalous back here. Not yet.

Thankfully we make it to my place with our hands still

in plain sight. Adam pulls his mouth away from the tender flesh of my neck with a little pop. I catch the driver looking back at us with the exhausted look of a parent. "Thanks," I squeak as I exit the car. I make sure to leave him five stars and fat tip on the app.

"Huh," Adam mumbles, standing on the curb. "Didn't realize you lived right across from the coffee shop."

"Yeah," I smile a little before taking his hand to lead him into the building. "I'm a regular there. Can't top the convenience. And the service. Davey is basically my boyfriend."

"So, I've got competition?"

"I dunno. Can you make a cortado?" I ask him before pressing the elevator button.

"I guess I'll surprise you in the morning," he tells me. I bite my lip as I realize he wants to stay over. Sure, we're hooking up, but staying the night is different. I know that's a big commitment for some guys, but I actually prefer when guys do, even if they're basically strangers. The nightmares aren't as bad. And it's nice to wake up to something other than my empty apartment.

The elevator arrives and once I push the button for my floor, Adam is back to touching me. He surprises me, wrapping his arms around my waist and pulling me in so my back is pressed against his front. He buries his face in my neck but doesn't nibble or suck at it like he did in the cab. He just presses his nose against my soft flesh like I'm a life size pillow.

It feels... romantic.

It also makes me realize how tall he is. No one in my family is over 5'10", and even that's being generous. Adam is over six feet, about half a foot taller than I am. It occurs to me that holding me probably doesn't feel all that different from holding a woman. Height-wise that is. I don't have hips or tits to grab onto. I wonder if he misses that.

The elevator dings and we reach my floor. We pause our touching and make it down the hall to my apartment. "Make yourself at home," I tell Adam once we're inside. I like to keep my apartment modern. I've been told my place looks like a catalog, but I think that's just because I keep the place pretty clean. Not that it's hard when I'm the one person living here and my only guests are hookups. Though some guys leave my bathroom a mess.

Adam doesn't waste any time walking into the kitchen. "Do you want anything to drink?" he asks.

"Isn't that my job?"

He smiles at me. "I just wanted some water. Figured while I'm here..."

"I'm good, thanks." That one paloma is enough for tonight. I want to remember Adam as much as I can.

I slip off my pink overcoat and place it over the back of the couch when Adam's voice grabs my attention. "What's this?" He's looking down at the stack of cards on the counter.

Shit. "Um... it's a tarot deck. You know, like fortune telling stuff."

"You believe in all that?" Adam asks. He doesn't sound dismissive. Just curious.

"Sorta. My mom practiced and taught me all the cards. Actually, you can use them like normal playing cards too. All the suits and major arcana line up with a normal deck of playing cards." I don't know why I'm trying to act like I play Rummy with tarot cards, like that's more normal.

Adam lets out a slow grunt, as if thinking. Then he flips over a card. I walked over, curious as to what he pulled. Death. "That can't be good," he remarks.

"Not necessarily," I assure him. "The Death card doesn't literally mean death. It means something is coming to an end, or more importantly, it signals rebirth." Adam blinks a few times before looking at me. Then back at the card. "Kinda scarier than death itself huh?" I tell him with a grin. "Death is just the end. But renewal and rebirth mean you have a whole lot of shit coming your way. Things you might not have expected or aren't quite ready for."

Adam just lets out a low whistle before he places the card back on top of the deck. "Remind me not to mess with that again."

I laugh. "No one ever told you not to mess with the occult?"

"Well, sure, yeah. I grew up in Virginia, which is just south enough that you sometimes come across those people who double dip into palm readings and baptisms."

"You ever have your palm read?" I ask, genuinely curious.

Palm reading isn't magic in the literal sense. Not the very tangible and dangerous magic I practice, but humans have their own sort of magic. With practice, a cold read can be just as illuminating as what I do. But even if palm reading was a real school of magic, as a caster you're limited, only looking at the major threads of one person's life. My family was much too utilitarian for that sort of focused magic.

"Yeah one time," Adam says. "Apparently my life line is all weird." He lifts up his left hand, then drags his index finger over the line closest to his thumb. "See, it breaks, right here." He gestures to the rounded line near his thumb. I lean over to get a closer look and he's right. It's not a straight shot. The line starts and stops, the two lines never running parallel but close enough that they're practically the same line. There's maybe a hair of space between them. But it's like he said, definitely a broken line.

"Huh," I utter, wishing I knew more. "What does that mean?"

"The woman said would have some kind of health issue in the future. But she also said I was in for a strange life." Adam rolls his eyes before taking a sip of water. "I think she just didn't like lefties."

"Can never trust a leftie," I tease.

Adam finishes the glass of water. "Don't you flip on me now." He puts down the empty glass before crossing around the counter to reach me. "We're just about to have fun." He wraps his arms around my waist and kisses me. I melt, letting him support me. His hands move to grab my thighs and he lifts me up so my legs are wrapped around his abdomen. I'm embarrassed to admit it, but I squeal a little into his mouth when he pulls me into his arms. I feel his lips curl into a smile against mine, which makes me feel better.

This time I'm the one pressing my tongue against his lips, letting the tip flutter and tease the inside of his mouth. I shut my eyes, appreciating the sensation of his lips on mine, his strong hands caressing my thighs. I wrap my arms tight around his neck for the extra support and to make sure his face is as close to mine as possible. Then I hear a rattling, metal against metal.

I open my eyes and find we're standing next to my locked magic room. "Oh," I chirp. "Um, the bedroom is past the kitchen."

"What's with the locked closet?" he asks. I quirk a brow, not sure why it's relevant or why he cares. "Just curious if it's like a dungeon or something," he shoots me a smug smile.

"Hoping I'll tie you up?" I retort, making it clear I'm not

all that amused. I know it's not his fault he had to stumble across my magic-trauma-closet, but I also consider it setting a boundary. Locked doors are locked for a reason. I thought a good southern boy would understand hospitality.

Adam swallows hard, either because he's realized he's upset me or because I've awakened some new fantasy in him. I'm not sure. "Maybe next time..." he says, voice trailing.

He starts walking back towards the kitchen. "On your left," I tell him before I start kissing his collarbone. A guttural moan builds from his chest as he carries me to the bedroom. Fuck the cards and palm readings; this is the real magic.

Adam drops me on the bed with a thud. I sit up a little, about to make some snarky comment accentuated with a pout, when I see him taking his shirt off. I've known since this morning that he's muscular, and I've been with enough guys like him to have a picture of what that might look like in my mind, but as soon as Adam has his shirt above his pecs, I'm obsessed.

The dark, thick hair trailing down his stomach catches my eye first. A little tease of what's to come. The dips along his hips are to die for, deep enough I know my fingers will have plenty to explore—and his pecs are the same. Finally, his shirt is off completely, and I see a tattoo on his left pec. A skull with a dagger through the eye. "I got it when I was eighteen," Adam says, catching me eyeing the design.

"Explains a lot."

He puts one knee on the bed before grabbing my shoulder and pushing me down. He's back to kissing my neck while his hand starts to undo the buttons on my shirt. I gasp and groan for a while before realizing he needs a little help with the buttons. He's only down to the third one when I start undoing them myself. Adam grunts, as if thanking me, before his lips trail down my collarbone, then my sternum. His tongue drags down my stomach to my belt. A tingle runs through my spine and all the way up my cock.

Adam starts paying attention to the bit of flesh below my belly button, kissing and nipping at it with his teeth. I shamelessly writhe and moan, not so subtly pressing my erection against his neck. A nip turns into a proper bite, and I yelp. Adam stops, looking up at me. "Too rough?" he asks, his voice gravely but his eyes much softer. I swallow before shaking my head. "I don't hear you..." His gaze turns stone like. "*Was that too rough?*" It feels less like a question and more like a demand.

"No," I tell him. "No, I like it rough." He grins and while my lips stay soft, I can't help but grin internally.

"Good." He sits up before leaning back on his calves, his legs now straddling me. Adam starts undoing his belt. "I need a good rough fuck." He pulls his pants down just enough I can see his erection pressed against his briefs.

Again, I take over stripping myself. I've just slid my belt out of the loop when Adam grabs my hips and turns me over so I'm on my stomach. My shirt hangs open, my chest exposed but back covered. Adam pulls my pants down along with my underwear, practically ripping them. "*Careful,*" I hissed. "These clothes aren't cheap."

There's barely even a beat before Adam has his groin pressed against my back side. He leans over me, his hand holding my chin while he presses his lips against my ear. "*You're more worried about your clothes than you are about what I'll do to you.*" With his teasing concern, he starts to kiss just behind my ear. Then my earlobe, then the very back of my jawbone. They're soft but attentive kisses. He takes his time with each one, paying each part of my face special attention.

Meanwhile his hips are grinding against me. His cock is still contained by his briefs as he rubs against my ass. It feels like we're horny teenagers, forceful and desperate. I sigh and rock my hips back. Adam groans at the new friction. The hand that was holding my chin now shoves two fingers into my mouth. I hum with approval as his pointer and index finger slide in and out of my mouth. Feeling his size against my ass makes it easy to fantasize about something else of Adam's being shoved between my lips.

"God, I don't know where to fuck you first..." Adam sighs. Then I feel him pull away, taking both his fingers and cock with him. The bed creeks and the sound of his belt hitting the floor tells me he's taking off the rest of his clothes. I take a moment to completely strip my bottoms but return to my hands and knees.

"There's lube and condoms in the top drawer," I pointed to the bedside table. I face forward, trying not to giggle as I hear Adam scramble to open the drawer. A moment later I feel his fingers press against my hole, slick with lube and spit. It feels a lot like when he slid his fingers in my mouth, my body taking him with glee. It's not long before he retracts his fingers and replaces them with the head of his cock. "Had me waiting long enough," I tease in a sultry tone.

Adam grunts the second he's inside me. I bite my lip, expecting him to push further, but he's paused. His hands grab my waist again, fingernails digging into my skin before he jerks me back and pushes his hips forward. I gasp, my eyes rolling back in my head as he shoves the rest of his cock inside me. Again, Adam takes a moment—this time longer. I feel his hands wander from my hips to the curves of my ass, his fingernails dragging across my skin the whole way. Then, he smacks my ass.

I gasp, and he spanks me again. My body tightens around him and my own length twitches. Adam caresses the red tender spot he's just created. I whimper, my thighs shaking ever so slightly. "Fuck, if you could see how cute you are bent over like this." He leans over me, his lower back pressed against mine as he finally starts grinding his hips again. "You're tight. I thought you were a bit of a whore, but fuck, you feel like a virgin." He admonishes in a husky voice.

I manage to speak in between heavy breaths, "I'm extra tight for big dick."

I feel Adam smile against my neck. Then his smile consumes where my neck meets my shoulder, his teeth digging into me. He starts fucking me faster and I grip my bedsheets. Even with his mouth preoccupied with my neck I hear him moaning. His jaw finally releases me, the warm, sharp pain of his mark starting to make my shoulder numb. I think I'm close when he stops. I shamelessly whimper, resting my head against my mattress in angst.

"Don't make me beg," I plead.

"Sweetheart, you started that yourself," he mocks before flipping me over so I'm on my back. Then he's back on top of me, pressing his slick length against my own. His hand wraps around us both and starts pumping. I'm already gasping when he starts to pump his hips as well, each thrust shaking me to my core. His blue eyes have my gaze trapped like a whirlpool. I see his pupils dilate, and he bites his bottom lip. "Fuck," he curses under his breath.

I push my hips up with a gasp, still looking right at Adam when I finish, splattering myself with warm cum.

"Fuck," Adam curses again, this time less under his

breath, with proper weight behind it. A heavy burst of white flies from his cock all over my chest. His hand still wrapped around the both of us, I feel him move slower and deeper, cum now trickling from his slit down our shafts. There's so much it makes my head spin.

Finally, Adam releases the both of us, panting like he's just won a marathon. I expect him to flop down beside me, both of us spent from our romp. Instead, he continues to hang over me, though he's no longer looking at my face. His focus is solely on my chest, decorated with white cum like a fine lady's lace. Adam makes a sound at the back of his throat. He says nothing, and I'm inclined to stay silent too, just enjoying the mess we've made.

CHAPTER FOUR

LANCE

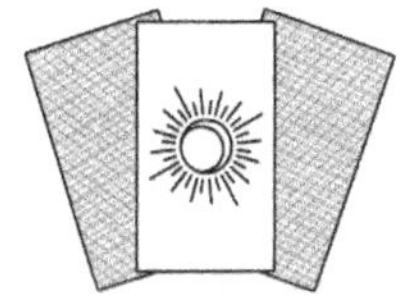

I slept without any dreams last night. The magic of good dick. Or, more likely, the presence of someone else in my bed keeps the nightmares at bay. But when I groggily reach over the other side of the bed, I find it empty. I sit up as fast as I can, which is pretty damn slow, blinking the sleep from my eyes.

My room comes into view. The sheets are ruffled, barely holding on to the edge of the bed, and Adam's pillow has been slept on. But no Adam. I fling my legs over the side of the bed, my head still heavy with morning lethargy. Then I see a note on my bedside table. I pick it up, reading in all too neat handwriting:

Went for a run. Be back soon.

I furrow my brow. A run in what clothes? I could see his religion in those jeans, I hardly imagine they're good for running. But as I get out of bed and look around, I don't see any of Adam's clothes. If it weren't for the note, I would have assumed he ghosted. Maybe he has. Maybe waking up next to a guy was too much for him. Maybe he's back home lying to some girlfriend or wife about getting wasted with guys from work. Why didn't I ever consider before now that he might have someone? A nice-looking guy like him doesn't stay single for long. I've heard for years that straight guys are the worst, but did I listen?

The sun is just peeking out, orange light making my bedroom look like it's being illuminated by a salt lamp. I checked the time: 6:00 AM. I start doing math in my head. Adam was at the coffee shop yesterday right at opening. He didn't look like he'd just gotten back from a run. Though I have to account for the possibility that he's a freak that goes for runs in skinny jeans. Still, he wasn't flush or sweaty. Nor did his hair look wet like he'd taken a shower. Does he go for a run at six? At five?

I huff and finally stand up from my bed, grabbing a robe before I waltz into the heart of my apartment. The living room is even darker than my bedroom, but even in the faint light of dawn, I see it.

The door to my magic room is open.

"Oh, you sneaky—" I whisper through gritted teeth. I tiptoe over to the room but stop just a few steps away from the ajar door. Do I need a weapon? Fuck, even if I had one, I know Adam can pin me down. It was fun last night, but now I'm wishing I'd picked a guy my size to take home.

This is so fucked. He must have had a lockpick in his pocket all last night. To rob me? Well, he's about to be disappointed. Unless he's got some eclectic collector he's selling to, most people would think my magic wares are junk.

I bite my lip. My cell phone is back in the bedroom. I should probably call someone, the police, or Jason. But Jason saw Adam and knew I went home with him. So, if I'm killed at least someone will be able to give a description. It only now just hits me that Adam *could* actually kill me. I feel sick, but somehow this also gives me the push I need to walk over and open the door.

The door creaks and I flip on the light. Lo and behold, there is Adam, standing over an open wood chest that holds my neglected magic books and crystals. He's got a book in his hands. He's clearly been flipping through it. "Didn't realize you were this into the occult," Adam muses, as if I haven't just caught him red-handed.

My jaw clenches, and I feel my face grow hot. "Get out!" I shout at him.

"Why do you hide this stuff?"

"I said, get out!" I stomp over, snatching the book out of his hands, and then holding it a little aloft like I might hit him with it. It's not exactly a light read. With the amount of red I'm seeing, I might just be able to knock the lights out of his pretty head.

But I don't. And Adam just looks at me.

"What the hell is wrong with you?" I shout, still holding the book high. "Get out or I'm calling the cops."

"Funny you mention that..." Adam leans down, reaching beside the wooden box. I can't see what he's doing, but he's bent over. Now is the perfect time to slam the book into his head like he's a spider. But I don't. I was always one of those people who released spiders anyway.

Adam stands back up, showing off what he's got in his hand. It's a ceremonial dagger. All the angry heat pooled in my cheeks falls away. I feel ghoulish; probably look it too. Adam holds the dagger sideways, the blade facing away from him, but his hand not wrapped around the hilt. Instead, his fingers hold the cross guard of the dagger, slowly tipping it back and forth like he's showing off its splendor.

He surprises me by offering me the hilt of the dagger.

"Pretty gnarly looking weapon you've got, Lance." I look at it like it's a snake he's trying to hand off to me. He's got no idea the things I've done with that dagger—the things I was forced to do by my family. I don't know why I kept it, except I do. To torture myself. To remind myself of the people I've hurt in an attempt to avoid being hurt myself.

I must be shaking because Adam says to me in a soft voice, "Take a breath."

I do, like I've just dove to the bottom of the pool and am finally coming up for air. "What do you want?" My voice is still shaky.

"I just need to talk to you about some things." *Talking. Okay, I can do talking.* "I need you to tell me about your Father, Arthur—"

That's when I grab the hilt of the dagger. I pull it away just to get it out of his hands. I didn't exactly trust him with it before, but now that I know he knows who my Father is, I can't dare trust him with any of the shit in this room. Adam hisses and I realize I've nicked him with the blade. Even from where I'm standing, I can see blood start to drip from the tip of his thumb.

"I—" I take another heavy breath, a fish out of water gasping air like that will make things any better. "I didn't mean to, I'm sorry."

"Hey," he says in such an unbothered tone, I actually feel myself relaxing a little. "It's alright. You just made my job a lot easier." He closes the gap between us, reaching out for my wrist while I still clutch the dagger. There was no way I could expect what he was going to say next. "Lancelot le Fay, I'm charging you for assault against a federal officer with a deadly weapon."

Adam's grip on my wrist turns tight. He twists my

whole arm so it's behind my back. I wince before dropping the dagger as a reflex. It clatters to the floor just as he grabs the back of my other arm and pushes me towards the door back into my living room. I realize Adam is speaking this whole time. Reading me my rights probably—but all I can hear is my own heartbeat, booming like it's trying to leap out of my chest and run away. I can't blame it.

There are a billion questions and thoughts running through my head but one in particular keeps repeating over and over: how did the feds find out about my Father?

I'VE NEVER BEEN a fan of crime dramas, but I know what an interrogation room looks like. I'm sitting at a metal table with a heavy bar below the tabletop, presumably for handcuffs, but I haven't been restrained. Everything is painfully gray. Even the mirror, which I assume is a one-way sort of situation, has a steely gray sheen to it. It makes me look like a sad orphan.

I wish. I wouldn't be here if I was a damn orphan.

I should have trusted my gut. Adam—or whatever his name is—has been playing me. Only for the past twenty-four hours, but playing me like a fiddle either way. I start to think about all the things I supposedly know about this guy I've slept with.

He's a construction worker: nope, not even close.

He's from Virginia: that might be true. It's close enough to DC, maybe he grew up taking trips to Quantico or whatever. I'd personally rather go to the zoo for a field trip, but I digress.

His name is Adam: also not true. Probably not even

close to the truth. God, what if his name is Carl or something? It's stupid, but I just can't get behind fucking a guy named Carl. How do you even moan that? Caaaaaar-ruuuuul.

He's left-handed: Would be a strange thing to lie about, but I've got to remember this guy knows more about me than I know about him. I can't imagine he knows my family are witches, like legit magic casting witches. But he could just write off all that as eccentric occult stuff. The palm reading thing might have just been a story to gain my trust. People used to think being left-handed was an infernal thing, so maybe that was his angle all along.

He takes cinnamon in his coffee: another weird thing to lie about but if he's been trying to get close to me... I don't know why it makes me sad to think that little detail is a lie. It's all been lies, but it really felt like there was something to us both liking espresso and cinnamon.

But this reminds me of something else—another potential lie. That I'm the only man he's ever slept with. Somehow, I know that's true. And it's weird to think he would go gay for his job, but I guess that's spy work for you. Is he a spy if it's on American soil? An undercover agent is probably more correct. I should be flattered. I bet they've got a file on me and everything. I bet I look good in candid shots.

The door opens and not-Adam walks in, like he could sense I was getting on edge. He's abandoned tight clothes for a proper suit: navy blue with a striped baby blue tie. With his eyes, it's all too much blue. I feel like a fashion novice compared to my coworkers, but I feel pretty confident in the assertion that it's way too much blue.

"Lancelot—"

"Lance," I interrupt. "For the love of God, call me Lance."

"Sorry..." He sits down across from me and says nothing further for what feels like a painful amount of time.

"You're wearing too much blue," I say finally.

Not-Adam looks taken aback, but he chuckles. It hurts to hear him laugh like he did last night, realizing it's his canned, manipulating criminals and crooks laugh. I feel my face curl in anger, which he notices.

"Look, let's start over. I'm agent Rooney, and—"

"What's your first name?"

Again, he's taken aback. I wonder if interrupting a federal officer is a crime.

"We've been keeping an eye on your family the past year," he explains, ignoring my question. "I understand you're not affiliated with the family—"

"Then why did you arrest me?" I'm over being polite. If they want to indict me for rudeness, so be it.

"For assaulting a federal officer—"

"Bullshit! That knife couldn't hurt a fly!"

Agent Rooney sighs before exposing his left hand. Gauze is wrapped around his thumb, which feels a bit dramatic. I'm sure a bandage would have done the trick. "Didn't need stitches or anything, but that wasn't a toy. And it certainly could hurt a fly. Maybe even..." He opens up a file he brought in with him and slides a glossy photo in front of me. "A woman in her early 20s?"

If I had eaten anything this morning, I probably would be sick all over the table. The girl from my nightmares looks back at me with a soft smile in what must be a photo for some kind of ID. I stare at her, and she stares back. It's a game I'm doomed to lose but I can't stop myself from playing. Finally I croak, "Please don't make me look at this."

Agent Rooney respects my request and slides the photo

back into the file. "Who was she?" I ask, the pain obvious in my voice.

"You don't know?" Rooney asks, his voice so clear and even toned, he almost sounds uninterested in his own question.

I hear myself stuttering but no words come out. I knew she was a witch. Probably covenless, otherwise my family wouldn't have chosen her for the ritual. Likely a latent witch, a person whose powers don't appear till adulthood—sometimes even later. But I can't tell Agent Rooney that for a whole host of reasons, number one being that he'll probably put me in some facility where the most exciting part of the day is *Jeopardy* reruns. "I know my family killed her. There? Happy?"

Rooney nods. "To be honest, yes." I scoff. "Not because I like the news, but we had her as a missing person. Can you confirm she's dead?"

I killed her, I think to myself. "Yes... she's dead'." That's when the tears come, so fast I can't wipe them away before they hit the metal table with a hollow *thwang.*

"Hey, hey it's okay." Rooney tells me, and I start crying more. "You did the right thing by being honest."

I bury my palms in my eye sockets like I'm trying to plug a dam. I've never said it out loud before. She's dead. A girl is dead because of me... If I say that aloud, I might just combust. I feel Rooney touch my hand. I look up and see he's offering me tissues, but I'm more interested in how he's looking at me. There is sympathy in his eyes. He's looking at me like I'm the last puppy in the cardboard box and it's about to start raining. I should hate it, but somehow, it does make me feel better. I take the tissue and blow my nose. An attempt to ruin any fuzzy feelings I have.

"Lance," I hear Rooney speak over the harsh sound of

blowing my nose. "You're doing the right thing by talking to us. I just need you to answer a few questions best you can—"

The door to the interrogation room slams open. "Don't say another word, Lance."

I look over to see Arthur. Not my Father Arthur. My twin brother, Junior.

CHAPTER FIVE

REAGAN

Lance's doppelgänger barges in, and I have to force myself to push a groan back down my throat. *You have to be fucking kidding me.* Arthur le Fay Junior. We've been trying to get him in an interrogation room from the moment this investigation started, but we've never been able to pin him for anything. Now here he is, ready to save his brother. It's so sweet I might puke.

The other le Fay walks over to his brother's side and touches his shoulder. "Don't say another word, Lance."

I take a moment to try and find the differences between them. Same light blond hair and green eyes, both short but somehow lanky. Like toothpicks. They've both got tall, round noses and thin lips with a deep cupid's bow. Junior definitely looks more put together. He could almost be part of the bureau, with a dark suit and his short hair slicked back. Lance meanwhile keeps his hair looking long and tousled, that fresh out of bed look. Junior has those same bushy brows, though his are in a constant scowl leaving a fine line between his eyes. To be honest, they're exactly identical.

But Junior has eyes like a snake and Lance... doesn't. Even now, with them standing next to each other, it feels like Lance is some poor mammal being slowly crushed to death by an anaconda—his brother. Obviously his family is a complicated web of killers and smugglers of unsavory things. But now actually in the room with one of the le Fays, I can feel just how slimy the whole family is.

All except for Lance.

"My client will be answering no further questions."

"Client?" Lance and I question at the same time.

"Yes, my client." Junior pulls some papers from his breast pocket and hands them over to me. I grab them like the pages might slice my hand further. It would be on brand for the le Fays, even if Lance's 'assault' was clearly accidental. I was just trying to get him booked for not declaring he owned a blade longer than three inches. The assault charge was just more watertight. Or so I thought.

"You were *assaulted* with an antique. Not a weapon."

I flip through the pages and find paperwork detailing the history of the knife. *Fucking hell, is it old.* I should have arrested Lance for not putting that thing in a museum. The paperwork, at least at a glance, all checks out. Arthur Sr. bought the knife at a museum auction in England twenty years ago, then gifted it to his son on his thirteenth birthday. My Dad gave me a hunting knife on my thirteenth birthday, but that was thirty bucks. Not a mortgage.

"Does it matter if it's an antique if it can slice me open?" I show Junior my thumb, but he is clearly disinterested. "It's still illegal to assault an officer.."

"That's for a judge to decide." He grabs Lance by the armpit and pulls him up like a cat grabbing a kitten by the scruff. He drags Lance, who stumbles to follow. The door to the interrogation room opens and I'm stuck just watching two marks walk out the door. But Lance looks back at me with deer in headlight eyes. I don't blame him. I've been in active combat, committed to some brutal training, but even I'm scared of the le Fays.

The door slams shut, and I'm left alone in the interrogation room.

"Fuck."

There is a tapping on the glass, and I turn around. I can't see my boss past the mirrored glass, but I know he's in there. He and I had a rundown of how this interrogation was supposed to go before I walked in. He's been watching this whole time. With a groan, I grab my papers and prepare myself to get chewed out like the cardboard gum you get with baseball cards. Spat out on the sidewalk and stepped on too.

"Reagan," my boss growls as soon as I step into the observation room. "I don't have to say it."

"I fucked up."

"Like hell you did!" He's past growling and is straight to yelling. Both of us have a military background, so we often fall into the drill sergeant and cadet roles. I don't like it, but it's familiar enough. "Twelve months of work down the drain."

"Sir that's a bit dramatic—"

"You calling me a fucking actress, Rooney!?" I can see the blood vessels popping in his forehead. "The le Fay family didn't even know we were investigating them til you got the bold idea to bring in the runt of the litter."

"Sir, if they sent in Arthur Jr. to bail his brother out, they probably knew we were onto them before now. Besides, we got confirmation that Lauren Lobo was in fact killed in connection with the le Fay family."

"Whoop-de-doo, they killed a college student. That's

not a federal issue, Reagan. The smuggling is." He looks at the ceiling and lets out another, "Fuck!"

I sigh. As much as this tongue lashing sucks, my boss is right. The le Fays have connections to a few other crime families and an international syndicate. They've smuggled in pretty much everything that can be smuggled, including people. They're the scum of the earth, and we've got nothing we can use to indict them. From what we've gathered, they leave the day in, day out dirty work to others. They're like FedEx for criminals, only better at keeping their paperwork in check.

I rub the stubble of my chin and purse my lips trying to think how I can fix this. "I'll talk to Lance."

"Like hell you will!" My boss shoves a finger into my chest.

"You saw how he acted in the interrogation room. He's not in the muck like the rest of his family. And he feels bad —about whatever it is they're doing. Guilt is one hell of a motivator."

"I know he's cute, Reagan," my boss drones, and I go stiff. Everyone knows I played honeypot, but they've got no idea how far I went. Nor do I think they care, or they wouldn't have if this plan had actually worked. "But as long as that slimy lawyer brother of his is around, you can't talk to him."

"Did Junior even go to law school? That's never popped up in any of our snooping."

"Don't. Talk. To the le Fays. Not Lancelot. Not the Arthurs. Not even the little sister. Though I'm sure you wanna seduce her too." He starts laughing like he's his own personal laugh track. I grit my teeth and say nothing. What is there to say?

Oh, that's right.

"Yes, sir," I salute before turning to leave.

It might have been my idea to bring a task force out west from Quantico, but there's nothing I hate more than the "task force" rooms they set up for us. It's usually just a conference room and white boards—sometimes our own coffee machine so we don't have to get caught up in the rabble of the precinct. What I hate about all of it, and it sounds egotistical, is not having my own office. Sitting at a conference table just staring at the same two documents feels productive when it's just me and four walls. Now, I've got other agents so close I can hear them stifle a cough.

I find myself sitting and just staring at two glossy photos in the file.

Logan Lobo: twenty-three, but only a sophomore in college when she disappeared one night from campus. Leaving the goddamn library at that. That was a decade ago. Some punk drug runner between the American and Canadian border spilled about her about six months back. Said he and some of his guys nabbed her for the le Fay family. Which sounds like a bad attempt at a plea bargain if it weren't *so* stupid.

The le Fays are smugglers, not killers. Our problem has always been the inability to find their source. Hell, even how they get things in the country. Just, poof, like magic; weapons, drugs, even people just appear. Magic has become a taboo word on this case. The last thing we need is to get renamed the Merlin wannabe case.

That's the one thing we actually do know about Arthur le Fay Sr.

Man loves the occult. At first, I thought it was a tax shelter thing. Buying all these artifacts like Mordred's shield, a supposed Lute of Orpheus, items that are trash unless you believe they belong to the person they supposedly belong to. Even then, who cares about Mordred or Orpheus? Were they even real people? The le Fay family seems to think so.

That did give some weight to that punk-runner's claim. Logan Lobo was studying occult anthropology and claimed she was a practicing witch too. It all reads like typical college girl stuff, but in connection with the le Fays, it's a pattern. Which brings my attention to the other photo.

Lancelot le Fay: thirty-three-year-old interview journalist and the estranged child of the le Fay family. If it weren't for his twin, we probably wouldn't have even known he existed. As far as we can tell, he hasn't interacted with the family since he came of age. You can't really call an eighteen-year-old a runaway, but that's what he is. Strangely, he didn't change his last name. I'd get it if his family name was Brown or Smith—but le Fay?

Turns out he's an occult nut too. The tarot deck was bad enough, but that room had plenty of junk. Expensive junk too, it turns out. According to the museum receipt, that letter opener that sliced me is 12th century Europe, another supposed relic of some Cloyes French kid. At least the hilt is from the 12th century Europe, with a lot of restoration. I could look more into this stuff, but I've been down that rabbit hole about a hundred times working this case. What all this means to the le Fays is irrelevant at the end of the day. Or so I thought...

It's just too convenient, these cards and knives and books. Lance wants out of his family's shadow—he's pretty effectively cut himself out of his family's life—so why keep all that stuff? All in a locked room, an almost literal skeleton in the closet. And he knew Logan Lobo... Shit, maybe there *is* a literal skeleton in his closet. No one ever found Logan's body.

But then I look at Lance's picture again, his ID photo for the office building his magazine operates out of. He's smiling, his eyes are bright, and the light catches those little veins of gold right around his pupils that expand into his green iris. But his eyes are hollow. Haunted. I know now from experience Lance is skittish, like a little dog. In your lap one minute and running off the next. He has regrets... The interrogation made that clear.

I realize I've been chewing on my lip so long I've torn off some skin. I lick my lips before breaking my trance and grabbing some coffee. I skip the machine we've got set up in our task force room. The local police rabble might be a bunch of nosey hot shots, but I need gossip. I haven't even said hi to the duo stirring too much sugar into paper cups before they're asking me about the neurotic guy I brought in this morning.

I immediately want to tell them to fuck off—except I need them. It's clear they think Lance is some kind of tweaked out rich kid. They know he's a le Fay, which gives me an in. "What's up with those guys anyway? They don't even live in the city proper, do they?" I know they don't. They've got an estate farther north where all the private yuppies have lake houses. But I also know they pop up in pretty much all the major cities around the Great Lakes. To say it's their territory is a bit generous, but the Lakes are definitely their home base.

The two cops start talking (mostly between each other, which is perfect for me). They chatter about the Mother. She's never alone but never with her husband. It's always one of the kids or some bodyguard, as if she's in constant danger. Besides that, the whole family sometimes is spotted leaving five-star establishments at 2 AM, always the last ones to leave a restaurant. They're private, like all rich people are. What strikes me is neither cop mentions anything eccentric. No purchasing museum artifacts or the Mother dropping thousands on crystals. She apparently likes gardens. Funding temporary art exhibits. Hosts galas at said art exhibits. Cover for the artifacts maybe... Or a genuine interest?

"Anything about the one I brought in. Lancelot?" I ask, trying to steer them back to the person I'm actually interested in.

They both laugh about the name. Lancelot and Arthur. No one in this building is a scholar but we all know that Arthurian tale. No one else seems to connect what the last name is a reference to; King Arthur's half-sister and a powerful sorcerer, Morgan le Fay. It's all very theatrical, like everything about the family. The hidden nature of it all, just behind a velvet curtain, yet no one questions it. The cops are still snickering about the names when I ask another question. "How did they get their money anyway?"

Finally, the two cops shut up. They've got no clue.

I walk away, leaving behind my untouched cup of coffee. Lance is all I've got. The occult lead doesn't even feel like a lead, just a door that leads to a mirror where I have to stare at myself and my own stupidity. But Lance maybe can navigate me though the funhouse. Even if I have to guilt him into it.

CHAPTER SIX

LANCE

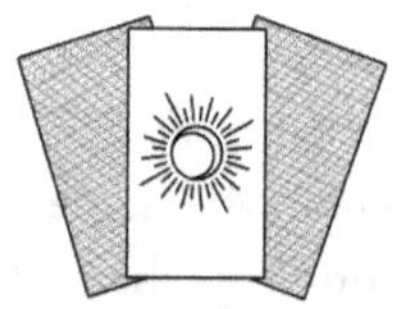

"Since when did you go to law school?"

"Lance, shut up." My brother drags me through the police station like we're outrunning a volcano. Not quite running, but 'we've gotta get out of here' footfalls.

We make it to the elevator, and I attempt to speak again. "Juni—"

"Shh," he hisses at me without even turning to look my way. "You don't think they have a way to listen in on us?"

"Uh, isn't attorney client privilege a thing?"

"Isn't assault with a deadly weapon a pretty heavy charge for a spineless thing like you?"

I already miss the interrogation room.

We make it to the ground floor and continue to march out. I haven't seen my brother in years, but we still manage to fall into a rhythm without a word. Our steps in time, the two of us standing shoulder to shoulder. 'Course, I'm in a gray shirt and sweatpants provided by the precinct and he looks like death itself in his dark suit. As always, we make quite a pair.

We make it outside, and I figure now is a good time to

talk. "What is going on?" He finally turns to look at me. "And just—please, the simplest version, with minimal detail."

Junior scoffs, "As if we'd trust a liability like yourself with any real information."

We.

So, Dad knows. There is a gurgle at the back of my throat, and for a second, I think I really am going to vomit bile. My brother must notice because he reaches out to hold my shoulder. "Lance, stay with me. We're not interested in..." he pauses. I know he's trying to find the best way to say that my family isn't interested in skinning me like a rabbit—which I appreciate. "I'm here because we can't have you giving the feds any information."

"I told them about the girl I killed."

"Well," he shrugs. "Maybe you'll make friends in prison."

I push his hand off my shoulder. "Seriously?!"

I see Junior purse his lips before adjusting his cufflinks. His jaw is tight, but he manages to speak. "Lance, listen to me carefully. You are as good as dead to our family. You have nothing on us. Even if you did, who the hell is going to believe you?" He's right, and I should be worried about that fact, but all I feel is relief. "They can't prove you killed that girl. They don't even have a body. And say you did decide to spill your guts about our dealings... We would take care of you."

"Now you've got me confused. 'Take care,'" I put the words in air quotes, "in our family means maiming and killing. But you actually bailed me out of there. Why? You even said it yourself, I don't really have anything on the family."

For once, Junior doesn't have an immediate reply, only

lifting a curious brow. I've finally stumped him. He slips his hands into his pockets and looks down at his shoes. He chuckles. I look down too and realize what he's laughing about. They gave me plastic flip flops at the precinct to match the sweats. Flamingo pink ones. "Come on, I assume they didn't feed you." With that, my brother starts walking down the street. I roll my eyes and groan up at the sky.

If I had just kept my dick in my pants, none of this would have happened.

WE FIND a diner far enough from the precinct that Junior is pretty sure no cops will be having a meal alongside us. "My treat," he tells me, as if the most expensive thing on the menu isn't fifteen dollars and our family isn't worth billions. I order oatmeal and a coffee, requesting a side of cinnamon for both. Junior gets the standard eggs, bacon, and toast. He would never drink the coffee at a place like this. I'm surprised he'll even eat the food..

"How's Mom?" I ask as soon as our waitress is gone.

"Neurotic as usual." I must make a face because he lets out an exasperated sigh. "She does a reading for you every day to make sure you're safe. You must have had a cold or something at some point because she drew... what was it? The Fool I think..."

"The Fool usually means a careless mistake." I can see the interest fade out of Junior's eyes. He's an alchemist, the scientist of witches. He likes reactions and numbers and things to fit in just right. Divination is much too floaty for him to take any interest. "She might have thought I was about to be in an accident."

"Were you?"

"I got stuck in the elevator at work last month. They had to call the fire department."

"Take the fucking stairs next time."

There's a long pause. The waitress arrives with our food. Steam rises from our plates, adding some extra drama. Junior finally breaks the silence. "You want to know why I bailed you out?" He leans across the table. "Because you have a bleeding heart, and you *would* say something to get us in trouble."

I furrow my brows. "You said I have nothing—"

"I don't know what it is the feds are looking for, *Lancelot.*" I wince and I can hear the whinging in his voice too. Something about using our full names with each other has always dealt psychological damage. He's Junior, I'm Lance. Arthur and Lancelot are... painful for obvious reasons. I suppose we did end up being rivals of sorts. Ones with a strange sort of loyalty between us just like the king and knight of legend. But it's just so silly. Twin brothers named Arthur and Lancelot.

Junior runs his fingers through his hair, messing with the gel and leaving it looking a little crooked. "Better safe than sorry. For all parties. Just tell me what they were asking you about."

I lean back into the booth, the worn plastic leather cushioning me. I look down at my hands in my lap, studying my palms. "You came in before Adam—Agent Rooney—could ask me any real questions. They just know that girl is dead."

"Which girl?"

My head shoots forward. "Which—the *girl.* The one I —" I don't want to say it. "You know the girl. The brunette girl that wouldn't stop screaming and Dad wouldn't gag her even though I begged—" The waitress comes back to check on us, refilling my coffee. I bite my tongue so hard I taste copper. Junior meanwhile looks unbothered, like I've just been telling him about work drama.

He glances up at the waitress. "Thank you." He gives her a smile. She smiles back. It sucks to see your own face being so fake. The waitress leaves and Junior's smile falls faster than dominos. "I remember the girl now," he says in a low voice. "So, you just admitted to killing her?"

"I told them she was dead."

"And that's all you told them."

"*Yes*," I stress.

Junior shrugs his shoulders. "Then we're all good here. I was hoping you could tell us what they're snooping around for, but no news is good news." Junior pulls out his wallet and drops a fifty dollar bill on the table. He slides his untouched plate of food towards me. "Give this slop to your dog or something."

My brother gets up to leave, and I look up at him. "I don't have a dog," I reply stupidly.

"Really? You should look into getting one." He buttons his suit coat and with that, he's gone. Good riddance, really. Except I have a feeling it's not the last time I'll see him. I'm eyeing my still hot oatmeal when I hear a distant, "Oh."

Junior sits back down on the very edge of the booth, his legs facing outwards telling me he's not planning on sticking around. "You haven't been in contact with *her* have you?"

It takes me a second to piece together who he's talking about. Even when I figure it out, I play dumb. "Who is *her*?"

Junior grumbles. "We both agreed to keep her a secret." I of course know who he's talking about. But for some reason, I can't keep myself from messing with him.

Still I concede, "Minerva."

"Shut—" he's on the verge of yelling when he catches

himself. "Shut up. Don't say her name, just tell me you haven't been in contact with her."

"I haven't. As far as I know she's at the same address, but I haven't—"

"Good." Junior stands up and marches off. "Keep it that way!" he calls over his shoulder before exiting the building.

The waitress, looking confused, shuffles over and points at the plate of food with her pen. "Would you... like a box for that?"

———

I TRY to ignore the odd looks I'm getting walking through the city, gray from top to bottom with loosely fitted clothes perfectly accessorized with the pink flip flops. I've probably seen people dressed like this at the grocery store and thought nothing of it. But if one of my coworkers sees me like this, I'll just curl up and die. The cherry on top of an already terrible morning.

I don't think I should go to my apartment. I mean, what if I walk in on agents finishing up bugging my place? How embarrassing. It's definitely not safe. So, instead, I keep walking to the historic district until my flip flops are about to come apart. I stop in front of an old, well-kept brownstone, a sign on the front reading Metropolitan Antiques in a swirly font. As I climb the stairs to the entrance, another sign gives the shop's hours. Closed on the weekends. Perfect.

I ring the doorbell. A few moments later, the door opens, a massive, broad man with copper skin and gray poking out of his beard greeting me. "Lance?" Taylor has his hair wrapped in a bonnet and he's wearing a Toronto Raptors shirt. I feel bad interrupting his relaxation day to deal with my problems, but it's too late to back out now. He looks me up and down with his warm brown eyes. "Did you get mugged?"

"Sure." My tone is curt, a little cranky after walking so far. "At least they were kind enough to give me these spare clothes."

Taylor opens the door wider, "Come in." He doesn't have to tell me twice.

The front foyer of the house is open with a dazzling chandelier overhead. The adjacent rooms are overflowing with vases, statues, couches, coffee tables— even some taxidermy. A velvet rope blocks the main staircase, a sign reading *Staff Only*. The staff being Taylor and his wife, Daphne. Taylor unclips the rope blocking the staircase. "I always feel like I'm having the red carpet rolled out." I tease.

Taylor gives me a genuine smile, his mauve lips framing perfectly white teeth. "Over the top *is* our style."

We both laugh as we ascend the stairs. "Is Daphne awake?"

"No, but she'll be happy to see you."

"So, I should go wake her then?" I'm already walking towards the bedroom at the very back of the house when Taylor moves to step in front of me.

"I would rather you let me." He gives me another sweet smile but this one appears more forced. "Bad idea to catch her on the wrong side of the bed."

"I thought vampires didn't actually sleep."

Taylor doesn't elaborate. He opens the bedroom door just wide enough for us to slip in. The room is pitch black, but I've been here enough times to know the layout. There's a massive bed with a canopy against the wall facing the windows that have been painted black in addition to blackout curtains. It's the one modern thing in the house, heavy slick black fabric juxtaposed with the intricate wood, rich velvets, and gold detailing of everything else.

My eyes are adjusting to the darkness while Taylor leans over the bed, speaking softly. "Love," I hear a murmur, his husky voice sending a particular shiver down my spine. There is stirring in the bed. "Lance is here. He's looking rather drab."

A figure slowly sits up in bed, back straight as a board. Taylor taps the base of a lamp next to the bed illuminating him and the figure. Long white-blonde hair falls down the woman's back almost brushing the sheets. She pushes it back from her face, then turns to me. Despite being vampiric, Daphne looks more like a cherub. Round face with eyes so large the skin beneath them makes little pillows for them to rest upon. Her whole body is soft, hips, breasts, and stomach overflowing. She once casually mentioned she was a muse for a lot of Baroque artists. Emphasis on the casual mention.

"Lance..." she breathes. "You look awful." Taylor takes Daphne's hand and touches her lower back, escorting her out of bed. Which feels silly, especially when as soon as she's on her feet she's standing right front of me in a blink. "You look so... gray."

"You're missing the shoes, darling." Taylor nodded down at my feet with the cheap flip flops.

Daphne raises her brows before looking down at my feet. "Oh, how... fun." I appreciate her trying to be nice despite her waking comment. "Perhaps we can find you something to wear. Unless you want to dress like this?" she asks, as if she's offended me. Daph looks back at Taylor. "You would know better than I, love. Is this fashion?"

I cut the fashion talk short. "I got arrested."

Taylor and Daphne both look at me like I've just burst into flames. "Oh, that's why you look dreadful!" Daphne pulls me into a very cold hug. It feels like falling face-first into a big pile of fresh snow. "Did they hurt you?"

"Not physically," I assure her.

A much warmer hand clasps my shoulder. Taylor looks down at me. "Are you comfortable telling us what happened? Maybe over some tea?"

THE KITCHEN IS MUCH BETTER LIT, the lamps all decorated with frosted glass flowers. The windows are still painted black, like all the windows on the second floor. Daphne really only ever goes downstairs at night or when it's overcast enough that she doesn't have to worry about the sun. On the second floor, she's free to move about as she pleases, though she usually sleeps during the day. *Hundred-year-old habits are hard to kick,* she once explained to me.

I finish retelling the past 24 hours and set down the empty cup of chamomile tea Daphne brewed for us. Vampires can handle liquids, and she brews the best cup of tea I've ever had. Daphne's brows are furrowed, and her round face scrunched, much too lost in her thoughts to be looking at me.

Taylor, on the other hand, leans back in his chair, calm as can be. "Why are the feds wasting time with your Father again?"

"Seriously? That whole story and *that's* what you're curious about?" Taylor shrugs like a teenager being called on in math class. "My Father works with mortal crime syndicates. Of course they're interested in him. No one knows that we're witches but the gangs don't care so long as their stuff gets into the country."

"Dear," Daphne coos, her face softening, "do you ever listen to our guests?" Her soft smile makes it clear she's teasing, but Taylor still lets out a heavy sigh.

"We have so many guests," he laments.

Daphne and Taylor's house doubles as an antique shop and a sort of home for wayward supernaturals. I know Taylor is a born wolf, but beyond that he's pretty private. Daphne on the other hand loves to talk about her past. She's been a vampire since the 1500s. More than that, she was on the Vampire Council for almost a century before she chose to retire. Retire to do this. Listen to people like me who have no other supernaturals to talk to. Vampire spawn abandoned by their masters and newly turned werewolves being pressured to join packs they know nothing about.

I think I'm their only witch 'client'—or guest, as they like to call it. They do everything for me, and I do little for them. I know I'm not in immediate danger like a lot of their guests, but I can't decide if that makes me more or less of a freeloader. I'm even wearing their clothes for goodness' sake, a black button up with white embroidery and pants, both Daphne's and both much too loose on my body. But if I'd worn anything of Taylor's I'd be tripping over myself, so we raided Daphne's wardrobe.

Taylor and Daphne look at each other, communicating in that silent voice couples always have with one another. It reminds me that vampires can't procreate. Unlike werewolves, who not only can procreate but usually have pretty big families. I guess for them, all the lost spawn, pups, and witches are their foster family. Still, I feel like I've taken enough of their time and clothes for one day.

That is, until Taylor speaks up. "Maybe it's best if you take your mind off it. Go out and have some fun."

"You want me to ignore all of this?"

Daphne chimes in a soft voice, "You're not ignoring it." She smiles, flashing her fangs. "Not forever, just tonight. Nothing is in your grasp. Not your brother, or this Adam—"

"Agent Rooney," I correct.

Taylor jumps back in. "Yeah, you can't change anything right now. Might as well distract yourself." He puts a hand on my shoulder. "I'll take you out."

"Out where?"

CHAPTER SEVEN

LANCE

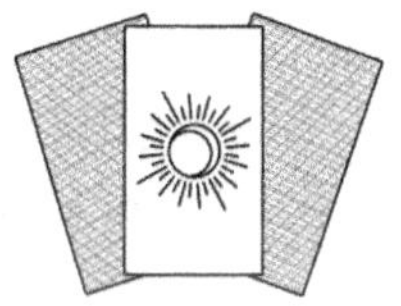

I'll give Taylor some credit. I haven't really been thinking about my problems at the bar. Instead, I've been thinking about all the two hundred pound bikers eyeing me up as we sit at the bar.

"Taylor." I say with every ounce of patience in my body.

"Hm?" He hums just before taking a big gulp of his beer.

"Why did you bring me to a dive bar?"

That's really the only way to describe it. The place is primarily lit with white Christmas lights strung up in the rafters. The walls are lined with license plates and road signs, most of which look pretty banged up. Not in the aesthetic pottery barn way either. The dents and rust are genuine. Everything is made of dark wood from the floor to the bar top. The loud clang of pool balls echoes behind us. At least the place is clean, but the air is hazy with cigarette smoke. Both Taylor and I are overdressed, me in Daphne's embroidered top and Taylor wearing a nice Burberry sweater. Taylor sets down his beer, some foam clinging to his mustache.

"Taylor—" I press. "Why am I here? I'm starting to think you just wanted to go out to a bar."

He chuckles. "Maybe, but I figured this bar is safe. So long as you're with me, everyone here has your back." As if to prove his point, he turns and waves to a group of guys playing pool. They all give some sort of acknowledgment, a wave or nod of the head. One of them even smiles. The juxtaposition is not lost on me.

"Why didn't you just bring Daphne if you wanted a drinking buddy?" Granted this place isn't really her scene either, but she's married to the guy. I didn't sign up for sickness and health and two-dollar beers.

The bartender speaks up. "No vamps allowed," she says while cleaning a whiskey glass. "Not even for the good ones like Daph." The bartender is so pale I could have mistaken her for a vampire herself. She's got long mousy brown hair all pushed to one side and cut in a side shave. Her lips are soft and rounded like a doll's, but her eyes are killer, in a perpetual scowl. She breaks her harsh expression to raise a brow. "I've never seen you around."

"He's just a friend who needed a night out," Taylor remarks.

"Alright." She leans across the bar. "Well, what shots do you like?" she asks me.

"Uh... spiced rum." Without hesitation she pours me a shot.

I look at Taylor for an explanation. "Sara owns the place," he tells me. "She's in here every night."

"Got nothing better to do," she says before sliding the shot my way. "I like to treat newcomers." With that, she walks to the other side of the bar to help another customer.

I down the shot figuring it shouldn't go to waste. The rum is a very welcome and warm burn. "So, your bar owner friend Sara hates vampires? Isn't that awkward with your wife?"

"Daphne and Sara are good friends too. The rule stands because this is a werewolf bar."

I blink, then decide I need another shot. "Why did you bring me to a werewolf bar?" I hiss. There is only one pack in the city I know of and that's the Blood Moon Pack. They're a proper biker gang: drugs, prostitutes, hell, they probably do hits too. My family never bothered with them though they've tried to bother us from time to time. Guess they thought there was only room for one supernatural gang in this city.

Taylor shakes his head. "Where was I supposed to take you? A witch bar? Most vampire establishments ban werewolves. And plenty of succubus hang out here too."

I roll my eyes. "It's not like most of the bars in the city are run by humans."

"Isn't your problem right now a human problem?" He pointed out, gesturing with his beer.

We just look at each other. I could be crying on Daphne's shoulder ruining her nice vintage blouse or I could have gone back to my bugged apartment and cried to Kate Bush all by myself. But instead, I'm the overdressed witch at a dive bar not meant for me. This isn't my space. "I need to use the restroom."

I don't actually, but the bathroom is a nice break from the smoke and noise. Instead of heading for a stall I just stare at myself in the scratched up, graffiti-covered mirror. I notice one part of the mirror has been scratched out and then blackened with a marker. But I can still see a round B and the tail of a P. I guess the Blood Moon Pack isn't as welcome here as I feared. Though, I should have known Taylor would never bring me somewhere dangerous. Taylor cares about his guests just as much as Daphne. He just shows it in his own way, like one of those parents that lets their kids climb to the very top of a tree so they can learn for themselves why you don't climb to the very tops of trees.

I splash some water on my face and walk back to the bar, only to find Taylor isn't sitting where I left him. I look over my shoulder and see he's struck up a game of pool with some other werewolves. Great. Now I have to share Taylor's attention and that I'm terrible at pool.

A smooth voice pulls me from my moping. "I can practically see their tails wagging." I turn and see a man with deep golden skin sitting in a booth alone. He blends in with a leather jacket, but I look closer and see a tight knit purple sweater with a white shirt collar poking out from the neck-line. He turns to me, his wide smile resting on a plush lower lip. His brown eyes twinkle with mischief. "Don't you think?"

I swallow before swiftly replying. "I don't want to say something I'll regret."

"Scared of the big bad wolf?"

"My friend over there is actually the one that brought me out here," I explain. I'm not going to gossip about Taylor to this stranger, especially when I'd rather talk about this stranger. Or talk about me. Or a hypothetical us.

"And how do you like it?" The man asks.

"The free shot is nice."

"Sara is a doll," he says with genuine admiration behind his words.

I raise a brow. "Owning a place like this? Maybe Biker Barbie, but otherwise..."

The stranger slides over in the booth making room for me. "Would you like another free drink?" I look at the stranger, then back over to the game of pool. Taylor and I catch each other's eyes. He gives me a thumbs up. I want to roll my eyes so hard they fall back into my head, but I don't want the stranger to think it's intended for him. "Hard offer to pass up," I say before sitting down.

"My name is Kas by the way." He waves over to the bar. "Sara!" As I expect, she scowls across the bar at him. "Two dirty martinis." I expect some rebuttal, but instead Sara just starts making the drinks.

"You two must be close..." I think aloud.

"Very. As close as I am with Taylor over there."

I blink. "Do you just... know everyone?"

Kas leans in a little closer. "I don't know you."

He finally gets a proper smile out of me. I know ogling a guy when I'm still reeling over my last hookup isn't the best idea, but healthy coping mechanisms suck and I've got a decade of bad decision making that isn't going to change tonight. "My name is Lance," I tell him. "Now you know me a bit better."

Sara appears with our drinks. "How long have you been eyeing this one, Kas?" she asks, but doesn't stick around for the answer, returning to the bar as quickly as she came.

"Since he walked in the bar," Kas replies, his eyes fixed on me.

I'll give Taylor credit— I'm not at all thinking about Agent Fake-Name now.

CHAPTER EIGHT

REAGAN

By the time I've changed out of my suit and left the precinct, Lance is very much in the wind. Still, I scope out the area, popping my head into cafes and restaurants hoping for a lead. I speak to a waitress at a diner who tells me everything— the nega-twins, she calls them. One who dressed immaculately and ate nothing while the other looked like he'd just rolled out of bed and finished his plate before paying in cash. She says Lance left about thirty minutes ago, heading north.

I take a gamble. North is the historic district and there are a few old brownstones bought up to turn into storefronts: one new-age bookstore, one store of occult odds and ends. I can't say I understand the difference between new-age and occult despite working this case for months. I don't know anything about this witch nonsense. It all gives me flashbacks to high school, kids getting suspended for dressing like Mötley Crüe, as if hairspray was satanic. Girls showing up to class with pentagram necklaces and skirts that hid their feet. I always thought they looked like Dracula with his cape dragging along the floor, just waiting to trip the old geezer. Teachers and parents were panicking, but I always thought it was just silly. Now here I am trying to piece together what appears to be a real ritual killing.

I wander around the historic district, sticking to the shops. There's no way I'll find Lance if I stop at every house with no idea which resident he might be visiting. Even if I did know, I can't risk getting a trespassing violation. My boss would dip my feet in cement and drown me in the lake. But the shops are a bust. Neither shop owner has ever heard of a Lancelot le Fay. Not a forgettable name, especially for this lot.

I'm ready to go back and stake out Lance's apartment, but as I walk back towards downtown, I look up and catch sight of a strong, blond profile. I scramble into the bushes. Through the dark green foliage, I see Lance and another man start to walk the way I just came. The other man looks like he could knock Lance over with just a flick of his wrist. They walk past my bush hideout, and I realize the man is a few inches taller than me. He has hints of gray in his hair that make him look more distinguished than old. He might have been considered pudgy, but I knew guys like that in the army. They've just got a little padding for the muscle underneath, and that fat is extra helpful when you're pinning some fucker to the ground.

I chew my cheek. Why am I bothered by this? I don't know Lance's relationship to the guy. Lance is just hanging out with a guy taller and stronger than me. A man he probably trusts and feels safe with... I literally shake my head, trying to focus as I remind myself I'm working a case. When Lance and his pal are far enough ahead, I slip out of the bush. Instead of immediately following, I walk back to grab the address of the building they've just left. Metropolitan Antiques... no shit. Of course he wouldn't go to some obvious occult shop. I wonder how many antique shops are fronts for some freaky magic shit.

I pinch the bridge of my nose. "This case is fucking with me," I mutter. *This is why Caroline left,* I curse at myself.

LANCE and his friend walk for a while until the sun is so low in the sky, its pinks and oranges are engulfed by darkness. We're out of the historic district. Homes and storefronts covered with boards and with yards that resemble jungles appear more and more. Eventually the scenery becomes more urban, the abandoned houses replaced with empty concrete lots surrounded by fencing. Lance and his buddy walk into a two-story bar on the street corner. A blue neon sign reads One-Eyed Dog Bar in the window. Motorcycles line the opposite side of the street, a few parked out back behind the bar.

I'm getting real sick of being thrown for a loop, but at least the bar is an easy entry, my jeans and decade old boots letting me blend in with the bikers. Still, I keep close to the wall in the shadows while Lance and his buddy sit at the bar. So far so good. I can't risk getting close enough to hear what they're talking about but maybe once they're gone, I can grill the bartender. After a while, Lance gets up from his seat and leaves for the bathroom. His friend hesitates but stands up and makes his way over to the pool tables. Perfect.

One of the guys playing pool shouts over the chatter of the bar. "Taylor! Hey, the ball and chain let you out of the dog house?"

Lance's friend, his married friend, lets out an awkward chuckle. "She lets me out whenever I want. I just don't like leaving her all alone at night. But a friend needed some guy time." He shrugs before smiling. "This game almost up?"

"Yeah, grab a cue." I watch the three guys finish up their game before starting another with Taylor. They all start chatting about their plans to go upstate next week. Something about a full moon. I wouldn't pin these guys as stargazing types, but a moonlit bike ride in the woods does sound nice.

I look past the pool tables and spot Lance sitting in a booth with *another* guy. Again, I chew at my cheek not even realizing it. I watch as the two of them inch closer and closer together until Lance is practically in the guy's lap. God, is that what we looked like last night? My teeth nip my bottom lip.

It's not like Lance is my first honeypot job. My recruiter even told me the bureau would use me like a cheap date. My then-wife wasn't a fan, but at that point she wasn't the biggest fan of me anyway. I'd already broken my promise to her. I think the only reason she didn't serve me divorce papers the second I told her I was being recruited by the FBI was for the benefits. Which I don't fault her for. I don't fault her for any of it.

I'm not going to lie, seducing and sleeping with people for information was kinda fun. Not all of them were Bond Girl Bombshells, but I didn't exactly have time to go on dates anymore. No one was waiting for me at home. Mindless sex was mindless sex, and I didn't let it bother me that I was fucking for information. Lance had been the first time my mark was another man. I figured I could phone it in like with all the other marks I wasn't all that attracted to.

But once we started kissing, I didn't want to stop. When I broke into the locked room of his apartment, I was really hoping to find some vial labeled 'love potion'— some explanation for these feelings. If Lance wasn't meddling with my emotions, then those feelings were mine alone.

Just then, Lance and his newfound date slide out of the booth and walk back towards the bathrooms. I wait a beat, just long enough for me to blink and feel a surge of jealousy, before I follow them.

CHAPTER NINE

LANCE

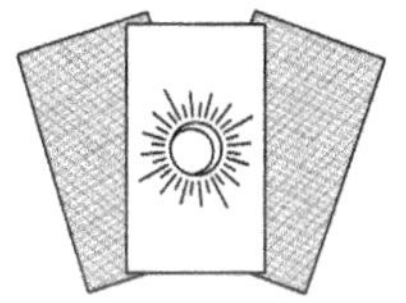

I push Kas against the wall of the bathroom stall, grateful for his jacket, the soft leather giving me the perfect handle to pull his lips to mine. I work my lips roughly against his smile. He chuckles before his lips relax and follow my lead. His hand reaches back behind my head and pushes me closer to him. It's nice—it makes me feel less desperate. My lips leave his and I catch my breath, still holding two fistfuls of leather. He looks euphoric, his pupil's dilated. His bright white smile returns. "I'd hate to ruin the moment, but there's something I have to tell you."

I hold back a groan. Communication is important, and I'm sure I'll be happy he said his piece later. But right now, I just want to be on my knees thinking about very little. "Everything alright?" I ask him.

"Perfectly alright. But I like my bedmates to know *what* I am." I blink. I hadn't assumed he was a werewolf. But I also never questioned what he could be. His smile curls in a devious manner. "I'm a succubus." He brings his hand to my temple, slowly dragging the back of his fingers along my face. "The classic, tempting, lustful kind."

And the most common type too, but I don't bring that up. Succubi are minor devils, pretty much the only infernal thing that other supernatural beings are comfortable with keeping around. They're attracted to and feed on sin. Lust, wrath, greed... the whole seven yards. "That doesn't bother me," I tell him without a second thought. He can feed on my lust all he wants.

"I didn't think it would, but I like to be transparent." His hand slips down to the edge of my chin and takes it between his fingers before he tilts my head back. I think he's about to lean down and kiss my lips again, but instead he goes right for my neck. First, it's just his soft lips, and then I feel his teeth drag against my flesh. I let out a slow exhale, my heart racing. What was it Jason said? Bathrooms have great acoustics? I moan and it bounces off the tile walls. Kas makes it to my collarbone before he stops and chuckles to himself. He looks up at me. "Does your friend want to join?"

What the hell is he talking about? It's like Kas can read my mind because he releases me and walks to the door of the stall. He pushes the door open. I see a familiar face standing in the corner of the bathroom. I couldn't see his feet from under the stall door and must have been distracted (for obvious reasons) when he followed us. Agent Rooney looks at us with big eyes, clearly caught off guard by us catching him in the act. Ironic considering what Kas and I were about to do to each other. "It's been a while since I've had a three-course meal," Kas teases, but I'm much too pissed to find the joke endearing.

I see Rooney take a microstep backwards, and I shout, "Don't you dare!"

I practically fly towards him before grabbing his wrist and dragging him into the stall with me and Kas. "Are you a fucking stalker?" I ask him before turning to Kas. "Did you help him with this?"

Now Kas is the one looking confused. "I don't know who this man is. I've just got a pretty acute sense of when people around me are aroused."

"I'm not into this shit." Agent Rooney barks.

I bark back. "What? The exhibitionism or the two men?"

Agent Rooney's mouth hangs open like a fish mounted to the wall. Kas, meanwhile, looks enthralled. "Oh, if you two don't mind." He leans back against the stall door, clearly intending on listening in. "Carry on," he waves his hand dismissively.

Rooney looks like he's about to tell Kas to fuck off but I'm faster. "What gives you the right to just follow me around? Aren't I allowed privacy under the law, *agent*?"

"Don't—" Rooney's voice is heightened, but he pauses and starts whispering. "Don't call me agent right now. Please."

I cross my arms. "I don't know what else to call you. Someone conveniently forgot to give me their name. Too busy shoving your tongue down my throat."

He sighed, running his fingers through his cropped hair. "My name is Reagan."

"Like... the president?"

"Yes," he replies exasperated. "Now can we just—"

"No, stop." I raise a hand, my other arm still tucked under my shoulder. "Stop. I need to process the fact I fucked a guy named after Ronald fucking Reagan. I need an enema for my brain." Kas snickers while *Reagan* looks disgusted. Somehow, it's his scrunched-up expression that pushes me over the edge.

I push past Kas and leave the stall. "Lance," I hear

Reagan call after me. I exit the bathroom and walk out into the bar, but stupid Reagan and his long legs aren't far behind, and he soon cuts off my egress. "Lance, listen can we just talk?"

"Not without a lawyer present." I announce.

As soon as the word lawyer leaves my lips, I feel a shift in the room. A bunch of bikers— enough to be a gang I'd hazard to say— look right at us. Some just peek over their shoulders while others turn their whole bodies to face us. These guys might not be Blood Moon Pack, but I get the sense they don't like the idea of law enforcement being in here. And who could blame them?

Just then a hand appears on Reagan's shoulder, turning him around. "Listen up." We both look down to see Sara, her scowl now a full blaze of rage and authority. "This is *my* bar under *my* law. You don't like it, I suggest you get out." She's in a staring match with Reagan now. "Or, if my regulars want to throw you into a pool table, that's fine by me. Just know the bill will be attached to your ass when I kick you out." She pushes her finger into Reagan's sternum. I can see and hear how tight her jaw is as she growls, "Got it?"

I see Reagan purse his lips, the wheels clearly turning in his head. "I got it." He walks past Sara, turning his body to the side so he doesn't brush her body as he walks to the exit. The whole bar watches him leave. He stops in the doorway and looks over his shoulder at me. I try to scowl but I'm not sure it's very convincing. I want to talk to him—to yell at him. Who's to say you can't get some good conversation from an argument? But Reagan eventually exits the bar without another word.

As soon as he's gone, the chatter of the bar starts up again. Taylor's voice snaps me to attention. "Was that the guy?"

"Yeah," I say, just now realizing how dry my mouth feels. "Reagan. His name is Reagan."

"Wait. Reagan Rooney?"

I look up at Taylor. "Yeah, you know him?" I can't imagine why he would.

"No... Just a funny name."

Kas's head literally pops in between Taylor and I. "Sorry to interject, but isn't your name Taylor Todnam?" He gives Taylor a cheeky grin.

"It is. It's a family name," Taylor raises a thick brow. "What's strange about that?"

"Please tell me you're joking, old friend." Kas sounds as exhausted as I feel.

I follow in Reagan's footsteps and start walking towards the exit. Taylor notices and pipes up. "Lance?"

"I need sleep," I tell him. "I feel like I've been awake for a whole week."

Someone grabs my hand. To my surprise I turned to see Sara. "Listen, is that guy a problem? You want me to get someone to walk you home?"

I'm taken aback by her offer. "Thank you, but I'll be alright," I assure her. I know I should accept the help, but I've already been such a burden, I can't bring myself to ruin some stranger's night. Plus, whoever walks me home will ask questions. It was one thing when I told Taylor and Daphne about what happened, but they hear stories of woe all the time. No one else needs to hear about my shitty day.

So, I walk home alone. The cold night air keeps me alert, almost as much as my paranoia. At one point a motorbike with a sidecar passes me, and I stop walking. I watch the bike pass and try to confirm it's not one of the guys from the One-Eyed Dog Sara has sent after me. Both riders have helmets on, even the figure in the side car, so I can't identify them. They continue down the road, and I tell myself it's probably just a coincidence. Probably.

WHEN I GET BACK to my apartment, I stand with my back pressed against the front door for longer than I would have liked. I take in my apartment, trying to remember if my couch was always that far back from the glass coffee table. I study the photos from the last few work holiday parties, checking to see if they're still in the order I left them. I consider tearing my apartment up to try and find any cameras or bugs. I consider tearing up my apartment just to feel something. I think, maybe, I should try laying on the floor and redownloading all the dating apps until I find a stranger to come over and fuck me better than Reagan ever could.

Instead, I find myself in my kitchen looking at my tarot deck from the day before. "Stupid," I mutter to myself as I look through the cards. Eventually I find what I'm looking for: The Page of Cups. My querent, the card that most represents me. Years ago, I chose the young romantic poet. Maybe now that I'm older, less optimistic, I should choose a new symbol, but I've got history with this card, and with my past coming home to roost, I figure it's a fitting choice.

I set the card down on the countertop and shuffle the deck considering what sort of reading I should do. I could focus on Reagan, but he's just a piece of my angst. It's everything; my family, my magic, my piss poor decision making— it's all ruining my life. Maybe more cards will give me an answer. I settle on a six-card spread.

I pull my first card and The Hanged Man looks back at me, almost mocking me as he sways from his tree. I'd been self-sacrificial, giving up my own morals for my family's sake. Hiding out and not making any waves. Not until the FBI showed up. But I had nothing to do with that. I've lost a lot, but I've gained something better that my family could never offer me: normalcy.

The second card is familiar, as The Moon in reverse greets me, the river at the base of the card now at the top. I pulled the card yesterday, but in reverse The Moon has a more cynical meaning. My intuition is now clouded by fear. Fear I need to release. Once again, I'm left disappointed by the card, but I move on.

I pull my third card, a brave knight riding atop a white horse charging into battle. It could be the illustration to accompany a fairytale. The Knight of Swords is focused, ambitious, and brave. So not me at all. I'm a lover, not a fighter, but maybe I should try reaching for what I want without fear of rocking the boat. Now if only I knew what I wanted...

Next card is The Wheel of Fortune, which means a change is coming. A good one too, based on the card and its placement in the spread. Though major changes are never easy in the moment. Especially when dealing with lofty ideas like destiny and purpose. I've been focusing on the forces right in front of my nose: my family, my friends, myself... but perhaps this issue goes beyond them. Maybe I need to reach out to someone I haven't spoken to in a long time.

Arthur's question at the diner rings in my head: *"You haven't been in contact with her, have you?"* Minerva is my half-sister. Well, our half-sister. We found out about her while snooping through Dad's files one day. We met her once, briefly. She had no idea who we were, and I doubt that's changed since. Maybe I need to reconnect with her.

She *is* family at the end of the day... But I'm getting ahead of myself.

I draw The Four of Cups. At this point in the spread, I'm looking at what will be an obstacle. So, apathy. Or some sort of crisis of faith. *Just believe in yourself, Lance!* I can almost hear the cards say in the tone of a children's morning program.

It's time for the final card. The outcome of all this mess. I face the image of a woman holding back a great beast. The Strength card has always fascinated me. The image features a woman for one thing, and while she is entangled with the beast, she never looks like she's fighting it. More like she's trying to help the creature. Compassion, confidence, and control. Not a bad ending in sight.

I look at the spread of six cards on the countertop, my querent in the corner. It feels like the cards are telling me to remember who I am, what I've overcome. I've tried so hard to just fade away and it changed nothing. So, now I have to get up and change things for myself.

No pressure there. No one to blame but myself if it blows up in my face.

I feel a tingle at the back of my neck like I'm being watched. I spin around, "Reagan," I say, proactively thinking he's followed me again. But it's not him standing in my living room. It's not even one person, but two, both dressed in dark and ratty clothing.

The shorter of the two men speaks. "Let's talk." He's got what I can only describe as a mullet and a distinct cut going from his bottom lip to his chin. The taller man behind him has long dark hair that covers half his face. He looks about as big and bulky as Taylor.

I somehow manage to speak. "Sure... Talk about what?"

"Not here." The mullet man takes a few more steps my way.

"Uh, yes here," I push, managing to put some pluck in my tone. "I'm not going anywhere."

"Yeah?" He asks me with a teasing grin.

I blink, and suddenly he's an inch from my face. He's only an inch or two taller than me, but it doesn't matter. He reaches back and grabs my hair. I can tell by the grip alone he's stronger than me. It finally clicks that he's not human. Figures. I let out a groan as his fingers threaten to rip out a third of my hair by the scalp. "Listen, little witch boy— you can either come with us on your own two feet, or we'll carry you out of here." His voice rasps but is somehow still soft like a whisper.

I spit in his face— surprising myself more than the stranger. He doesn't even wipe the lob of saliva off his cheek. I feel him push me down onto the counter, my temple slamming into the granite. I'm on the ground, the room spinning. I hear the shorter man say something but can't make out the words. Next thing I know, I feel myself being lifted off the floor, limp like a cloth doll.

I should scream. I should do anything— but I can't. Everything just fades away...

CHAPTER TEN

LANCE

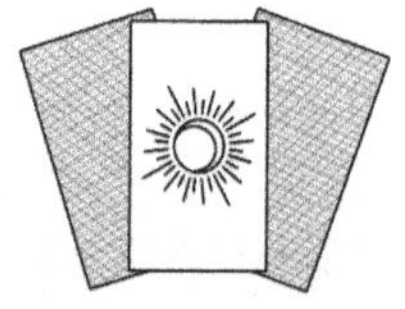

As I start to come to, all I can make out is a blinding yellow light. I shut my eyes tight. Opening them again, the yellow light persists. I begin to blink, and more things come into view. A bald man stands guard over me, so checked out he doesn't even notice my eyes are open. Shifting my hips, I find myself sitting on a metal chair. My hands are tied around the back. I look down, my ankles tied and wrapped around the legs of the chair as well.

The man in front of me walks away without a word. Guess he finally realized I was awake. I hear him knock against a metal door. Within a few moments the door groans open and I hear marching footsteps. There's an *actual* gang of biker-looking men in the room now. All of them stand at the edge of the light. One of them steps forward. It's the shorter Mullet-man from my apartment. "Hey, witch boy. Let's talk."

"What do you want?" I can be some hero another day. Whatever this guy wants, I'll give to him.

One of the goons hands him a chair. He flips it around and sits across from me, like we're school friends chatting in detention. "We're hoping you could give your brother a call and get him down here."

I groan and roll my eyes but end up rolling my whole head instead. The soreness in my temple makes me groan even more. "You want my brother?"

"Yeah, Junior. Give him a ring, will you? We saw him with you this morning."

"Wh-what?" The edges of my vision are starting to go black again.

He grabs my face, the cold metal of his rings helping me stay lucid. "You can pass out again if you want, buddy. We'll wait. This isn't the Four Seasons though."

I do my best to speak past my stupefied state, Mullet forcing me to look right at him. "You'll let me go if I get Junior here?"

Mullet shoots me a wolfish grin. "Exactly."

My life for my brother's? Sounds like a fair trade to me. Maybe these guys weren't even going to kill him. But if they did it wouldn't be much of a loss. "Yeah... yeah I'll call him."

"Good." Mullet lets go of my face. Without the support, my head falls forward, the sudden strain on my neck making my vision double. Mullet pulls an old flip phone out of his back pocket and begins dialing. I watch him press the speakerphone button before holding the phone up to my face.

It rings once. Twice. "Hello?" The bored voice of my brother comes through the phone.

"Junior?" I speak with obvious terror.

"Lance? Who gave you this number?".

Wow, off to a great start. "Listen, I need your help—" I plead.

"Does this involve a certain government organization?"

"No, but listen—"

The line goes dead.

I can see the muscles in Mullet's face tense. I worry he might smash the phone into the side of my head but instead he presses redial. Junior picks up faster this time. "Junior seriously!" I manage to shout despite my pounding head. "These guys—this gang, Blood Moon—want you to come otherwise—"

The line goes dead again.

Then, silence. Like we're all waiting for the damn laugh track, only for the silence to be broken by a dry chuckle. I recognize the other man from my apartment, that beast of a man with a proper mane to match. "You idiot," he mutters. I'm sure if he's talking to me or his buddy. When I turn my attention back to Mullet, he's literally baring his teeth at me. I tense, but Mullet turns to his bigger friend.

He moves fast despite his height. Within a blink of an eye, he's standing in front of his friend, reaching up as if to grab him by the hair. Mullet yanks the large man down to his level and he lets out an anguished grunt. "Listen to me loud and clear, Malcolm." Mullet tosses something aside, the object skidding towards me. "I DON'T WANT TO FUCKING HEAR SHIT FROM YOU!" I looked at the object, an ear, still bleeding, lay on the ground in front of me.

I gag, bile bubbling up my throat. I shut my eyes tight as I swallow my puke down, regretting that shot of spiced rum. The burn is not at all good the second time around. I can't stop myself from looking back at the men. The big guy, Malcolm, must be his name, is holding the side of his head. His face is curled in pain, but he remains silent. Meanwhile, Mullet is still fuming, huffing so hard his whole body moves.

One of the other goons attempts to soothe their leader.

"Boss, it's alright. Come morning, we'll just send a scout to tell the le Fays our demands."

That appears to settle Mullet, their unlikely leader. I don't know why I assumed he couldn't be the head of a biker gang. Maybe it's the height or the 8os fashion choices. He looks young too, maybe a few years younger than me. I don't know much about The Blood Moon Pack, just that they've been around longer than I've been alive, and obviously they're werewolves. I know wolves age slower than mortals— slower than us witches too. But I'm still pretty sure this little guy wasn't a founding member.

Mullet breathes. "Yeah... Yeah, that'll be fine." He turns to me, his back still hunched over in rage. "Give me a bit of time to decide what piece of this *witch* we're gonna give as an offering."

How original.

And unnecessary.

My brother isn't going to shed a tear over my pinky toe. "Until then. Do what you want with him." Mullet finally stands up to his full, underwhelming height. "I encourage you all to play with your food."

My heart skips a beat. My Father taught us that in the hands of abductors, we were basically cargo, and it was in their best interest to keep us in good condition. But that was when we were literal children. Now, here I am, a dozen eyes looking at me like meat on a hook. I know none of them care that I'm a man. I can't fight back. And if I do, they have every excuse to beat me. That's what they want. Violence and a helpless victim.

Mullet leaves without another word. Malcolm leaves as well, muttering something under his breath, still holding the side of his head. The other men chuckle amongst themselves. Some of them get closer to the light but don't step into it, remaining in the shadows. I should have stayed with Taylor. Or with Daphne. Hell—I could have called Jason, but if these guys nabbed me at my apartment, they would have hurt him too.

The men circle me for some time before one of them laughs. "Dodger, you've been watching this guy the longest." I see one of the men clap the bald man who was guarding me on the shoulder. Maybe if I time it right, I can puke all over his cue ball head. The rest of the men file out till it's just me and baldy. I wish I had some quips, some last words of dignity before it happens. Whatever *it* is. But my mind is blank. I lean into that emptiness, wondering if I just retreat into myself if I'll remember any of this later. If I'll feel anything if I refuse to acknowledge it's happening. I shut my eyes and imagine the deck of tarot on my kitchen counter, drawing a card one by one and admiring the familiar illustrations.

The Hermit, a hooded man guided by lantern light.

The Magician, a young figure holding a candle aloft their head

Death, who rides a pale horse.

The Knight of Swords, another pale horse, but this one valiant, with a handsome hero.

A soft voice pulls me from my mediation. "Hey..." It's not the voice I expect to hear from my captor. I open my eyes to a familiar deep blue. "Are you hurt?" Reagan asks.

CHAPTER ELEVEN

When I leave the bar, I notice a new bunch of motorbikes parked on the edge of the property. The bikers don't seem all that interested in me, the four of them with their backs to the building smoking cigarettes. I walk past them, trying to see if I recognize any symbols or colors of local gangs. The only matching patch across the four men is a black wolf with blood dripping out of its maw and the words *sanguis lunae* written underneath. I get too close and end up bumping my shoulder into one of the men.

"Sorry," I say to a guy with dark hair blocking half of his face. He says nothing.

Unlike his short friend, who pipes up with, "Got a problem?" His hair has more curl to it, but it's the same dark black as the guy I bumped into.

"Just curious about the bikes." With a shrug, I move on, relieved when none of them follow me. Especially when I just settle into an alleyway across the way, giving me a good vantage point to watch the bar doors. I watch Lance walk out of the One Eye Dog. Alone. I should run over and offer to get him a cab or something, but I stay put watching him walk away. Just then, the four bikers scatter. Two bikes go one way while another bike with a sidecar heads in the other direction up the same street as Lance.

Shit. I can't shake the feeling that this isn't a coincidence. I follow the bike with the side car best I can, but I'm useless on foot. I'm ready to give up and head back to the hotel with my tail between my legs when I spot them again, this time heading west out of town. This time with an additional person in tow.

The bikes halt at a stop light giving me the chance to really look the three over. Based solely on size, I can tell the man who covers his face is sitting on the back of the bike, holding onto its driver. A slumped over figure wearing a bike helmet sits in the side car. The slumped figure slides further down into the seat. The big guy on the back of the bike grabs the figure by the collar and pulls them upright like something out of an old comedy skit.

I should call someone. Whoever that passed out person is, they're in danger. I have no way to tell who they are with that helmet on. I tell myself there's no way it's Lance under there, but then I check the street signs. Just five blocks ahead is the back of Lance's building. I scoped the place out weeks ago, trying to find all the easy exit and entry points. The back was definitely lacking in security, the door always being opened for cleaning and maintenance staff.

Looking right into the black visor of the motorcycle helmet, I just know it's Lance under there. The light changes and the bikes drive off, leaving the smell of gasoline in their wake. I stop pretending that all of this is for the case. Lance is being abducted, and I can't let that happen, not because he's an asset, but because he deserves better. Even if not-being-abducted-by-motorcyclist is a pretty low bar.

I hail a taxi and tell the guy to take me west to the

outskirts of the city. He tells me there's nothing out there but abandoned warehouses and factories. Exactly what I'm looking for. It takes about half an hour for us to get to the edge of the city, but I don't let him drive a block past city limits. I pay him, tip well, and tell him to stay safe, hoping some of that good karma helps me out tonight.

Thankfully these bikers are idiots and they leave their bikes out in front of a warehouse. The building has a very worn manufacturing logo on the side, but I doubt this place has been used for any legit business in years. Right now, I just need to find a way in. Hopefully one that's close to wherever Lance is being kept. I've got no idea what I'm walking into. It could be a damn maze in there or a completely open room with everyone watching Lance squirm.

Who even are these guys? *Sanguis lunae.* I'm shit at Latin, but spend enough time in the military, heard enough catchy little phrases, and you pick up a few things. *Lunae* is obviously the moon. *Sanguis* is blood. Blood Moon. I don't know of any gangs that use the moon as a calling card.

I fucking hate not knowing what I'm walking into.

I find a dumpster situated under a window and climb on top of it. I catch my first real stroke of luck. The window is right over Lance, who appears to be tied up in a chair. It's just him and one other guy. Perfect. I slide my fingers along the bottom of the window, finding a bit of give. When I look back inside, I see more men fill the room. I tug the window open and hope their footfalls cover the sound. I consider jumping down right now, but there's no real cover down below. I lay in wait, holding my breath as I watch the men surround Lance. I can hear snippets of the conversation. The short man with a dark mullet from the outside bar does most of the talking. If Lance is talking, I can't hear him. I hear cursing. I hear the le Fay name spoken. These guys know about the le Fay, but I don't know who the hell they are?

The men file back out of the room. Now is my chance. I hop down, my feet hitting the concrete with a thud. The bald man playing guard locks eyes with me. I race over and clothesline him with my elbow, catching him before he hits the ground. I wrap my arm around his neck and hold him against my chest. The bald guy sputters and tries to catch his breath, but his eyes are starting to roll back. He goes limp, but I hold onto him a few more moments to make sure he's really passed out. Once I'm satisfied, I set him down on the ground and finally go to Lance.

"Hey..." I breathe. "Are you hurt?"

I can see a bruise on the side of Lance's head. His eyes look hazy, and I worry he's got a concussion. But then his eyes focus on me. He speaks in a raised voice, "Why did you—"

I panic and cover his mouth with my hand. "Hey, shh, seriously, come on." Still covering his mouth, I get down on my knees and start inspecting the rope tied around his legs. "I know you're pissed to see me," I whisper. "But I promise I'm just here to get you out."

I look up at him. He looks annoyed but nowhere near as upset as he was back at the bar. So, we're making some sort of progress. I take my hand off of his mouth and start untying the knots around his ankle.

"I don't appreciate you stalking me," he hisses, his green eyes really emphasizing his contempt.

"I—okay, I'm sorry I'm following you, but is this really the time to get into that?"

There is a sharp inhale and I'm ready to cover his

mouth again, but Lance stops himself with a huff. "Okay... Let's just get out of here?" he murmurs.

I nod and untie the ropes around his legs, then shift ones around his wrist. "Okay, we have to find an exit."

"We don't have an exit?"

"Not unless you can get us fifteen feet up to that window I jumped through."

"Do you have a gun?"

"No," I tell him. Finally finished with the ropes, I take his wrists and rub them to make sure blood flows evenly back into his fingers.

Despite the gesture, Lance sounds annoyed. "You didn't bring a gun?" A thick brow meets his hairline. "What kind of agent are you?"

"The kind who disobeys orders and stalks a mark even though my boss told me not to." I grab his wrist and drag Lance out of the chair. I start looking for an exit besides the main door the gang has been using. Lance is silent. I look back at him. His heart shaped lips are agape, and his eyes are fixed on me like I'm a statue that's just come to life. "What?" I ask, afraid he has some injury he's just now feeling.

His voice is so gentle it makes my heart break. "I'm confused."

"I'll explain later—"

"I'm not confused about why you're here," he tells me. His eyes fall to our hands, mine still wrapped around his wrist. He pulls his hand ever so slightly back and I let him, thinking he's pulling away. His hand slides into my palm instead. I give his hand a squeeze, hoping to ground him. "I don't know if I should kiss you or punch you..." Lance says, barely a whisper.

I know now isn't the time, but I grin. "When we get out

of here, you can do both." I'm pleased when he doesn't glower at me.

I find a door and open it, cursing under my breath as I see it's just a storage closet. "Maybe the window is our best bet..." I think aloud. The room is so quiet I hear the clicking of pins from the main door. In a moment of panic, I pull Lance to me, and he collides into my chest. "Sorry," I tell him before shoving him into the closet and shutting it.

I race over to the passed out bald man and grab... well there's no hair to grab, so my hand sort of just rests atop his head while I shove his face into the cement. I put my knee onto his back. "Tell me where he is," I shout in a gruff voice. Heavy footfalls fill the room, and two guys pull me off baldy.

"What the hell?" A voice shouts.

Another voice calls out. "Boss! Dom!"

I don't try too hard to fight back, instead watching the door as the Mullet man walks into the room. His eyes grow wide when he sees the empty chair in the center of the room. Then he looks at me. "Did that witch fucking dissolve? Where is he?" I can tell the question is aimed at everyone in the room, not just me.

"That's what I want to know," I lied. "I've been tailing that guy for weeks now, so where did you put him?"

Mullet man, the boss—Dom—starts pacing back and forth, rubbing his chin, his fingers heavy with iron rings decorated with engraved skulls and wolves. "No, no, no, this doesn't make sense..." I hear him mumble. "How'd he get out? How the *fuck* did he get out?"

"Boss," one of the guys calls, nodding at the window I just entered from.

Dom looks up, makes a note of it, then looks back at his men. "Good eye there, Boone. Now answer me this: did the witch sneak in a broom up his ass?!" He gestures wildly at the window "HOW THE FUCK HE FLY FIFTEEN FEET INTO THE AIR?!"

That's the second time this guy has called Lance a witch. Witches. Wolves. Moons. I feel like I'm in a teenage soap opera, one my little sister watches and explains five seasons worth of love triangles and plot twists to me. I swear I try to listen because I'm a good brother, but it's all a bit much. Maybe I should have listened closer and gotten a few tips since I've gotten myself stuck in melodrama.

"I'll help you find him," I tell Dom.

"Oh, how charitable. I'm guessing for your services you want us to let you walk away with him too?" He approaches me, his brows knit closer and closer together with each step he takes. "Or maybe... *you* let him go? Just to *fuck* with me?"

I speak the truth for the first time. "I don't know you."

He laughs. "Where are my manners? I'm Dominic. This is my pack." He grabs the hair at the back of my head and pulls. I feel his nails scrape my scalp but they're much sharper than any nails I've felt before. "And I'm about to ruin your fucking life. No hard feelings."

CHAPTER TWELVE

LANCE

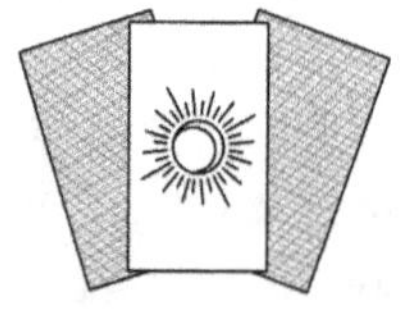

I TOLD MYSELF NOTHING WOULD EVER MAKE ME GO back into the closet again. Granted, my closet had always been made of frosted glass, but there were still a few years I told everyone I was straight. Now Reagan's shoving me into a broom closet. How ironic. "Reagan—" I hiss before he shuts me in. I grab the door handle but the sound of shouting from outside makes me pause. We're too late. The gang will find Reagan, see that I'm no longer tied up, and eventually open up this closet. Then I'll probably miss the 'punishment' I had been promised.

Maybe if I'm lucky, they'll just kill me. Or they'll try to turn me.

I know the transformation process isn't pretty. A bite from a werewolf might as well be a kiss of death. Plenty of people just die from it, while those that survive the virus live the rest of their lives tethered to the moon cycle. I'm not sure who wins in that situation, but I'm not the one in a room full of werewolves. Reagan is. Reagan, who thinks my Father's obsession with the occult is just eccentric. He's got no idea the danger he's in. If he's bitten, he might just try to walk it off like some big tough, dumb man.

I might be pissed at him, but I don't want him dead. I don't want his humanity stripped away. With everything he's put me through the past two days, I should at least get to be the one to kill him. But if I leave this closet, I'll just be taken hostage again. I start looking at the stored supplies.

Witches are nothing without tools, without some sort of conductor. There are several materials that can be used as a conductor: pure and precious metals, herbs, cards, crystal balls, bones... All those things aren't for theatrics. We need at least two conductors to tap into the magic around us. Wands are an easy conductor to create but also the most obvious. At this point, though, I don't need to be subtle. Not for Reagan's sake.

I find some wire and take a quick lick before I can consider where all it's been. The taste is obviously copper. No idea if it's pure or not, which will throw some things off, but it's something. Copper is an excellent conductor and amplifies other magic. I find a dust brush and start wrapping the wire around the handle. It's going to be the ugliest wand known to man, but it's better than nothing. Now, if only someone had dropped some quartz in here.

I remember the rings on Mullet's hand. They looked to be made of iron. Silver is a touchy sort of metal when it comes to lycans and vampires. Silver protects against supernatural beings, so wearing silver dampens a wolf's power. Iron doesn't have that sort of side effect, but it's still a protective metal. One used more to defend against fae and other witches, but it should work especially with the copper I already have.

I exit the closet before I can convince myself to do

anything else. I see Reagan's arms pulled behind his back, two goons with their backs to me holding him down. I step out just in time to see Mullet lean down like he's about to kiss Reagan's neck. I know better. I rush over, just managing to slip past the two goons and grabbing their boss by the shoulder.

"There you are," he growls. I grab at his hand, somehow managing to wrap my fingers around the grooves of a ring with a carved wolf face. Mullet pulls his hand back, and the ring slips off his finger and into my palm. There isn't a moment to celebrate before he backhands me across the face. He slaps the same side of my head that he slammed into my kitchen counter. I fall to the ground, clutching the ring and my makeshift wand.

"You are such a little bitch!" He yells at me like we're sisters and I just borrowed his shirt without asking. I lift my head off the ground, ears ringing. That doesn't stop me from sliding the ring onto the handle of the dust brush.

But I'm not fast enough.

Mullet doesn't hesitate, forgetting about Reagan's neck. He grabs Reagan's elbow and pulls his arm out from his goon's grip. Mullet brings Reagan's arm to his mouth. I watch in horror as Mullet's back arches and his eyes start to glow, like a dog's in the nighttime. I see now that his nails are razor sharp points—proper claws. The hair on his head grows longer and thicker, including the stubble on his chin and cheeks.

He bites down, and there is a squelching of blood before Reagan screams.

Reagan pulls his arm back, his flesh tearing, leaving behind a good chunk in the mouth of Mullet— now a far cry from being human. Mullet smiles, his teeth cherry red with blood. Even with the horror show, I can see his mouth struggle to hold his elongated canines. Every tooth is pointed at the end, the mouth of a carnivore.

It's not too late. I slam the butt end of my makeshift wand into the concrete floor, the stone chipping and cracking. The impact creates a wave of force out from me. All the gang members fly backwards—Reagan included, his body rolling away as if he were going down a hill. Several gang members hit the walls of the room, the others lose momentum and land in a heap on the floor. I sit up and see Reagan is just a few yards away, groaning on the floor as he starts to bleed out.

I crawl to him, desperate. "Reagan," I choke. "Reagan." I force myself to my feet. Thankfully he's closer to me than the rest of the men. I reach his side and see his eyes are only half open, his eyelids heavy. "Stay with me," I tell him. I grab the bottom of his shirt and rip the fabric horizontally trying to create a makeshift bandage.

As I'm tying the fabric tight around the bite on his forearm, Reagan's head slumps sideways. "Lance..." he mutters. I look over my shoulder. Mullet is starting to stand back up, his teeth still sharp and skin still hairy. I pause our game of doctor to wrap my arm around Reagan's waist. I slam the base of the wand against the concrete again, sending out another wave of force. This time Reagan is close enough to me that he's unaffected. Mullet and any of his other goons who have managed to regain their footing are pushed back, rolling away from us.

I decide I don't have time to patch up Reagan. "Come on!" I shout desperately before taking his wounded arm and wrapping it around my neck, keeping it elevated. I stand up and realize Reagan is too heavy for me to carry on my own. I groan, "Use your feet, agent!"

"Don't..." Reagan doesn't finish his thought as he starts shuffling his feet towards the only obvious exit.

"Don't what?" I ask him, trying to keep him conscious.

"Don't... call me that..."

"Oh, sorry, do you prefer Adam? Mr. President?" We make it to the door and exit the concrete room, not that this hallway is any more cozy. I can see another door at the very end of the hallway. Hopefully one that leads to the outside. Where we'll go from there, I have no idea.

Reagan still manages to speak. "You're trying...to piss me off..."

"And if I am? What are you going to do about it? Bleed on me?"

To my surprise, Reagan chuckles. "You're something else..."

We're maybe five steps away from the door when out of nowhere the big guy who I watched get his ear ripped off reappears between us and the exit. I look up, seeing he's attached some gauze to the side of his ear with medical tape. Up close and in proper light, I can see past the hair that blocks his face. Pale raised skin cakes the side of his face like spiderwebs reaching for the healthy, unharmed skin on the opposite side. If he wasn't intimidating before, he sure is now.

"Please," my voice shakes like a leaf in the wind. "Let us go..." I still cling to the dust brush, but with him standing so close to us, I'm not sure if the spell would hit all of us or none of us. "If you want my brother—"

"Fuck off." He says before pushing past me. "We'll be seeing your friend soon enough."

My blood goes cold. Meanwhile, Reagan's hot blood is starting to drip down my neck, having soaked completely through the borrowed blouse I'm wearing. The big man is right. Either Reagan will die, or he'll be turned.

And I have no clue which fate is worse.

CHAPTER THIRTEEN

LANCE

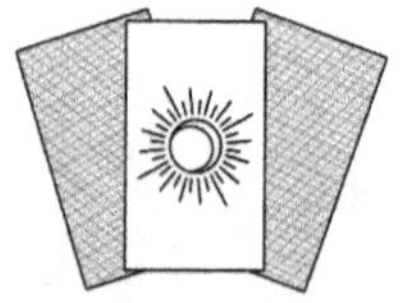

I drag Reagan through the alleyways between warehouses. I know we can only get so far. Not only is Reagan losing blood, but I'm losing stamina, adrenaline not enough to carry around a man a head taller than me with a good fifty pounds worth of muscle. I stumble over a raised crack in the asphalt, almost sending us both falling face first into the ground. That was enough to shut off my fight or flight and just default to flail. I bend my knees and manage to lower Reagan onto the ground.

I kneel down beside him, holding his face in my hands. "Reagan," I hiss.

He groans back, letting me know he's still conscious but not at all in a state to speak. I know I have nothing on me we could use to get help. I grab Reagan's shoulder and turn him on his side. Both his back pockets are full. I grab his phone and swear I hear Reagan let out a weak chuckle as if he's amused I touched his ass. "I ought to smack you," I grumble. Maybe it was the lack of blood reaching his brain that made him act immature. He just manages another weak laugh. I remember that any sound leaving his lips is better than silence.

I dial Taylor's number, one of the few I have memorized. He picks up almost immediately. "Taylor— shit, okay—"

I give him all the info I can manage to string together. He assures me he's on his way, and to look out for a white van with blackout windows. Taylor stays on the line with me, but I don't have much to say. Not to mention I'm afraid if I talk too much, a stray gang member might find us. I just sit next to Reagan, clutching his phone in one hand and his wound in the other.

I looked at his ass—not to check him out, but curious about his other full pocket. It's wrong to snoop, but Reagan has never given me that courtesy, so why would I? I set down the phone and pull a worn leather wallet from his pocket. If Reagan notices, he doesn't say anything, his breathing labored but steady. I don't check the contents of the wallet. Not now. I hide it in my back pocket.

Soon, there are headlights in the mouth of the alley. I speak into the phone. "Taylor?" A van stops in front of the alley entrance. The side door swings open, and Taylor hops out, running to meet me.

"Lance! Are you—"

"Reagan is hurt." I stress.

Taylor wraps Reagan's arm around his shoulder and hoists him off the ground. "We'll take a look at it in the van. Sara knows these streets better than me, anyway. She'll get us out of here." In a flash, we're in the back of the van. Taylor lays Reagan down in a seat, parking himself in the walkway between the van seats. "Sara, I need you to head north."

"You really want to bring them all the way out there?"

"I didn't even tell you where we're going?" Taylor bites back like a boss who's just been questioned by a subordinate.

Sara starts driving the car faster than I would be comfortable with if we weren't literally running for our lives. "You want to send them up to the campground? Why? So that idiot," she nods back to Reagan, "can sweat and convulse in the beauty of nature?"

Taylor doesn't look away from Reagan's injuries but lobs a stern voice at Sara. "He's going to have to head up north soon enough."

It feels like they're talking about sending Reagan up to the 'farm.'

I look at Taylor. "Isn't there some place closer? Don't you guys have a safe house?"

"It's not really safe for you two in the city, now is it? You have two gangs on your tail, Lance. You need to get out."

Sara glared back at us through the rearview mirror. "I hate to say it, but Taylor has a point. You're pretty popular."

I glare at Sara via the rearview mirror. Except one of the gangs is my family, so they don't count, and Reagan needs to be in a bed, not jostled in the back of a van. "Please, just take us to the safe house."

"Not my call. I don't know where it is." Sara keeps her eyes on the road. We'll hit the highway soon, and Sara needs to know which route to take.

I look at Taylor. "*Please.*" Taylor's lips form a hard line as he shakes his big square head. "If you take us up north, will you stay? Will anyone be there to help?" I grab Taylor's shoulder, giving it a squeeze. "I don't think I can do this alone."

He looks at my hand atop his shoulder. I look too and realize it's covered in dried blood. I'd completely forgotten about in the dark, but as we drive, the street lights blink in and out, illuminating the crusted, almost blackened blood. Finally, Taylor speaks in a solemn tone. "Take us west down by Riverside. Just spitting distance of the border."

AT SOME POINT during the drive, Taylor and I switch spots, me now hunched on the floor next to Reagan while Taylor sits and gives directions to Sara. I can tell it's killing him to not be in control of the vehicle, his hand clutching the front passenger seat. It doesn't help that Sara claims she knows a better route to the waterfront. Their bickering is distant, my focus solely on Reagan and his injuries. I tug at his makeshift tourniquet to find that the bleeding has stopped. I'm relieved that I don't have to worry about him bleeding out, but his eyes are still half lidded and I notice his face is slick with sweat.

The transformation is already starting.

We arrive at a duplex right where Taylor said it would be, where the lake meets the river, maybe a fifteen-minute drive to the Canadian border. Sara skids the van to a halt in the driveway, and Taylor jumps out the van like an action star. It's a touch tampered by him just running up to punch the code on the garage. Sara pulls the van in and hops out just as fast.

The door to Reagan's side slides open and Sara reaches for him. "Careful," I tell her, but she doesn't hesitate to princess carry Reagan out of the car. I blink. I haven't forgotten that Sara's a werewolf, but her petite frame carrying Reagan is still a sight to behold. I follow everyone, Taylor leading us inside to a downstairs bedroom. Sara lays

Reagan on the bed, then starts to undo the tourniquet on his arm.

I grab her hand. "Stop."

Sara looks at me. I expect her signature glare, but instead she just has a face like I've handed her an obviously fake ID. "Seriously, mother hen?" I drop her hand. "I want to see how it's healing." She goes back to undoing the dressing. I know Reagan has stopped bleeding, but still I don't want her touching him.

I see Reagan's wound for the first time in proper lighting and without oozing blood. I cover my mouth with my hand. Deep puncture wounds dot his arm, the edges bruising purple. A lot of the surrounding skin is shredded with some strips of flesh just missing and leaving indentations. I recall the hunks of flesh hanging in Mullet's maw, and my stomach churns.

Taylor walks into the room with a bowl of water and a towel, his hands already covered with latex gloves. Without a word, he starts blotting the injury. Reagan groans. Then groans some more, until his lips start to actually move. "Stop..." he breaths. "Stop," he speaks again, pleading now. "*Stop—*" I see Taylor wince, but he doesn't let up his caretaking.

"Stop!" Reagan howls like a dog cornered in an alleyway.

"Reagan, he's helping," I assure him.

"Fuck!" he snaps at me, shutting his eyes tight with pain.

"Ignore him," Taylor says in an even tone. "Rage is part of the change." He continues to work as he speaks. "Go shower... please." He clearly just needs me out of the room, but a warm shower can't hurt anything. "There are clothes upstairs," he tells me as I exit the room. "We'll need some for Reagan as well."

"You're not stripping my ass!" Reagan objects, but Taylor ignores him.

"Go," Sara tells me with a curt nod as she moves to hold Reagan down by his shoulders. "I doubt you'll want to see this temper tantrum."

I don't want to leave Reagan, but the sight of his wound is enough to have me fleeing the room. His blood caked over half my body isn't helping either. Still, I run back to the bed and give Reagan's calf a squeeze. "I'll be back," I tell him. He says nothing, which is perhaps the only kindness he can manage right now.

I go upstairs and find the other bed and bath with no problem. I turn on the shower and let it run hot before even attempting to get in. I've scrubbed blood off my skin before. Hot water is best. As I strip off my clothes, I find Reagan's wallet in my pocket. I'd almost forgotten about it. Holding the soft leather between my bloody fingers, I ask myself if I really want to open it.

At minimum it would have... what exactly? Credit cards and an ID? I guess it's possible Reagan is still lying about this name— though Reagan Rooney is one hell of a pseudonym. At most, it might have some revelation. A business card, club card, something that will let me see more of who this guy really is. I shake my head. Reagan and I have been through too much these past two days for him to be *some guy*. For better or worse, we're stuck together.

Trauma bonding at its finest.

I open the wallet and find what one would expect. Reagan's DC license confirming that Reagan Rooney is indeed his legal name, and that he's a Taurus. An April

Taurus, specifically. I pull out some of the cards. Two bank cards, a loyalty card to some store I've never heard of, and a punch card from Marble Ax with one hole in it. Six more and he'll get a free drink. I always forget about these things. The last thing in the wallet is a photo. And that's when my heart sinks, the way one's heart falters at the end of a tragedy. Just because everyone saw it coming doesn't make it hurt less. Why else had I taken his wallet, if not to validate my suspicion?

The photo is of him dressed in a tux, cheek to cheek with a blonde woman in a wedding dress. They look happy. Of fucking course they looked happy. I'd probably be smiling as much as her if I had trapped a hunk like Reagan in holy matrimony. I slam the photo onto the bathroom counter, noticing a muddy smudge at the edge of the photo where my grubby fingers handled the film.

I need to shower to clear my head. The hot water runs over my face, and I feel my whole body turn hot. So what if Reagan is married? I knew he just slept with me to get intel. He probably followed me to the warehouse for intel too. Unfortunately, none of it was worth it. He might have made me scream, but at the end of the day, I'm the person fucking him over. I scrub away the blood until my skin is red, raw, and tender. I force myself to shed a layer of skin, as if washing it all down the drain will change anything.

CHAPTER FOURTEEN

LANCE

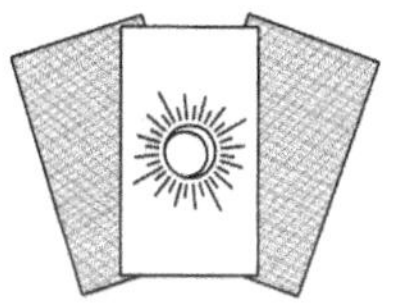

I FIND SPARE CLOTHES IN THE BEDROOM CLOSET LIKE Taylor said. It's all shirts and sweatpants, things that can adjust to any body size. I grab myself a medium shirt and pants, then a large for Reagan. I change into my new clothes and return downstairs into the bedroom. Sara and Taylor are in the kitchen, speaking to each other in soft voices. We ignore each other as I scurry to the bedroom.

Reagan is still in bed with his shirt stripped from his body. I decide to free him from the jeans and belt he's wearing and slip on the clean clothes. Reagan huffs but says nothing, his eyes closed despite clearly being awake. Once I've managed to slide the pants onto his body, I move on to his chest. "Hey," I whisper. "Can you uh... sit up?"

"No idea..." he grumbles. I guess he doesn't really need a shirt anyway.

I pull up a chair and just watch him. His breathing isn't as labored as it had been in the car, but he's still sweating, his face and chest flushed. I push some of his hair off his sweat-drenched forehead. Sara and Taylor return to the room, serious expressions on both their faces.

"Here's what's going to happen," Taylor says, crossing his arms over his broad chest. "Both of you need to stay here for the time being. Don't leave the house for anything. Use the landline to call me for anything you need." I nod in agreement. I don't think Reagan is even in a state to leave the bed, let alone the house. "Lance," Taylor says in a voice that makes me feel like I've done something wrong. "That includes the phone you used to call me."

"Oh, right," I say, feeling stupid. I take Reagan's phone from my pocket and hand it over. It wasn't my phone to give away, but if Reagan got a hold of it, he might call the damn Coast Guard on us.

"Alright, now that we have that settled," Taylor says, slipping the phone into his back pocket. "The change will take a few days. As the virus infects his entire body, he'll have flu-like symptoms. Then, his body will have to adjust to the change itself."

I raise a brow. "Adjust? What do you mean?"

"Think of it like a second puberty."

Sara makes a sound, half a chuckle, half a scoff. "I was a rage monster after I turned. Broke a bathroom sink with my bare hands."

I'm the reason he's gotten bit. Will that rage transfer to me? When he's finally able to sit up, will he just strangle me?

Taylor clears his throat. "The pituitary gland will grow and begin to produce more... everything. Sara felt rage, but Reagan might feel invincible, depressed, or uh..." Taylor rubs the back of his neck.

"Horny," Sara elaborates on Taylor's behalf.

Taylor clears his throat, "Right, thank you, Sara." I swear I see crimson rising to his cheeks. Sara rolls her eyes as Taylor continues. "Just make sure he takes it easy when his fever breaks. He might feel fine, but his body is still changing. Not to mention the full moon is in nine days."

"Okay, slow down," I tell them. Sara finds a new way of looking annoyed while Taylor looks bereft. Which he has no right to. It's not his *fault* this is happening. "Does Reagan even understand what's going on?" I turn to him and realize he's finally fallen asleep, breathing deep and slow. "What about his bite?"

"That'll heal on its own," Sara informs me. "But it won't be pretty." She pulls down the neckline of her shirt to reveal her left shoulder; a valley of raised pale skin taut against her bones. Scar tissue looks like spiderwebs to me, layers and layers holding together what little flesh remained. Despite her horrific scar, I want to look at it more. To find the punctures left behind by wolf teeth like I saw on Reagan's injury. But understandably, Sara is rather quick to cover back up.

I purse my lips. "But it's going to get better, right?"

"Lance." Taylor speaks my name like it's weighed down with cinder blocks. "Reagan might still die. If his heart or brain can't take the virus—"

"Hell, even his kidneys," Sara interjects. "Or his stomach. Organ failure is a bitch, I hear."

"I just want you to be prepared for that," Taylor tells me.

I just stare at them, my mouth partially agape. "*Prepared* for *that*?" My voice is a broken whisper. "How in the hell am I supposed to prepare for a man dying? How am I supposed to accept that he might just die and there's nothing I can do?" Neither of them offers me an answer. I look at Sara. "You survived. How?"

"Luck," she says without hesitation.

"Bullshit."

"If I had advice, I'd give it to you."

Taylor clears his throat a second time. "Sara will also give you her number in case you have any questions." Sara glares at him and he looks back with a smile on his face and a plea in his eyes. "After all, she knows how hard this all is."

Sara lets out a little growl from the back of her throat, but then she turns to me and confirms Taylor's words. "I'll give you my number. Call whenever, but I'm pretty busy at night."

I nod. "Thank you." Sara isn't someone I would want to go to with my problems, but I need her snarky guidance right now. For Reagan's sake.

THE FIRST DAY at the safe house is boring. Taylor comes by in the morning with groceries and asks if there was anything he missed. It's a pretty solid array of food, but I do have one request. "Cinnamon." After that, it's just me in the house.

Reagan has been dead asleep since last night. Throughout the day, I check on him, apply a cold compress to his head, measure his temperature, and even force myself to change the bandages on his bite wound. Sara said it would heal on its own, but I'm paranoid. The wound still looks awful. but the swelling has gone down.

I just want to be able to do more for him. I spend the rest of the day watching crap TV, which ends up being a bit of a minefield. *Real Housewives* reminds me too much of my childhood with all the shouting and money. Cop shows are also hitting a bit too close to home. Eventually I find a cooking channel and settle. I never make myself a proper meal, just snacking on the crackers and fruit Taylor brought.

Despite having nothing to do, I'm up long past the sun.

All the windows in the house are frosted for privacy, but I find myself trying to take a peek up at the moon. The crescent sliver of darkness is now ominous. When I finally am ready for bed, I go to check up on Reagan one last time. To my surprise, he's facing the doorway, his blue eyes open but hazy. I rush to his bedside. "Reagan? Reagan, tell me you're alive and haven't died in the creepiest way ever."

"I wish I was dead..." he groans.

Immediately I feel tears prick at my eyes like the big baby I am. "Don't say that!" Of course he wants to be dead. He's in a lot of pain and surely confused about what's happening, but I can't stand to have any more blood on my hands. "Reagan, please. I need you to live." He raises his brows and attempts to sit up but winces as soon as he's upright. I grab his shoulders and help lower him back down onto the bed.

"Why... Lance why do you need—"

"I told you. I killed someone. And I'm about to kill you too." The tears fall down my cheeks. I feel so stupid looking like this in front of Reagan.

He shakes his head. "Lance, I chose to go after you."

"You didn't know what would happen."

"I knew it was dangerous." He manages a smile, cocksure and charming despite everything. "I'm kinda drawn to danger."

It's my turn to shake my head. "Reagan, you still might die. In bed. Wearing sweatpants. It's not exactly going out in an explosion."

"I'll sweat it out."

"Reagan, do you even know what you're sick with?" His smile falters. "You're infected with lycanthropy. You're going to become a werewolf."

"That..." He blinks. "That's not..." He blinks again, this

time shutting his eyes tight like trying to wake from a dream. "That guy bit me..."

"He's a werewolf. He infected you, and now you're either going to die or become like him. And it's my fault."

He musters up all his energy. "Stop saying that."

"No," I default.

We stare at each other, two stubborn auras knocking into one another. Reagan can act like everything is okay, but blind optimism turns my insides out. Just smiling in the face of horror, like that changes anything. I reach over to cup his clammy cheek with my hand. Reagan, for his part, leans into my touch. We sit like that for some time, my thumb lazily running along his stubble-covered cheek while he looks at me with sleepy blue eyes.

"Sleep with me," he commands in a low rumbling tone. "I don't want to be alone."

"You're not in the state for—" I stop mid-sentence, realizing he just wants me to rest in bed with him. "Oh... Yes, of course." I get up and slip into the bed from the other side so his back is pressed against my chest. I lay on my side and let my arm rest on his chest with my hand on his heart.

He chuckles, his body shaking. "You thought I wanted to get laid? In this state?"

I shrug. "It would be a nice distraction?"

Reagan hums, "This is enough of a distraction..."

I feel his chest rise and fall as he drifts back to sleep. I rest my head on his shoulder for some time, knowing that if I left now and slept in my own bed, Reagan would have no idea. He'll probably sleep like death again tomorrow. But I don't want to leave. Despite the bed being drenched in sweat and Reagan radiating heat, I don't want to leave. Eventually I uncouple myself from Reagan and turn onto my own pillow, falling asleep faster than I thought possible.

REAGAN IS STILL fast asleep when the morning sun beams through the windows, little rainbows dancing across the comforter. I'm surprised I slept past six. Looking at the clock on the bedside table, it's almost 11 AM. I guess I needed to sleep off the last few days worth of stress.

I get up and walk to the kitchen to attempt my first meal. Nothing fancy. Toast, eggs, and cooked tomatoes I just leave in the pan. I add bacon last minute. I have nothing to base this on, but Reagan seems like a meat and potatoes guy. Also, werewolves probably like meat. I brew some coffee as well, which reminds me of my cinnamon request. I peer out the front door and sure enough, there's a little baggie on the stoop. I open the door just enough to swipe the bag and open it to find a bottle of cinnamon.

I plate our meals and return to the bedroom with everything on a tray. I rub Reagan's shoulder, trying to get him to wake. "Hey... I have breakfast." Reagan's eyes open and he lets out a groan. "Sorry to wake you, but you should probably have some water." He just grunts in agreement. I bring the glass of water to his lips, and he drinks, finishing the whole glass without stopping. He licks some water off his lips. I find myself licking my lips as well. "Do you want some more water?"

He shakes his head. "Did I... imagine breakfast?"

I feel the corner of my lips pull into a smirk. I grab a plate and show him the spread. "Nothing fancy."

"I hate fancy," he mumbles.

I grab a fork and start to cut up some eggs. Reagan, meanwhile, grabs the pillow from my side of the bed and uses it along with his pillow to prop himself up. I scoop some eggs up onto the fork. When I catch Reagan's eyes, he looks a little bewildered. "Are you... going to feed me?"

"Um..." I can't think of a response. It just sort of happened after I gave him water. I just bring the fork to his mouth, which he accepts, taking a bite while looking at me with knit brows.

After humoring me, he takes the fork. "I can feed myself, I promise." He takes the plate from me and lays it on his lap before going in on the bacon. Just one bite and he moans with content. "You're sweet," he talks with food still in his mouth. I begin to eat as well, and we both fall quiet. I don't think either of us realized how hungry we are until we have good food in our stomachs.

Setting our plates aside, I find myself lying beside him in bed again. This time Reagan has his chest facing mine, his cheek pressed against my shoulder. I run my fingers through his hair. "You need a shower," I tell him.

"That sounds nice... Standing, not so much."

I just keep running my fingernails along his scalp. Reagan breathes rhythmically, relaxing. "Are you going to fall back asleep?" I whisper, though he's already slipped back into slumber. I stay with him, my fingers interwoven with dark chestnut hair. This is better than TV for sure.

CHAPTER FIFTEEN

In my dream, there's a full moon. Only, it's bigger than it's supposed to be, taking up half the skyline like that game on the Nintendo. I keep walking towards it as if I can reach the base. As I walk, I change, becoming larger, fur growing out of every pore, my nails cracking my cuticles as they expand and become pointed. My gums fail to accommodate new canine teeth so large I have to keep my jaw open. Soon, I no longer feel human. I see best in the dark. Hear better too.

That's when I hear a beat like thunder. I race towards it, falling on my hands and sprinting. I fail to recognize the thunder for what it really is: my heartbeat reaching my sensitive ears. Then there's a figure in the distance. I see them before they can see me with their normal eyes. It's Lance. He's looking right at me, but he does nothing, like a doe in shock. Instinct takes over and I pounce.

And then I wake up. Blinking slowly as the room comes into view, I turn my head to see Lance sleeping peacefully beside me. I breathe a sigh of relief I didn't realize I needed. Of course he's okay. He's been the one taking care of me the past two days. Three days? How long has it been? That bartender— Sara —said it would take three days, didn't she? To be honest, I was in and out of that conversation. Not by choice. I would have loved to understand what's happening to me, to ask questions. As if answers would satisfy me.

It's impossible, the things people are saying. I go back and forth on believing their words. Everything I remember about the warehouse feels impossible as well. Just like everything surrounding the le Fay case. I just have to accept it. Witches, werewolves, the supernatural— they're all real. And I'm now one of them.

I reach out and touch Lance's cheek. He stirs and opens his eyes. "How do you feel?" he asks, still blinking sleep from his eyes.

"I think I'm ready for that shower." I'm not feeling great. and my body being sticky with day's worth of sweat isn't helping me feel any better. Not to mention I want out of this bed, even just for a few minutes.

Lance nods before he crawls out of bed, walking into the bathroom adjacent to the bedroom. I hear him turn on the shower before returning. He comes to my side and wraps his arm around my upper torso. "On three?"

I know I should take it easy, but being so feeble in front of Lance is... embarrassing, like tripping in front of your middle school crush. "Sure..." I listen to him count up to three and together we manage to lift myself out of bed. As soon as I put weight onto my legs, I'm grateful Lance is there, my joints feeling like they have a decade's worth of rust. Hopefully a hot shower will help.

We get into the bathroom, and I start undressing, glad to be able to do *something* for myself. Lance checks the closet of the bathroom and mumbles something. "What?" I ask.

"I was hoping there would be a stool or something in

here. You should probably sit. I don't want you slipping in the shower."

I sigh. Falling and bashing my head on the tile isn't a good look. "You could always shower with me." I offer, not thinking much of it.

"O-oh." I notice his cheeks are turning pink. "If you're okay with that." I just nod and he starts stripping his clothes. I watch him pull off his shirt and catch myself nibbling at the inside of my lip. Lance catches me staring. He's blushing hard now, his cheeks rosy. I'm much too warm already to tell if I'm visibly flustered, but Lance's red round cheeks are undeniably cute.

Both of us now nude, Lance takes my arm once more and helps me into the shower. The feeling of warm water splashing across my chest is a welcome one. Lance holds my hips as I let the water wash down my head and body. With one hand still holding me steady, Lance turns around to grab the body wash off the shelf built into the shower. I shamelessly check out his ass. Lance doesn't comment, either because he doesn't care or doesn't notice.

I expect him to hand me the bottle, but instead he pours the gel right into his hand and starts rubbing my shoulders. Just as he's getting into it, he pulls his hands away from my body. "Sorry— do you want me to stop?" He sounds scandalized.

I recall him feeding me eggs in bed. I'm quick to respond, "No. Could you maybe... massage my back?" Guess it's my turn to go all pink in the face, finding it hard to look Lance in the eye. His hands return to my body with a firmer touch. I sigh as he helps relieve the tension in my back. Slowly he moves down my body, rubbing suds and pressing his fingertips expertly into my muscles. "You're really good at this," I compliment him.

He's on his knees now. "It's not my first time helping another man out in the shower," he admits while rubbing my calves.

"Probably not the first time you've been in this position either."

Lance looked up at me from the floor of the shower. A grin spreads across his lips. "You must be feeling better if you're cracking jokes."

"Let's hope so."

As the water washes the suds from my body, Lance grabs shampoo. Before I can say anything, he lifts his hands to rub the shampoo into my hair. I chuckle and lean down so he doesn't have to reach so high. "I'm not that short," he mutters.

"Yeah? What are you, like 5'4?"

"*I'm* 5'8," he tells me, his thick brows furrowing and his bottom lip showing just a hint of a pout.

Fuck, that's adorable. I keep teasing him. "I was halfway right."

"Jerk..." Lance mutters as he continues to run his fingers through my hair. "Just for that I won't use conditioner."

"Please?" I request. "It feels nice, your fingers in my hair..." Lance makes a face like he's considering something. I lean down a little further to press my forehead against his. "Please?" I ask again.

We stand like that for a few moments, giving me ample opportunity to admire his deep green eyes before he finally gives in. "Fine," he agrees, then grabs the conditioner.

Once all the suds are washed from my body, we spend a little more time in the shower, letting the warm water help the soreness radiating across my frame. Eventually, Lance helps me back out of the shower. He grabs a towel and wraps it around his waist before grabbing another for me to use. I'm drying my chest when he gets back down on his knees and starts rubbing my legs with a towel. "Why don't you sit in the living room while I change your sheets?" Lance offers.

"You're really doing everything for me."

"Well, you can't really change the fitted sheet on a bed right now, can you?"

"I can barely do that when I'm well," I admit. Lance chuckles to himself as he finishes drying my legs. "But still, you are literally toweling me down right now." Lance just brings the towel to the top of my head and starts ruffling my hair.

Watching Lance play caretaker is quite the sight. After helping me into a fresh pair of sweatpants and a shirt, he parks me on the couch and rushes off to change my sheets. I know for a fact he grew up in a mansion with maids. Though I guess he's been separated from the money for so long he had to become self-sufficient. It couldn't have been easy leaving all that luxury behind. Then again, if Arthur le Fay is as ruthless a Father as he is a criminal, maybe it *was* easy to leave it all behind.

I turn on the TV and flip right to the news, curious if there's any mention of me or the incident at the warehouse. It's just business as usual in the city. A few robberies, a house fire in the early morning hours, a new city ordinance being voted on... Normal. Nothing odd or mystical at all. I already feel so distant from it. I can't help but question it, like if that fire had been, I don't know, some spell gone awry like the one Lance cast at the warehouse. If I've gone my whole life without knowing about the supernatural, what else am I oblivious to?

Lance appears behind the couch. "You want me to make us some food?" I nod and soon Lance and I are eating together on the island in the middle of the kitchen, a simple but satisfying pasta dish. I manage to stay awake for a good portion of the day. After we eat, we settle back onto the couch to watch some crap TV. Lance insists we watch a crime show with an FBI agent so I can point out all the inaccuracies. I remind him I'm still sick and that is a very mean thing to subject me to, but I play along anyway, groaning when the team finally solves the case in the last five minutes of the show. Every single time. They're doing a marathon.

At some point, I reach my arm around Lance's shoulder and instead of him moving away, he leans into me, resting his head on my upper chest. "Is my head too heavy?"

"You? Heavy?" As we watch, I run my fingers through his hair, much like how he shampooed and conditioned my hair. Sometimes I want to lean over and kiss the crown of his head. I don't, afraid of what a kiss might lead to. I don't need to seduce Lance anymore, and despite the doting, I don't feel like he's trying to seduce me. Yet here we are, cuddling on the couch.

Unfortunately, as the fifth episode is winding down, my head starts to grow heavy, my body following its lead. I insist on walking myself to the bedroom, which Lance agrees to, but he follows behind me like a puppy. I slip back into bed, happy to have some clean sheets. "Thank you, Lance."

Lance shakes his head a little. "You don't have to thank me."

"Well, I did anyway." I reach out and take his hand in mine. "If I wake up in the night, you'll be here, right? In bed?" He doesn't speak, instead just nodding his head in agreement. "Good," I tell him, nodding as well. I'm ready to roll over and fall asleep, but before I let sleep overtake me, I bring Lance's hand to my lips. I kiss his knuckles, not sure if

I want him to see it as a thank you or a plea for him to climb into bed with me right now. I just release his hand before saying. "Goodnight." I assume I'll pass out again until the next morning.

Lance's voice is soft like a lullaby. "Goodnight, Reagan."

CHAPTER SIXTEEN

LANCE

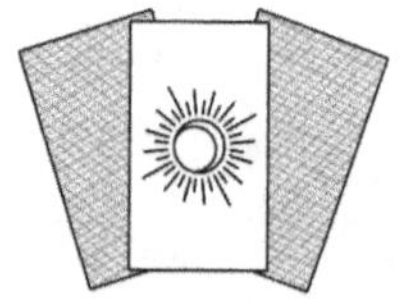

IT'S THE SECOND MORNING I WAKE UP TO REAGAN laying on his side, looking at me, which is a pretty nice way to wake up. His blue eyes sparkle in the morning sun, and there's something cute about his short but tousled bedhead. His lips curl into a smile. "Good morning…" he breathes. My heart could explode right then and there. He's looking a lot better, his eyes clear and face no longer red. It's the morning of the fourth day… Sara was right.

Before I can wallow in the fact I'll have to give Sara a very genuine thanks for her advice, Reagan brings his body closer to me. I don't know what I was expecting, but it definitely isn't his lips meeting mine. I wrap my arms around his neck, one of Reagan's hands cupping the back of my neck while the other slides over my body to reach around my waist. His hand rests on my lower back just above my ass.

Reagan pulls out of the kiss, and I whimper, not ready for this nice moment to stop. But then he pushes my hips into his own, creating a whole new moment as I feel his length press against my legs. His lips find my neck and I gasp, my body tingling all over as Reagan's lips work my neck and he pushes me against his erection. I just keep gasping for air like he's literally stealing my breath away.

Reagan releases my neck and grabs my shoulder, pushing me down so I'm flat against the mattress. He gets on top of me, looking at me with lusting eyes and a wolfish smirk. His hand teases the waistband of my sweats, dipping two fingers in and tugging. "I bet I could rip this off..." he growls. "I just keep thinking about how good you looked in the shower... naked and pale and all for me."

His hand leaves my pants and goes to his own, pulling down the sweats just enough to free his cock. His length bounces, almost hitting his stomach. He looks bigger, but maybe I'm misremembering. To be honest, I probably couldn't answer what color the bedsheets sheets are right now. Reagan leans down and presses his body against me, grinding his cock along my hips and stomach. I let out another whimper and realize Reagan didn't just look bigger, he has definitely grown a few inches since the last time we shoved our tongues down each other's throats. I guess every part of him is now werewolf sized.

Reagan grunts and growls in my ear, but I can only make out a few curses and the word, *"mine."* I'm so hard, and Reagan's thighs rub against my cock, which is barely contained by my own sweatpants. In a moment of weakness, I reach down to pull my pants past my ass. Reagan notices and shifts his body so our erections are pressed together. He starts rutting his hips again, the friction against my cock making me cry out.

"You like that?" he rumbles in my ear. Reagan's hand reaches between us, wrapping around both of our lengths before he continues to pump his hips. "I want to hear you say you like it."

"I love it," I breathe. My head rolls back onto the pillow. "I love it, Reagan."

"That's right. Tell me how much you love it." His lips are back on my neck, now sucking at the most soft and sensitive parts.

Where did this come from? Yesterday he needed me in the shower and now he's grinding against me like we're horny teenagers in the back of his Dad's truck. To my dismay, Taylor's voice echoed in my head: *there's a few days where his body will adjust to the change itself...*

Is this how Reagan shows his rage? He has plenty of reason to be pissed at me, and even as he sucks at my neck, he's growling like he might bite off my head. Then I remember hormones. Taylor said the transformation was like a second puberty. Reagan is *literally* a horny fucking teenager. If I wasn't around for him to grind his cock against, he would have just used his own hand.

I place my hands on Reagan's shoulders, pushing him slightly. "*Reagan,*" he lifts his head and looks at me. He stops moving his hips while his hand is still wrapped around the both of us. "You're not in your right mind."

"I want to fuck those pretty pink lips of yours."

"Fuck— listen to yourself." I gently push his shoulders again, and this time he lets go and rolls onto his side, grumbling the whole time. Sure, I would love for him to fuck my mouth and grunt like an animal the whole time, but it just feels wrong to do it when he's a hormonal werewolf teen.

"I'm sorry," he mutters, but keeps going. "I want you. I want to warm my cock in your mouth." He winces as if the words aren't his. "I'm sorry." He doesn't look at me.

"I want you too, just... now isn't the right time. You're still recovering. I mean, look at your arm." His bite mark is still raging red, but the puncture wounds have closed up with that spider like scar tissue. I'm starting to get used to it more. The purple bruising surrounding the bite is now just a shadow. It's remarkable how quickly his body is healing, but it's still far from the pale scar that marks Sara's body.

"That's bullshit," he grumbles some more before rolling out of bed. "I need to shower." He walks to the bathroom by himself, slamming the door. There's that rage Sara mentioned. But he's saying sorry... And he's really only being mean to the doorframe. He could slam me like that if he wants. Fuck, I want him to rail me so bad. But I'll forever feel guilty about taking advantage of him while I act as his caretaker.

Not to mention there's that wedding photo in his wallet. Now is definitely not the time to bring that up, but eventually... I need to confront him about it for both our sakes. Until then, I have to focus on keeping a wolf's rage at bay.

Somehow.

CHAPTER SEVENTEEN

REAGAN

THE WATER CAN'T WARM UP FAST ENOUGH. I SHUT MY eyes and let the lukewarm water run over my face. My cock still twitching, dying for some relief. I huff, just wishing it to go away. It's like I'm in high school again, praying my dick would calm down while Mrs. Mae explained our book reports to us. She had great tits but was literally 50 years old. It was a very confusing time for me and every other boy in her class. Probably a few girls too.

The water finally to my liking, I take my cock in my hand and start stroking it slowly. Ever since Caroline and I broke it off, I've gotten pretty used to fucking my hand. I find it best when I let my hips do all the work and don't let myself finish the first time I'm close. Normally, I would just think about fucking in general, not anyone in particular. But right now, all I can think about is Lance.

I think about the way his cock twitched against mine, so needy... And then about his pale ass turning red while I spanked it and railed my hips against him. He'd taken my dick so well in his ass, I can only imagine what his mouth is capable of. I groan and place my palm against the wall of the shower for support. Closing my eyes, I think about those lips of his, the angelic curve of his top lip wrapping around my cock like a bow. Him looking up at me with those emerald eyes, his moans vibrating against my shaft. Maybe he'd touch himself while he sucked me off. Maybe I'd tell him only I'm allowed to touch him. Yeah, *fuck*, only me. No one else is allowed to have him. He's *mine*.

As I stroke my cock, I feel something different at the base. Looking down I see round, pillowy flesh where my shaft meets the rest of my body. I give it a little squeeze, surprised by how firm it is and how good the pressure feels. I should be horrified by this new appendage, but all I care about is climaxing to the fantasy in my head. I palm the head of my cock, pretending I'm hitting the back of Lance's throat and imagining the noises he would make. Gagging on me, whimpering around my length, struggling for air. "Take it," I speak under my breath. "Fucking take it..."

Drops of cum start to drip from the head of my cock. I begin stroking the rest of my shaft, stopping at the round flesh at the base. My breath catches in the back of my throat, and I know I'm close— so I stop. I pant, my dick twitching as warm water washes down my body. I start massaging my balls, slowly warming up to touching myself again. I consider if I would finish in Lance's mouth or finish all over his pretty face. It's my fantasy. I can picture both.

I start stroking myself again, thinking about Lance's tongue running along my length. My body tenses, feeling myself coming close to climax. I think about finishing in Lance's mouth, the look of surprise in his eyes and him swallowing my load. "Oh, fuck," I breathe, then grab the new thick flesh around my cock.

My knees buckle for a moment, the sudden shock of pleasure almost too much. But still I keep going, thinking about the tip of my dick pressed against Lance's closed lips before spilling my cum all over his face. I pump my hips and hand a few more times before finishing, moaning shamelessly the whole time. I grab the base of my dick again, more spurts of cum hitting the tiles of the shower and making my whole body shake.

I don't think I've come harder in my life.

I LEAVE THE BEDROOM, still drying my hair in a towel. I find Lance in the kitchen, having smelled the food he was making all the way from the bathroom. Without thinking, I slip up behind him, pressing my body against his. "Can you make more bacon?" I murmur in his ear.

A pressed voice leaves Lance's pretty lips. "Reagan."

"I can settle for just eggs."

"Reagan, your dick is touching my ass."

I look down. "We're both wearing clothes..." I had the decency to put sweats on before leaving the bathroom. No underwear though.

Lance just sighs. "Go watch TV, breakfast *with* bacon will be done in a little bit."

I grumble but do as he says, leaving him to his cooking. I'm not even sure why I'm so annoyed, but I am. I want to be next to him, to have him at grabbing distance, to be able to bury my face in his neck and smell him. He always has this slightly floral scent. Not overpowering or synthetic like a perfume, just a soft earthy, floral smell. I can't pinpoint the exact flower, nor do I really care that much. I just know I can't get enough of it. I sit on the couch and find myself bouncing my leg, antsy but not sure why.

Eventually breakfast is served. My plate is empty before

Lance has even finished eating his eggs. He blinks, looking at me while holding a piece of toast. "You seem to be feeling a lot better."

"I feel great," I agree. "It doesn't feel like I was sick at all."

Lance sets down his piece of toast, his face serious. "But you were sick. You *are* still sick. The transformation is still happening, Reagan."

I purse my lips. "So... we should just lay in bed together all day?"

"Okay, that," he points at me. "That's the sick. The werewolf sick."

I furrow my brows, confused. "How is that me being ill? I just want to cuddle a bit." And pin him down and hear him whimper while I fuck him into the mattress.

"*Reagan,*" Lance huffs and steps away from the kitchen island. I see him rub his eyes with the palms of his hands. "I don't know if now is a good time to talk about this."

"Talk about what?" I can tell he's not referring to me turning into a werewolf. Lance abandons his plate and walks over to the landline hanging on the wall. "Who are you calling?" Lance doesn't respond. I feel something ugly bubble inside me. "Who are you calling?" I don't just want to know. In that moment, I need to know. "**Lance,**" I stress while gripping my fork. The metal crumples in my hand like cardboard. I drop the fork, the crushed metal clattering onto the countertop. Something about the sound made me realize I didn't mean to destroy the utensil. I didn't know I could do that.

Lance looks at me, looks at the fork, then back at me. "That," Lance gestures at the fork, "is why we're not talking about it."

"I don't even know what *it* is," I grumble.

"Then you have no reason to worry about it." Lance shoots me an overly sweet smile like he's some customer service rep. I want to wipe that smile off his face, and I realize that ugly feeling from before is still lingering.

I get up from the counter. "I need to go for a run."

I start walking for the front door only for Lance to chase after me. "What? Reagan—" He blocks my path. "Taylor said we can't leave. This is a safehouse, we're... I mean, you're a federal agent. I don't have to explain safehouses to you."

He doesn't. I understand that Taylor had put us here so no one could find us. More than that, I understand that if anyone did find us here, Taylor could never use the place as a safe house again. I'm not such an asshole that I'd blow someone else's cover. With a huff, I change course and walk into the living room. Lance lets out a much softer, relieved puff of air before walking back to the phone in the kitchen.

In the living room, I get down on the floor. As much as I want to feel the wind in my hair and get out of the stale air of the safehouse, a full body workout would have to do. I can hear Lance on the phone speaking with Taylor, though I don't pay much attention as I start a rep of push-ups. Eventually, Lance walks into the living room. I feel his eyes trail along my body, and I smirk to myself.

"Wanna give me some extra weight?" I turn my head, not pausing my exercise for a moment. Lance's thick brows raise in surprise. "You can sit on my back," I explain.

He shakes his head. "That sounds like a terrible idea."

"You don't think I can actually do it? Come on, try." Somehow my childish teasing works because Lance comes over and settles on my back while I lay in a resting position on the floor. "Okay, one," I count out and raised my arms. I hear Lance squeak a little as my core rises off the floor, taking him with it. I keep my arms extended a few moments before slowly lowering my body back to the floor. "Two," I count off again before going through the same motions. And again, "Three." This time, when I'm in my raised position, I look over my shoulder at Lance. "Having fun?" I ask in a—I'll admit —cocky voice.

"It's like a hunkier magic carpet ride."

I snort, almost losing my form before quickly bringing myself back to the floor. I finish out a rep of ten push-ups with Lance on my back before deciding I change up my exercise. Which would be a lot easier if I had any actual equipment. I could always try to bench press Lance... but he'd probably be too squirmy. And I'd be much too distracted by his blushing.

Lance slides off my back, his gaze focused on the kitchen. "Just try to remember your own strength okay?"

"You said I'm still recovering," I remind him as a tease.

But Lance's reply is dead serious. "You're recovering and changing still. And if you push yourself... I don't know what I'll do."

It hits me then that Lance would blame himself for any ill that befell me. I could jump off the roof and he'd somehow twist the story so he pushed me. I decide I do need to take it easy. For Lance's sake. Which I guess includes keeping the flirting to myself. I don't agree with Lance that I'm not in my right mind. I want him, why is that so surprising? Sure, he's a man, but that's not that big a deal. I've decided it's not that big a deal.

CHAPTER EIGHTEEN

LANCE

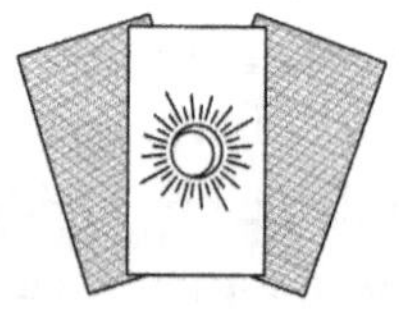

THE NEXT FEW DAYS HAVE BEEN MUCH THE SAME. Every night there's a knock at the door and I find a bag left on the stoop, then a white van or a motorcycle drives off into the night. If we need anything specific, I call ahead. Reagan is elated when a set of dumbbells is dropped off for him. Physical activity probably helps with the rush of hormones. Not to mention Reagan definitely works out every day. That deep V at his hips and the firmness of his pecs don't come from nowhere. We watch TV together. I cook and then insist on cleaning up— though Reagan usually helps out. It's all very domestic.

Minus Regan still undergoing the change.

Every once in a while, Reagan will forget his own strength and break something. Door handles, a few more forks, or, the worst, when he smashed the alarm clock on the bedside table. I just thought it would be good for him to wake up at a reasonable time, establish a routine. My mistake. But he did clean up the plastic and wires and promised he would buy a new one. He certainly isn't the rage monster I was afraid he would be, but it's impossible to forget what is inside him.

One morning we wake up to find the sheets of the bed shredded. Reagan insists he has no idea how it happened. I believe him, but I've seen how sharp werewolf claws are. It's pretty obvious to me how the bedsheets got turned to ribbons in the night. That's the other thing. We keep sleeping in the same bed. Every night and every morning, Reagan cuddles up to me, burying his face in my neck while he presses his half-hard dick against my body. Fucking tease. Like I don't just want to crawl under the covers and hear him howl while I give him head. But I know all this affection is just the change…

The wedding photo in his wallet might as well be a five-foot-tall portrait hanging in our bedroom.

I can't get it out of my head, and I finally crack. While Reagan showers, I plate our breakfasts and set down Reagan's wallet next to his plate. I make sure the photo will be the first thing he sees when he opens the wallet. Reagan walks into the kitchen still a touch wet, water glistening off his neck. "Looks great," he tells me before sitting down. I made a veggie omelet, skipping the bacon for once.

Reagan shoves a big bite of omelet in his mouth before he even notices his wallet. I watch his chewing slow down as he picks up the worn wallet and opens it up. He swallows his mouth full of food, hard. "Where did you find this?"

"I took it off your body the night you were attacked." I expect anger, but Reagan just looks at me with a befuddled expression. He drops the wallet onto the countertop and returns to eating. I don't know why I let the silence hang between us, but eventually I blurt out a damning question. "Don't you have anything to say?"

"What? You want me to compliment you on your pickpocketing skills?" He doesn't even look up from his plate. "I get it. You wanted... leverage or something to hold over me."

"No," I insist. "I wanted to know who you were. I think that's fair since you have a whole file on me."

Finally, he lifts his head. "Lance, I..."

He doesn't finish his sentence, but I just know he was going to say he'd never lie to me. But both of us know that's bullshit. "Besides my name and my job, everything I told you that night at the club is true. I'm from Virginia, I like cinnamon in my coffee—"

I interject, "You've never slept with a man."

I see him chewing the inside of his cheek. "Is that what this is about?" he asks in a low voice.

The game is up. "Who is the woman in your wallet?"

Reagan blinks, then slowly shut his eyes tight. He lets out a burdened sigh. "That's my ex-wife. Caroline."

"How long have you two been separated?"

Reagan rubs his temple. "Legally? Six... eight months I think?"

I walk away, running like I always do, but Reagan catches my wrist. "Lance, listen, please."

I don't want to listen. I mean, half a year apart from his *wife* and here he is, grinding his dick against me every chance he gets. "What am I to you?" I muse out loud.

Reagan replies without hesitation. "You mean a lot to me." His hand slips down from my wrist to hold my hand. He runs his thumb along my knuckle. "We should talk." It feels a bit late for that, but I let him lead me to the living room couch. Even as we sit next to each other, he keeps touching and toying with my hand, holding my palm up like he's trying to read it. "I met Caroline when I was nineteen, fresh out of basic training and about to do my first tour. I told her we should get married immediately."

"Wow. Really living up to the stereotype." I know it's bad to be interrupting already but it had to be said.

He shrugs. "If it's true, is it a stereotype? You get a lot more benefits in the military if you're married. But she told me no. That she wanted to make sure I was actually going to be there for her. So, we did long distance for a while. Letters and care packages."

That was some paperback romance shit. How am I supposed to compete with care packages and love letters sent into an active war zone? This past week has to be a cakewalk compared to months of separation and anxiety. Reagan continues. "When we were twenty-one, we agreed to get married on the condition that once my mandatory service was done, I'd stop taking foreign missions. That I'd stay domestic, work some office job for the military, or just go civilian."

Caroline currently isn't my favorite person, but I see where she was coming from. I'm not exactly thrilled to be drooling over some ex-military guy— though the muscles are a big plus. Sitting at home fretting over Reagan was... Well, that had just been my first day at the safe house. That was just one day, but waiting for months? Years? She's a better person than me.

"I agreed. We got married, got a house on base. I did a few more tours but also had time back home with her." He pauses for a moment, as if he's really considering his next words. "We talked about starting a family once I was out. We both agreed we didn't want me away from our hypothetical kids. But as I got closer to finishing up my service obligation... I realized I didn't want to quit. The idea of working some office job..." He shakes his head. "Not being out there in the field... It killed me on the inside."

I start to see the cracks in the foundation. "But you told

her that, right?" I don't know why I ask when I know the answer. Forget cracks, the foundation might as well be built right over a sinkhole. Nothing about playing spy sounds domestic to me.

"I thought the FBI was the best of both worlds. I'd work domestic affairs, spend the day out in the field and be back home for dinner." He runs his fingers through his hair and huffs. I shake my head, surprised by how blind Reagan was. How selfish he could be. "I was pretty naive in my late twenties."

"Okay, stop." I pull my hand away from him finally. "But you were telling her these things, right? You didn't just come home one day and say, 'Darling, your husband is a federal agent now,' right?"

"No, I mean..." He keeps scratching at his scalp. "I told her they were scouting me as my release date got closer and closer. And I told her what I just told you. I'd work during the day, but I'd come home each night. Quantico isn't even that far from where I grew up, so she'd have my parents and sister to help out with the kids when I *was* busy." Reagan starts to chew the inside of his cheek, which I've come to realize is his obvious tell when something is bothering him. Right now, it's as if his words are leaving a bullshit taste in his mouth. As they should.

"Reagan, you had to know that wasn't going to work. You're not exactly in Virginia right now, are you?"

"I told you... I was naive." He leans back, taking up half the couch now. "I don't know if Caroline was naive like me, or just hopeful... She's a civilian too, so she probably had no idea what all the job entailed. But no, I didn't come home every night for dinner..." I could picture Caroline alone in some cute little southern cottage, sitting at an empty dinner table waiting dutifully for her all-American husband to come home.

This sucks. I'm feeling bad for some woman I've never met. This poor woman who had been strung out for a decade waiting for the day she could have that white picket fence life. Reagan seems worth the wait... I can't fault her for hoping, can't blame her for waiting for him. But clearly Reagan had his own agenda, and clearly there was no end to the waiting.

"She divorced you?" Good for her.

"Not immediately," Reagan explains. "We tried for a year to make things work, but it just wasn't. She said she needed time, and she'd given me *so* much time. She went to go stay with her parents in Florida and just... never really came back."

It's hard to pin down the exact emotion in his voice. Hollow, but tinged with sadness, because he misses her or because he realizes what an ass he'd been. I'm not sure.

"We had to live apart for a year before she could even file for separation. Then it was a little messy figuring out compensation and whatnot. Military spouses have a lot of benefits and I had to figure out how not to leave her high and dry. When it was all said and done..." He purses his lips then sits up again. "Legally, it's been half a year since we've been separated. But emotionally? Way longer. I don't even know exactly when that split happened."

Of course he fucking doesn't.

"I mean..." His voice sounds so lost. "When she told me she wanted a break, I just accepted it. It felt... I felt..."

"You still have her photo in your wallet," I point out, bitter.

"I know..." he admits, defeated. "I guess I like to remind

myself of what an asshole I was. I am." Admitting it is the first step, I guess. But I don't buy it.

I can either accept that Reagan has a past and move on or hang it over his head for the rest of eternity while he tries to get into my pants. We can just give in to our mutual lust for each other and I can wonder from time to time if I'll ever be the most important thing in his life. I can even lay in bed and wonder if he sees me as I am or as some other copy, a more masculine version of Caroline. I can also just reject him and we'll both die alone. Which is maybe what we both deserve.

"Lance..." Reagan's voice pulls me out of my wallowing. Before I can try to parse out what he wants, he leaps forward and pulls me into a kiss. I expect a soft, sad sort of kiss but it's not that at all. He holds my face firmly in his hands so I can't move an inch, his lips forceful and moving mine with ease. He drags his teeth along my lips, and I shiver against their sharpness. But I don't return the kiss. It's hard, but I force myself to stay neutral, statuesque. Finally, Reagan realizes the kiss is one-sided and he pulls his face away from mine, his hands still holding my cheeks.

I guess it's my turn to talk. "I don't want to be some rebound." Reagan's eyes go wide, but I speak again before he can object. "I don't know if you've fooled around with guys before. Reagan, but I don't want to be your fun little sexual exploration before you come to your senses and realize you still want that family with Caroline."

"Caroline and I are over," he assures me, and I believe him.

"But there are plenty of Carolines." My hands take his wrists and gently pull his hands away from my face. "There are plenty of women you could start a family with. Live that perfect picket fence life—"

Reagan lets out a dry, humorless chuckle. "I'm not even human anymore."

"Werewolves are known for big families," I inform him. "Lycanthropy will pass on to your kids— even if their Mother isn't a werewolf."

"Well, fuck." His face scrunches in disgust. "I'm not putting anyone through that."

"But you could easily find a lady-wolf to shack up with."

Reagan shakes his head. "Lady-wolf?" He tries to make it seem like he's objecting to the concept and not the word itself. But I know better.

"Wanting a domestic life doesn't just go away because... because you got divorced and turned. How long have you wanted a family? Probably longer than you were in the army."

He furrows his brows but there is a softness in his eyes. "Do you not want a family?"

My mouth goes dry. I swallow trying to make my tongue feel less like a desert. "Of course I do. One day, but—"

He raises his hands in confusion. "Then what's the issue?"

I don't know if there is a word for the sound of tires screeching to a halt but that's what I feel in that instant. Did he just tell me he wanted to have a family with me? No, no he didn't. He just sort of just pointed out that we both want the same thing. I'm noticing a pattern. Reagan is bad about outright saying things. Everything feels veiled, like everything desired is sealed away in a top secret file. Except for lust, which he's happy to make obvious.

Reagan takes my hand. "I think you'd be a good Dad."

What am I supposed to say in response? 'No, you're right, let's adopt a hundred little werewolf babies and live in this tiny safe house forever while we wait for a vicious were-wolf gang and my Father to stop wanting us dead.'

But I need to step away from the supernatural bullshit. I've avoided magic for years anyway, and Reagan is so new to being a wolf, it's not like he's attached to the idea of were-wolf pups. If he hadn't been turned, if I had never been born a witch, we'd still be sitting here arguing over what we could be. Magic isn't the issue.

"Are you straight?" I ask point blank, and Reagan even looks at me like I'd just shot him in the chest. "I'm the only man you've been with. I'm guessing I'm the only man you've ever been attracted to, if you're even attracted to me."

"*Of course* I'm attracted to you. Haven't I made that obvious?"

"You're attracted to the idea of having sex with me," I point at him, accusatory. "But sex is a little itty-bitty part of relationships, Reagan. Being with me means being with a man. Have you even thought about the comments your army buddies will make? Or how your family will react? Do you think you could ever come out?"

I can tell by his expression he hasn't thought about any of that at all. He shakes his head before rubbing his eyes with his fingertips. "Lance, I've had a lot on my mind since we've met. No, I haven't thought about all of that, but I can handle it."

I cross my arms over my chest. "Go on then." Reagan looks at me confused. Then it dawns on him what I'm asking.

The funny thing about the closet is it never goes away. Just like in a real house, you can clean all the junk out, but the closet is still a part of the house. Even in my frosted glass closet.

Dressing in pastels and bold patterns, going exclusively to gay bars, and having never looked at a woman except to admire her outfit—I have to come out all the time. And I remember every reaction to my bold, brave debut as a gay man.

Jason had just grinned, his silent way of telling me he'd known from the moment we met. Then he came out as well, even if he was just as obvious as me. My mom cried a little the first time I told her I liked boys. I knew she supported me but still she cried. Junior complained that everyone was going to think he too was gay by proxy. We were eleven, so I don't hold it against him. I've got plenty of other instances to prove he's a shit brother. Daphne has always been supportive and has mentioned off-handedly that she's slept with women. But when you're a vampire whose age reaches into the hundreds, that's sort of to be expected. It was the least coming out, coming out I've experienced, but it still counted.

I just don't think Reagan is ready for all that. And, maybe selfishly, I'm not sure I can be the person to hold his hand through all that. I'm scared of the words and looks that will be lobbed at us when we're together. I know better than to start fights with homophobes, but Reagan probably doesn't. It's one thing when words are thrown at me because, whatever, I'm a gold star gay and that's never going to change. Reagan has no idea what it's like– he's never had to think about it. I've come into his world and ruined his charmed life. No longer is he the golden boy any woman's mom would die to have as her son-in-law. Now he isn't even human– never mind him being gay. Bisexual. Straight-with-an-exception.

Lance," Reagan speaks again. "I... I can't lose you. I don't know why but I can't imagine being without you."

"Because you were hopped up on hormones, half dead, and have been trying to fuck me the past week."

His face scrunches, looking at me annoyed. "Did you forget that I ran after you? That I tried to protect you?"

"So you could get dirt on me for your case," I remind him.

Reagan huffs. "Sure, yes that was why I broke protocol and followed you to the bar. But the second I thought you were in danger—" He shakes his head. "What can I do to show you I mean it? That I care about you?"

"Well, what did you do for Caroline to show her you meant it?"

Reagan stiffens. "That's not fair."

"It's a genuine question." I worded a little mean, but I'm serious. At least from Reagan's story, it sounds like he's the type of person to jump head-first into things. He could tout all he wanted about benefits, but he wanted to marry Caroline at nineteen. He broke protocol and stalked me through the city. Hell, he broke into a warehouse by himself to rescue me— which was as stupid as it was heroic.

Reagan is past hiding his nervous nibbles inside his mouth and is now biting at his bottom lip. "I was always there for her. Even when I couldn't be there physically, I would always find some way to be there. That's all I'm asking, Lance." I feel my head start to shake. "Just let me be here for you. Let me keep you safe. You're in a dangerous position. The unwanted son of a crime family. Even if Blood Moon Pack gets off our backs, who's to say there won't be others that want to hurt you? And now, I can protect you now more than ever. Just let me stay by your side."

I don't know what to believe. Maybe Reagan means what he says, or maybe the hormones are still making him feel things that aren't real. He could still be trying to get close to my Father, planning to eventually bring him in on his own accord. Or he's just so lonely without his wife he's latched on to me, the first person who's doted on him in God knows how long.

"You don't have to give me an answer now," Reagan assures me, as if he can read my mind. "Just consider it. Consider what I'm telling you: I want you, Lance. I want us."

Us sounds nice.

CHAPTER NINETEEN

LANCE

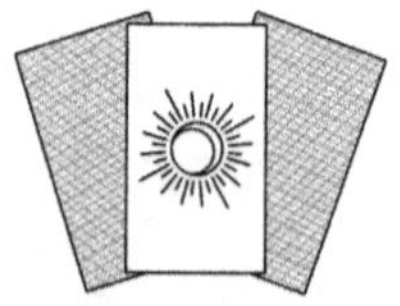

THE REST OF THE DAY IS UNEVENTFUL. TV, FOOD, AND lots of pacing around the house. I'm starting to get a little stir crazy being cooped up in this place for a week. I'm also starting to miss dressing myself, my closet filled with pieces I've collected over the years replaced with nothing but gray sweats and shirts. Not exactly fun to style, and certainly not my aesthetic. Either my gray shirt is tucked into the band of the sweatpants or it isn't. I just want to try on all my pants to find the perfect pair to match my top— sue me.

I wonder if Reagan is getting homesick. At least I'm still in my city. He's hundreds of miles away from home and stuck here for who knows how much longer.

I notice the sun beginning to set and I make my way into the kitchen to start dinner, only to find Reagan already heating up a skillet. I walk over to get a better look at what he was making when he stops me. "Let me," Reagan gently pushes me away from the stove with his hip. "You've done the cooking and dishes all week. It's the least I could do."

"I just wanted to see what you were making." Like I would object to him doing work around the house. Okay, so maybe I would have at the beginning of the week, but things are very different now. I look at the countertop and snicker when I realize what's on the menu. "Grilled cheese, huh? I didn't realize you were a Michelin star chef."

"It's not just grilled cheese." He lifts up a plate with apple slices so thin it's actually impressive. "There are apples too. And bacon. Trust me, it works."

I settle onto the kitchen island and watch him work. Soon it's in front of me, and despite the meal being basic, it does taste very good. The sweetness of the apple and the savory of the cheese and meat is a comforting combo. I finish dinner pretty quickly, pushing my plate away when I'm done. "I'll start dishes—"

"No," Reagan objects. "No, I've got it." He grabs my plate and brings it to the sink before grabbing the pan and everything else he's dirtied.

I quirk a brow, wondering if this all has something to do with our conversation this morning. "Alright. Then I'm going to head up to bed."

Reagan perks up as I stand to leave the kitchen. "You want to sleep in separate beds tonight?"

"It's probably healthier. Right?"

I can tell Reagan doesn't agree, his lips forming a thin line. But he says nothing and returns his attention to the dishes. At least he's respecting my boundaries. Even in the thick of his change, in his rage, understood the word **no**. I guess werewolves are a lot more polite than I'd been led to believe. That, or Reagan was just raised right.

I go to the bedroom upstairs. I honestly haven't spent a lot of time on the second floor, opting to stay close to Reagan. I sit on the edge of the bed, wondering how I'll sleep tonight. The nightmares stopped when I was sleeping in the same bed as Reagan. But that was to be expected. I always sleep great when I have company. It's only when I'm alone, feeling helpless, that the nightmares plague me.

I strip off the loose clothes I've worn all day, ready to pick out a nighttime version of the same outfit. I grab a random shirt from the closet when the door opens. "I just wanted to say good—shit," Reagan averts his gaze when he sees I'm naked. "Sorry, I just wanted to say goodnight. I'll go."

"Why are you acting like you've never seen me naked?" I struggle to hide my amusement, a giggle bubbling up from my throat.

"Um..." Reagan covers his eyes now that he has to make conversation. "Because I didn't know you'd be naked, and you didn't know I'd see you naked?"

I burst into laughter. "What a gentleman."

"Is that sarcasm?"

"What if it is?" I tease. Still covering the top half of his face, Reagan gives me a toothy smile.

"Thank you for coming to say goodnight." It was sweet... A little gesture that tells me he isn't angry even if things between us are complicated. Reagan just grunts in acknowledgment.

I approach him, still naked as the day I was born. I take his wrist and pull it away from his eyes so he can look at me. Almost immediately, Reagan licks his lips like I'm acting all sexy when really, I'm just standing there. This is a bad idea. I've been good this past week and good this morning standing my ground. But deep down, I'm still scared, selfish, and worst of all, horny. In denying Reagan. I've also been denying myself. And I'm not exactly known for my constitution.

I stand up on my toes to kiss him. He hesitates before wrapping his arms around me, pulling my naked body to him. I have no hope of escaping his grip once he has me, like a fox in a trap. So, Reagan's the one to pull away and ask, "Are you sure?"

"No," I admit. "But I'm getting sick of all the teasing."

"Fuck," he breathes, exasperated. "Me too." With that, he goes for my neck, skipping kissing and going straight nibbling along where my skin is taut against my collar. I shiver, my heart racing. I know he won't hurt me, but my body doesn't seem to understand, my intuition screaming that Reagan is dangerous. I'm prey and he's the hunter.

He grabs my hips, his nails digging deeper into my skin than human nails ever could. I hiss as I feel one of his nails puncture my skin. Reagan doesn't notice until a bit of blood starts to drip down my hip. He looks down, pausing his attack on my neck. His hand releases my hip, and he gets down on his knees to investigate further. He licks the line of blood up to the wound itself. I take a deep breath, finding this both erotic and terrifying. Reagan kisses the wound; the softest kiss I think I've ever received from him. "I'm sorry," he speaks into my skin. "I'm still learning..."

His husky voice makes my cock twitch. Not to mention the sight of him on his knees in front of me. I reach to touch his head, running my fingers through his hair, not unlike petting a dog. "Maybe you should make it up to me," I suggest, feeling my length grow harder with each passing moment.

Reagan begins to trail kisses along my hips, starting at the little cut on my hip then along my stomach, stopping right at the trail of peach fuzz that leads to my crotch. "I have a lot to make up for..."

"You don't have to," I assure him, and I mean it. He begins to trail further down my body until his face is in front of my half-hard cock. He takes my girth in his hand

and brings the tip of my cock to his lips. Another soft, light kiss that makes me dizzy, like I'm a princess finally being touched by her prince. I guess it is the first time Reagan has ever touched me like *this*.

He takes the head of my cock in his mouth and immediately his tongue runs circles around the head. My whole body tenses and I gasp, his touch almost too much, too fast. I grab Reagan's hair and pull him back. "S-slow down," I breathe.

"I've never done this before," he says with a hint of embarrassment.

"Reagan... it's a dick. You know it better than I think you realize."

I see the wheels start to turn behind his blue eyes. In his next attempt, he takes me into his mouth and just lets the head of my cock rest atop his tongue, warm and wet and inviting. I release his hair, my fingers now lightly brushing his scalp. "Keep going," I breathe. Reagan takes more of me into his mouth. I let out another, more relaxed gasp. I look down and marvel at the sight of Reagan swallowing my cock. He looks so good on his knees.

Reagan's lips slide further and further down my shaft until he pauses, gagging slightly. A twisted part of me wanted to shove his head forward so he takes the rest of me in his mouth. I remember to be nice, seeing as this is his first time. Reagan pulls away and I moan, feeling his lips slide off my cock. "You're doing good," I praise him.

"You don't have to lie, Lance." He tells me before he starts lapping at the head of my dick like it's a popsicle. Then he pops my dick back in his mouth and attempts again to take it all, getting farther down the shaft this time.

"You're doing so good," I tell him again, hoping this time he'll realize I mean it. He starts to slide off my dick once more but stops at the head before bobbing his head forward again. "So good," I whimper. He bobs his head slowly and purposefully. The farther he gets down my length, the more he gags, but still he presses on.

Finally, his nose presses against my hairs and I feel the tip of my cock hit the back of his throat. I decide to be a bit of a dick and grab a handful of his hair, keeping him pressed against me so he can choke. "I fit perfectly," I tell him, the sound of him gagging on my girth music to my ears. "Your mouth is perfect for my cock."

I release his head, and he pulls back, gasping for air. Spit dribbles down his cool pink lips and down his stubbly chin. I wipe the drool from his chin with my thumb then rest the pad of my thumb against his bottom lip. "Good boy."

The pet name feels odd on my tongue, and Reagan seems to notice, chuckling. "Now that's just mean. Calling a werewolf a 'good boy.'"

"But you are a good boy," I tell him, the term of endearment feeling more natural now. Usually, I'm the one being teased with praise, but it's nice to be the one doling out the compliments for once. Someone has to show Reagan the ropes. Show him how to give good head.

He takes me in his mouth again, slow but deep, swallowing me completely. The little choking sound he makes when I hit the back of his throat is intoxicating, made all the better when I remember this is his first time. That I'm the only person he's ever touched like this. I match my breathing with his bobbing head, inhaling as he slides onto my cock and exhaling as he slides backwards.

Reagan's hands start to explore my body, first rubbing the outside of my thighs and then reaching back behind me. He moans as he cups my ass and gives it a tight squeeze, the vibrations resonating through my entire body. Reagan pulls away again, catching his breath. I think he's finally spent when he speaks up. "Do you want to face fuck me?"

I'm taken aback, both by the suggestion and the turn of phrase. I can't imagine any scenario in the world where I would respond 'no,' but with Reagan, I hesitate. "It's your first time, you don't have to…"

He appears to take this as a challenge, adjusting the weight on his knees before taking my hands and placing them on the back of his neck. He opens his mouth wide, just an inch away from the head of my cock. As an extra tease, his tongue flicks forward, lapping along my slit. My fingers twitch and I take a handful of his hair at the base of his neck, my other hand moving to the top of his head. "Tap my thigh if it's too much," I tell him, not really wanting him to suffocate even if it would be a hell of a way to go.

Now, with a good grasp on his head, I buck my hips. Once I start, it's hard to stop, the back of Reagan's throat making me shiver. It's not long until I'm moving his head in time with my hips, his nose grinding against my waistline. Reagan's muffled choking and moans alone are enough to make me finish. But I try to hold on, not wanting this to end. I feel my knees and thighs quiver, my breath shallow as I struggle to hold back my orgasm. I look down at Reagan, his blue eyes wide and wet with tears. I maintain eye contact with him as I take my last thrusts. I hold his head against my body when I finally finish in his mouth. A waving moan leaves my lips, my grip on his hair only tightening as I ride out my orgasm. Finally, I let go of his head, my legs still tingling.

Reagan doesn't miss a beat, standing up and scooping me into his arms. I'm too worn out, still basking in the post-orgasm glow, to even react. I just rest my head on his chest, feeling the soft gray shirt against my cheek. He sits down on the bed, letting me rest in his lap. His sweatpants do a poor job of hiding his erection. I make a note of that, but right now I just want to lay in his lap and admire how pretty he is. He looks down at me and starts stroking my cheek with the backs of his fingers.

"I do alright?" He asks, and I think he must be teasing me. Like I wouldn't be lying here looking at him like he's made of constellations if he hadn't done a good job. But when I don't respond, he cocks his head a little to the side.

"You're amazing," I tell him. I start to palm the bulge in his pants. "Give me a few minutes to recover and I'll reward you." Reagan shuts his eyes, lifting his hips as I touch him over his sweatpants. Now that I'm not on his chest, he takes a moment to slip his shirt off, letting me appreciate his body. I lay on his pec like a pillow, eye to eye with the skull tattoo on his opposing pectoral. One hand teases his dick while my other hand trails along the peaks and valleys of his muscles. Reagan groans and I stifle a laugh, thinking back to the past few nights of him spooning me.

"Lay down on the bed," I whisper to him. Reagan slides me off his lap, then pulls down his pants, discarding them on the floor. Only when he's naked does he lay back onto the bed, his cock sticking straight up. I swallow, having forgotten he's bigger now than before. The head is already slick with precum, and I notice a ball of flesh at the base of his length. I've heard about knots but have never seen one, nor do I know how I'll fit it in my mouth. Or if I even can.

Reagan grabs some pillows so he can lay at enough of an incline to watch me work. I lay my body along his legs and start at the base of his length, curious about Reagan's new knot. Holding his shaft, I start kissing his knot and immediately Reagan groans. "Fuck," he curses.

"Sensitive?" I tease, my hand starting to pump along his length.

"Really, *really* sensitive." I wonder if he realizes I am absolutely going to use that against him. I bring all my attention to his knot, taking a round section in my mouth and sucking lightly, my tongue rubbing against it. Meanwhile, my hand keeps moving up and down Reagan's shaft. His groans turn to singing moans, and he arches his back against the mattress.

My mouth and hand switch positions. I take the head into my mouth, savoring the taste of his precum as my tongue swirls around his dick. My hands start to fondle Reagan's knot, feeling it begin to swell "Lance..." He breathes my name, and I take him deeper into my mouth. I take as much of him as I can, the tip of his dick sliding down into my throat. I try to fit in more, but I start choking and have to pull back.

"I don't think I can fit it all..." I say between breaths.

Reagan has a look of utter bliss on his face, my hand still massaging his knot. "It's so fucking hot when you choke."

"Likewise," I slip in. He's looking down at me rather amused, and I take the opportunity to slip my tongue out of my mouth and tap the tip of his dick against it.

"Yes..." he growls. "Fuck... I want to finish on your face."

I give his knot a squeeze. "How long have you wanted that, you horn dog?"

"Every little expression you make..." He takes a second to catch his breath. "I think about how cute you would look covered in my cum." The husky desperation in his voice makes my whole body spark with joy. I keep caressing his knot while his cock rests against my lips so when he's finished it'll be all over me. Fresh beads of cum pooling along his head tell me he won't last much longer.

Reagan starts gripping the sheets. "Oh fuck," he breathes before ejaculating all over my lips, thick warm cum dripping down my chin. I tilt my face so the next spurt lands on my cheek. More and more cum spurts from his dick, landing on my face and hands. Reagan watches me with a dreamy look in his eyes, like he can't believe this is real. His hand reaches up to stroke my hair.

"Beautiful," he purrs. "Even better than my dreams..." I start licking his cum from my lips, thick and white like a salty cream. I start licking it off my fingers as well, and Reagan grins. "Fuck you're filthy."

CHAPTER TWENTY

REAGAN

I swear, none of this was planned. I didn't think Lance would want anything to do with me after our conversation this morning, let alone let me finish on his face. Nor did I think I'd offer him to fuck my mouth, but it just felt right. I was so hot and bothered for him, I'd let him fuck any part of me he wanted. But I have no experience. I'm just glad I didn't ruin the moment by choking so bad I needed to stop, or, god forbid, vomit all over him... But even if that had happened, I know Lance wouldn't be upset with me. He'd probably be upset with himself despite him doing everything in his power to make sure I was comfortable.

Everything feels good in a way I can't put into words. I'm not so sure it's the act itself, but watching Lance unravel that really does me in. I probably would have finished in those sweatpants if Lance had decided to just fondle me. Instead, I got the pleasure of him covered in my cum, got to watch him lick it off his lips like melted ice cream. I may have been half-hard for the past four days, but at least Lance can match my filthy fantasies.

As fun as it is watching Lance struggle to catch every

drop of my cum dripping off his body, I slide my legs out from under him and pop into the bathroom to grab him a towel. Back on the bed, I start wiping his cheeks. I don't know if it's the texture of the towel or just my act of cleaning him up, but he giggles. It's adorable even when he's still got cum on his face. Once he's cleaned up, I wrap my arm around his shoulder and pull him to my chest, then lay us back down on the bed. I kiss his temple but find I want to kiss the rest of his face, my lips trailing down his cheek to his chin and finally, a soft peck on the lips.

Lance's deep green eyes sparkle, his body so small against mine. "Did you enjoy yourself?" I ask finally.

He laughs, and I feel his whole body shake. "Did it seem like I didn't?"

"Communication is important," I point out. "And I wasn't sure if my dick was too... weird."

He lifts a brow, amusement still dancing in his eyes. "Your knot? I'll admit, I'm kinda glad it wasn't going inside me..." He glances down at the space between my legs. "But it was very fun to play with."

I almost don't want to speak, the sight of Lance looking down at my dick with such reverence making my ego expand to jerk levels, but a question is nagging me. "It's uh... called a knot? That bump at the bottom?"

"That's what I've heard," he informs me. "I've never slept with a werewolf. To be honest, I don't really know much about them. But people talk about that sort of thing."

"About werewolf dick?"

"Well, it's a pretty interesting dick, isn't it?" He gives me a cheeky grin.

Lance says he's glad he didn't take my knot tonight, but I'm already thinking about the future. About our future: Lance riding my hips until my knot pops inside him and he cries out. Us laying together, just like this, and talking about our day. Talking about our plans together. Maybe it's because we've just been stuck inside doing nothing but cooking and watching TV, but I want to run errands with him. Try the domestic thing. I failed miserably with Caroline, but maybe with Lance things will be different. I don't consider the fact that I still have no idea how to maintain my old human life alongside my new ailment. I don't even know if it's possible. But I'll find out, with Lance at my side.

I bury my face in his neck. "I want you to tell me everything." I speak into his collar. "I want to know what you know... I want to know how you grew up." I feel Lance's body become rigid. "You know this world better than I do." He says nothing. Very intentionally.

I don't want to argue. This moment is too precious to sully with discussions of witches and wolves and whatever else there is. But I want him to know I'm not going anywhere. "Can I sleep here tonight?" I ask, seeing as Lance came up here so he could sleep alone. But that was before we got a taste of each other.

"Of course you can," he breaks his silence, but his body is still tense. Lance kisses the crown of my head. I know something is wrong... but sleep is starting to make my eyelids heavy. I let out a weak yawn and settled myself back in the crook of Lance's neck. He rubs my back. "Goodnight, Reagan..." I've gotten so use to his voice being the last thing I hear for the day, it's like my own personal lullaby.

THE BED IS empty when I wake up. I slowly sit up before rubbing the sleep out of my eyes. I don't think much of Lance not laying in bed beside me. I think he might be showering. He was a mess last night, but I don't hear the water running in the adjacent bathroom. I give myself a few more seconds to wake up before crawling out of bed. I lumber downstairs in the nude, wondering if maybe Lance is making us breakfast like usual. Eggs, meat, and coffee with cinnamon. But I don't smell anything cooking or hear the sizzle of oil.

Standing at the halfway point of the kitchen and the living room, a light breeze reminds me I'm standing in the nude. I go to the downstairs bedroom to grab clothes and double check that Lance isn't in there for some reason. Nope. The house isn't very big. I don't know where he could be hiding. Or even why he would be hiding. "Lance?" I call into the kitchen as I slip a shirt on. "Honey?" Did I just call him honey? Was that really the pet name I was going with?

I take another tour of the house and find nothing. Lance is gone and immediately my heart starts pounding in my chest. Was I so tired last night I failed to hear anyone break in? But Lance would have screamed if he was being abducted... I start checking the doors and windows to find they're all locked from the inside like they should be. "Fuck," I curse under my breath. I rush to the landline, intending to call Taylor but realizing I don't know his number. There's only one number written on a sticky note next to the phone and it's Sara's. Better her than nothing.

I dial the number, tapping my foot as I wait for her to answer. The phone rings once. Twice. "Hello?" A bored, female voice says over the phone.

"Sara? It's Reagan."

"Hey," she responds, still sounding bored even though I know I've got tension in my voice. "You sound good. Fully recovered from all that nonsense?"

I don't have time to update her on my weird werewolf body. "Lance is missing," I tell her. "He wasn't in bed this morning."

"Don't get your panties in a twist," she tells me, and I can practically hear her roll her eyes.

"Look, just get Taylor—"

"He's out of town," she cuts me off. "Sorry." It's like she Knows she's difficult. Actually. scratch that. She definitely knows she's difficult, and she's probably really proud of that. I knew a woman in my platoon who told me that she could smile and twirl her hair like a schoolgirl and intimidated men would still call her a bitch—*so fuck it.* "He had to head upstate to get things ready for us," Sara explains.

"Us?"

"Full moon is in two days, Reagan. Well, one more night."

I freeze. I might not know much about being a werewolf —hell, Lance knows more about my anatomy than I do—but I know what a full moon means. "When were you going to tell me this?"

"I'm not your nurse," Sara scoffs, "Lance is. Even if he's skipping out on the job."

"We need to find him," I press, not really liking her speaking ill of Lance.

"Give me thirty minutes and I'll be at the house." She hangs up without any further details.

I eat some bread, not even toast. I just don't have the patience to make anything right now despite literally waiting for Sara to arrive. I also dig around the closets to see if I can find anything other than sweats and a shirt. I'm starting to get sick of lounge wear. Eventually I find what must be a pair of Taylor's jeans based on how they fit me, looser around the waist and the hem wrapping around my ankles. I manage to find the belt I wore that eventful night and roll up the legs of the pants past my ankles. I try to ignore the little drops of blood still clinging to my old boots.

I wait by the window for Sara to arrive. She roars up on a motorbike in twenty minutes instead of thirty. At least she's acting serious even if her words aren't the most comforting. I leave out the front door and realize I don't have keys to lock it on my way out. But maybe Lance does... I start to spiral. Did Lance choose to leave or is he missing? Why would he leave without telling me? Did I get fucked and dumped by Lancelot le Fay of all people?

"Didn't think you'd be so pissed to see me," Sara remarks. I must not be wearing my best poker face while thinking about Lance.

"Sorry. Just a lot on my mind."

Sara acknowledges my apology with a hum and then hands me a motorbike helmet. "Bitch has to wear a helmet. I don't make the rules."

"I know the law," I assure her as I slip the helmet over my head.

"Oh, I know. I still haven't decided if I should let you into my bar." Ignoring her, I hop onto the back of the bike. Sara revs the engine. "You might be one of us, but law enforcement and I don't get along."

"Can we just go find Lance?"

"Sure," she says in a sickly-sweet voice before looking over her shoulder at me. "Just tell me where to find him." When I don't respond her sweet demeanor falls apart like a sugar cube in water. "That's what I thought."

We drive off and I realize I have no idea where she's taking me. Then again, I don't know where to go. I know this city in theory, know the landmarks and where the neighborhoods end, but I'm not a local. Lance might be at his apartment or at a friend's. Maybe he needed some air and went to the park. I just want him safe, and he's not safe if he's not in front of me. I spend the whole ride watching people, looking out for the short blond man I can't stop worrying about.

The surroundings start to look familiar, and next thing I know, we're stopped in front of the One-Eyed Dog Bar. "I thought I wasn't allowed at the bar?"

"I said I was still considering," she corrects me, kicking down the stand and turning off her bike. "Plus, we're closed right now." She doesn't wait for me, instead just walking right up to the front door and fiddling with a ring of keys. I follow her, leaving the helmet with the bike.

The bar is much more well-lit during the day, sun streaming in from high windows I never noticed at night. Sara walks right up to the bar and starts prepping a drink.

I furrow my brows and join her at the bar, sitting on a stool. "We need to find Lance."

"What we need is to wait 'til Taylor gets back." She's cutting up limes.

"Lance is gone—"

"Yeah, he probably left." She sets the knife down and looks at me. "You seem to think he's some princess that needs saving. That guy is a le Fay."

"You don't know anything," I tell her.

Her brows raise, amused. "And you do?" We're both quiet, then Sara breaks the silence with a snort. "Come on, start asking." She returns to cutting limes.

"What?"

"I know you've got questions. About the full moon, about the gang, about your dick," she gestures at my crotch with a paring knife. "So, shoot."

I don't like this. Lance is missing and Sara is trying to

play buddy with me. It starts to dawn on me that maybe she's the reason Lance is gone. She knew where we were staying, and she easily could have come up with some story to get Lance out of the house of his own accord. Taylor conveniently being out of town doesn't help. Though, I'm not a hundred percent sure Lance is that naive. But if she did want to hand Lance over to the Blood Moon pack, she had an easy in.

"The Blood Moon Pack. What's their deal?"

I watch her face carefully, ready to catch any little slip.

"Some of them are lost souls. The rest are grade-A assholes." She slides the cut limes into a metal bin then returns her attention, fully, to me.

"Your situation isn't that uncommon. A gang member bites some poor person, and desperate for answers, they stick around with the very people that made their life hell. They tell you, we're a family—we're a pack, so you got to pull your weight."

I notice she says *we*. "Then they're in too deep."

"Right." She nods. "You get some addict to sell you their blood or deal the old fashion way." I raise a brow and Sara elaborates. "Vampires can't get high the way normal people can. Has to already be synthesized in the blood. I got real chummy with folks down at the methadone clinic." I can hear in her voice how disgusted she was with herself. I'm starting to think she didn't nab Lance and hand him off to the pack. I think she wants as little to do with Blood Moon as I do. "Anyway, maybe you think laying on your back is easiest and end up selling yourself or you just think recruiting girls is somehow better. But it never stops. There's never a point where you've paid off your debts and they let you leave."

"But what do they even offer?"

Sara just looks at me. "They offer what I'm giving you now. Someone who understands. You like rum?"

"Isn't it like, nine in the morning?"

"It's nine-thirty." She corrects me while pouring herself a drink. "What? You've never put Baileys in your coffee?"

"I prefer cinnamon..." I considered having a drink... When in Rome, right? But I don't really want to be intoxicated in case something goes south. Which it probably will, based on my luck the past few weeks. "I'm good, really, thanks."

"Your loss," Sara says, topping off her rum with some orange juice, I guess to make it more breakfast-y. She takes a long drink before continuing. "You know alphas don't exist right?"

I shake my head a little, taken aback by her sudden and frankly confusing statement. "What?"

"Like wolf alphas. The scientist who came up with that only looked at captive wolves." She takes another decent swig of her drink. "In the wild, packs are just families. Mom, Dad, and pups." Sara brings the glass to her lips again and sucks down the whole goddamn drink. There's a little bit of immature, fresh out of basic training part of me who still thinks a woman who can out drink me is hot. As if being able to hold your liquor means anything other than being a functioning alcoholic.

I'm ready to stop Sara from pouring herself another drink but she just tops off the ice with more orange juice. "Blood Moon makes us captive wolves. We answer to their bullshit alpha because we don't know any better. Worst of all, during the full moon, folks are compelled to listen."

"How does that work?"

"Listen closely," she points right at me as if calling me out. "Tomorrow night you're going to turn for the first time.

You'll be feral, a real tornado of destruction. But if everything goes as planned, Taylor will make you submit."

"Um..." I'm not sure how I feel about submitting to a man I barely know.

"Or you could submit to me," Sara offers, looking past the rim of her glass right at me as she takes another sip of juice. A few seconds later she's snickering. "I'm teasing. I don't want that responsibility." She sets the glass down. "Submitting to Taylor just means during the full moon you'll listen to him. He'll be your alpha or your advisor—whatever you want to call it."

"And what if I don't submit to anyone?" I'm secretly hoping that's an option. No offense to Taylor, he seems like an alright guy, I'm just not ready for my sergeant to be a man I barely know without any real credentials beyond being a werewolf himself.

"Well, then you'd be a lone wolf. You won't have any sort of pack during the full moon. It'll just be you and your rage. Sounds cool, but trust me, I've seen lone wolves, and it's not pretty."

I chew the inside of my cheek. "Why should I believe you?"

Sara snorts again. "Well, shit, if you don't want to, be my guest. Figure it out on your own." She finishes off her juice and pops the glass into a nearby sink.

She really doesn't care. Which makes me wonder what her loyalty is to Taylor. "Was Taylor the one who... submitted you your first full moon?"

"No," she replies. "My first full moon I was with the Blood Moon gang. I submitted to their old leader, Colm." She let out a humorless laugh, shaking her head. "Mean fucker he was. I thought he was going to kill me my first night. Almost tore my throat out..." For the first time Sara seems small, as if talking through the memory brings her right back to that night being brutalized by the other wolf. "I submitted, and for the next few years, I was his pet, regardless of the moon."

I grimace. "But... you're not now."

"No... Colm got axed by another member about three years back. I'd already wanted out by that point, so when Dominic took him out, I took the chance to bolt." She scoffed, "Guy is an absolute maniac without dressing like it's 1985 and he's trying to sneak into some hair band's set. He was just a kid when he killed Colm, I mean, he's still a snot-nosed kid, but you know." It clicks that Dominic, the new alpha, was the man that turned me. I let my nails dig into my palms. "Anyway," Sara continues, returning to her assertive self. "Taylor sent me upstate for a few months 'til things cooled down."

That's why she's loyal to Taylor. It seems like sheltering supernaturals is his M.O. Maybe he just does it out of the goodness of his heart. Maybe he does it so he'll have a bunch of people in debt to him. "So, if I go with you and Taylor, what comes after that?"

"Wolves usually go upstate for the moon. There's no space to run in the city, and while bullets won't kill you, they still hurt like a bitch."

I guess if I saw what looked like a werewolf in the streets, I'd fire my gun too. "So, for the rest of my life I have to take camping trips with you two?"

Sara let out a belly laugh. "No, no. God, can you imagine? The three of us taking a six-hour round trip in our sixties? I'd jump out of the car."

"Which wouldn't kill you," I point out. "You'd just be acting dramatic."

Sara laughs again, lighter this time, like a bell. It's funny.

Under all that biker bar chick exterior, I can tell there's a softness. I know if I pointed that out, she'd probably make sure I never saw anything ever again, my final memory of sight just a flurry of her fists. I wonder what she was like before she was bitten, if all this toughness was a remnant of trying to survive with Blood Moon.

I sympathize with what they took from her. What they took from us, really.

"In a year or two, you'll have enough control over your wolf to not need someone like Taylor to keep you in check. But to be honest? We're meant to be in packs. Maybe not ones with strict hierarchies, but werewolves have always stuck with their families."

"So, you two would be my family?"

Sara's face scrunches like I've just burped in it. "Don't make this a mushy-gushy thing, yeah?"

"Oh, come on, sis."

"Fuck off." She pulls a dish towel from behind the bar and throws it at my face.

CHAPTER TWENTY-ONE

LANCE

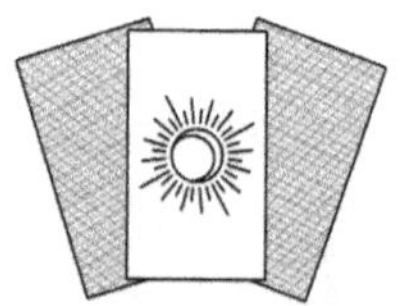

I DON'T KNOW HOW MUCH TIME I SPEND STANDING over Reagan, watching him sleep before I abandon him in the house. Slipping out of his sleepy hold is hard enough, like the most challenging game of Operation with the highest of stakes. But I manage to weave my way out of his grasp and slip out of the bed without waking him. I dress in the same baggy clothes as yesterday. It's still dark outside, but I don't know the exact time, Reagan having destroyed the one alarm clock in the house.

Reagan looks so peaceful sleeping. I'm afraid this is the last peaceful night of sleep he'll have. It's two days before the full moon, two days before the change. I'm not sure he's ready. I know I'm not ready, but there's nothing I can do about that. Maybe Reagan will be fine. He's brave and strong and has never shied away from what's happening to him. The opposite of me, trying to deny the life I was born into.

Finally, I pull myself away from Reagan and leave the safe house, locking the front door with the key Taylor left me. I walk back to my apartment, which I know is a bad idea, but I'm not about to confront my demons while wearing sweatpants. I want to at least look presentable. It takes me a little less than an hour to walk from the riverfront to downtown. I don't waste time at my apartment. I come in, go to my closet, pick out one of my standard work outfits, and leave.

Well, start to leave, before wondering where my wallet and phone might be. I realize I haven't had them on me since hooking up with Reagan. Thankfully I find both still in my discarded pair of pink pants. How nice of those jerks in Blood Moon to not rob me. Just abduct me, fail to ransom me, and then decide to use me as a chew toy. At least I still have my data plan.

I return downstairs to the street. Looking across the way, I see Davey at the counter inside Marble Ax. I wave to him, but there is a city street between us and he's busy with a customer. I have time to grab a coffee, but I don't feel like I can. The time I spent with Davey, playfully flirting and appearing like a morning person as I tried to forget my nightmares, feels unattainable now. Those were the days of me trying to act human, as if one day I would reach a certain threshold and would just... *be* human.

IT'S the second time I've stood in front of this duplex shaking in my shoes. I have to think really hard to remember how long it's been. Fourteen years. That doesn't even seem possible. But Junior and I were eighteen when we found out about Minerva, when we snooped around our Father's files and found a copy of a birth certificate not belonging to us or our sister. It was the first time Junior and I ever really shared an interest in something, though I doubt our hearts were in the same place.

After we contacted Minerva, we agreed never to speak of her to anyone. But how was that fair to her?

I blink and find myself standing at her front door. The paint is starting to chip, peeling in long white strips. It's sad to see. The place had been near-perfect all those years ago. But like a lot of neighborhoods, the house is falling into disrepair. What hasn't changed is the long strip of fabric hanging from a nail in the door. The fabric is pointed at the end like a sword, tiny glass beads of blue, red, and amber stitched up and down the fabric. Cowry shells line the edges like a fence to keep the glass beads in place. I know a talisman when I see one, even if this one is different from the kinds I grew up with. Nowhere near as flashy.

I knock at the door, half-hoping no one answers, but I hear a feminine voice chime from inside. "Coming!" About a minute later, the door opens. A woman, around five years younger than me, with warm brown skin and full curly hair that frames her face like a halo appears. She looks at me, her eyes emerald green and gold, the most damning evidence that we're related.

She starts speaking "I..." It feels like I'm a trapped rabbit in a snare. "I feel like I know you..."

"We've met once before," I tell her. She nods, but I can see in her eyes she still can't place me. "My name is Lancelot le Fay." Her eyes pop open, and I fear she recognizes the more unsavory part of my name.

Instead, she chirps, "Oh, that's right! The twins!" I instinctively wince, the way I always do when people from my past associate me with my brother. But I force a smile and she smiles back, which puts me at ease. "How could I forget the twins that brought me that scholarship."

How did I forget? We hadn't shown up empty-handed a decade earlier. It was pretty easy to just write a check for a couple thousand dollars for Minerva's education. I wish I could say it was my idea, but it had actually been Junior's. "Did you end up using it?" I ask stupidly.

She laughs, "I did. It paid for a good chunk of college, and then I got enough scholarships to go on to grad school."

My brows raise, impressed. "Wow. Look at you go." She was smarter than me, that was for sure. "Can I... come in?"

I don't know why I ask. I wouldn't invite myself inside, just a walking piggy bank. One half of a pair of twins back after a decade of silence. Nope, sorry, that's just too strange.

But to my surprise, Minerva opens the door wider. "I don't really have anything to offer you other than a couch to sit on."

I give her a smile. "That's enough for me." I step past the threshold for the first time. Junior and I never got past the stoop. She ushers me into the living room off the side of the entryway. Immediately, I'm drawn to the bookshelf holding a lot more than just books—though there are plenty of well-worn spines looking back at me. One of the shelves holds a copper bowl with intricate designs carved into its face. Four dolls made of scraps of fabric and shells of various shapes and sizes sit in the corner of the shelf. Remnants of red and yellow candles cling to the wood by melted wax.

My feet bring me to the altar like I'm being possessed. The closer I get the more I smell burnt wax and something else I can't quite place. Not sage but something similar. "Oh, please—" Minerva rushes to my side.

I interrupt her, "I won't touch." My attention shifts from the altar to her. "I know better than to touch an altar." Minerva blinks, cocking her head to the side. I can see myself reflecting in her eyes, can tell she's just now asking herself why I'm here. I sigh. Now or never. "You should sit."

"I'll stand, thank you." She replies, a hint of defiance in her voice.

I wish I could just say no like that. I take my own seat on the couch with Minerva standing over me like a teacher watching a student retake a test. "I know it's been a while," I start. "And uh, I never really explained anything all those years ago."

"You asked a lot of questions," Minerva recalls. "And I answered. For some reason..."

"We just... wanted to know you were okay." At least that's what I had wanted to know. Junior never has anyone's best interest at heart. When we met Minerva, I asked her about who lived with her, if she liked books—if so, what kind—and other little things. I was curious about my new sibling. Junior, I'm pretty sure, just wanted to make sure she wasn't a threat.

Minerva cocks a brow. "Okay?"

I look back over to the altar, finding it strange that there are four dolls. "We were being intentionally vague back then, but now I don't see a point." I return my attention to my sister. "Minerva, I am a witch like you."

"O...kay..." Her one raised brow lowers, now glowering at me.

Of course that wouldn't soften her up. She probably knows plenty of witches, ones who better understand her altar and her talismans. Witch lineage could be traced all the way back to the same place, to the crux of civilization, but witches scattered thousands of years ago. Fled before names like Athens or Cairo had any meaning. Practices changed overtime to reflect the environments and cultures around us. A game of resources and blending in. We might have all started out the same, but that was ancient history.

"Did you think I was a witch?" I ask.

She shrugs. "I knew that you weren't human. Just a hunch... But I didn't see why two guys would want to know what books I read if they didn't want me to reply to magic scrolls."

I chuckle, both of us aware that witches don't write down their magic. "But you told us you liked romance books."

I see a hint of red blossom beneath her cheeks. "Right..."

"Hey, at least you read. The last thing I read was the back of a frozen box for cook time." I see her lip twitch into a smile, but she quickly resets her face to be more neutral, more serious. This Minerva is a lot more hardened than the one I met fourteen years ago. "I'm... struggling to say what I want to tell you. I've never really said it out loud, I'm realizing."

"Then say it now," Minerva says, as if it's that simple. "Close your eyes, pretend I'm not here, and say it to yourself."

It feels like too simple a solution to actually work, but the other option is continuing our awkward small talk. Or I could jump out the window. I let out a slow, heavy breath like beginning a meditation, then I shut my eyes. Without sight, I can smell the mysterious aroma even better. The only smell I can compare it to is the smell of the trumpet vine flowers my Mother kept in her garden. "Minerva is my sister," I speak as if she's not there. "We share the same Father..." I could go on and on about our Father, but I think better of it.

When I open my eyes, Minerva looks... surprised, of course, but there was more behind her expression. The more I look at her, I recognize her face flipping through a rolodex of emotions. Anger, sadness, confusion... Again, all things I expect.

I stand up from the couch. "Minerva—"

She steps back like a spooked animal. "Get out." She speaks firmly.

"Minerva, can we please just talk?"

I take another step towards her, and she shouts, "Get out right now before I call someone!"

A deep voice calls from another room, making me jump. "What's going on?"

I turn and see an old man with a walker, his brown skin a much deeper hue than Minerva's but clearly the same golden color. Thick coke bottle glasses make it hard for me to make out his eyes, but from the way they shift down his nose, I can tell he's scowling. "Minnie, who is this?"

"No one, Gramps," she assures her Grandfather. "*He*," her voice is dripping with spite, "was just leaving."

I purse my lips, not wanting to leave. Ironic. I've been avoiding this place, avoiding Minerva, for so long, but now that I'm here, I feel a need to stay. I remember my wallet in my back pocket. "If you ever want to finish this conversation."

I pull out a business card and hold it out to Minerva. She just looks at the card between my fingers. The longer she stares, the softer her expression becomes.

Another hand snatches the card from my fingers. I turn to her Grandfather who's holding the card inches from his thick lenses. "Lancelot... le Fay?" Minerva's Grandfather mutters as he reads aloud. "Like the book character?"

"Unfortunately," I lament before turning to leave. To my surprise, Minerva follows, running past me into the entryway to open the door for me. I just nod in acknowledgment and step out of the house. She lingers in the doorway. I pause my exit and look at her.

I try again. "Minerva…"

A familiar cawing sound interrupts me. In the branches of a tree in the neighboring duplex yard, a crow is perched in the branches, looking right at us.

It caws a second time before flying off. Minerva is the first to speak. "Was that yours?"

"No," I admit.

She shuts the door in my face. I hear the deadbolt turn. I curse under my breath as I leave the property. Of course that went terrible. Like she was ever going to be ecstatic about finding out some stranger is her half-brother. Not to mention that crow making it look like I'm spying on her. We both recognize the bird as a witch's familiar. Not mine of course, but I do know who it belongs to.

A block away from Minerva's house, I finally find him. Or I should say he finds me, Junior jumping from a dilapidated house, grabbing me by my shirt. He pulls me a few steps onto the lot before pushing me against a foundation wall. "*Unnecessary*," I hiss. Clearly brother dear and I need to have a chat.

"You are one to talk," he bites back, speaking with such force his glasses slide a touch down his nose. "Coming back here, *unnecessarily*."

"You're here too," I point out. "Not to mention, you were the one who brought her up last time we spoke. You're the one with your damn familiar outside her window."

"Please." He rolls his eyes and releases my collar. I dust off my shirt while he runs his fingers roughly through his slicked-back hair.

I match his tone, quick and vicious like viper strikes.

"So, *he is* planning something? Are you really going to help him kill his own kin?"

"She's not our kin."

"How can you be so cold?" I ask despite only ever knowing Junior to be exactly that.

"How can you be so delusional?" He retorts. "We don't know her. She doesn't *need* to know us. Clearly she has a coven of her own. They'll protect her."

I clench my hands, nails digging into my palms. My Father is going to kill Minerva like he killed that college student all those years ago. Maybe Minerva's coven will protect her, but I can't take that risk. I'm not going to just let more people get hurt like I did growing up. But I also don't know how to help beyond warning her about our Father. Which I failed to do.

I push past my brother and walk back towards the street. "Lance, stop," he orders, and I ignore him. "Lance!" He repeats. I feel him grab the back of my collar again, but I'm on guard now. I turn and use my balled-up fist to clock him, my knuckle making direct contact with the flat on his nose. His wire glasses go flying off his face.

Junior, for his part, stumbles back but manages to stay upright. He holds his nose, hissing as he doubles over in pain. He glares at me, and it feels like staring down a dragon. Removing his hands from his face, my heart sinks as I see his nose looks relatively fine. No blood, some bruising, but certainly not broken.

"You're rubbing off on me, brother dear." His voice warns, and I think he's about to punch me back. Instead, he pulls a folded piece of paper from his pants pocket. It takes me a second too long to realize what it is as he opens the paper square and blows something in my face. The fine dust smells sweet and I swear it has glitter in it.

"I can't stop you from meddling any further... Take that risk if you want." Junior says ominously. More and more dust fills my eyes, and my body goes limp. I crumple to the ground, just barely able to watch my brother step over my body and leave before I pass out.

CHAPTER TWENTY-TWO

REAGAN

"Are you still worried about Lance?" Sara asks me. She's finally convinced me to have a drink, fireball with cranberry juice. I tell myself I'll sip at it to satisfy her, but the drink is gone in fifteen minutes.

I grumble, "I just want to know he's okay."

Sara snorts and grabs my glass, filling it up again though I know it's going to go to waste. "Puppy love," she comments as she's fixing the drink.

"We've been through a lot together the past week," I point out. "Most people would get attached."

"That's what I said," Sara rebuts.

I shake my head. "Puppy love is for tweens and their boyband posters. Lance is my responsibility."

Sara looks at me, her expression silently asking if I really just called Lance my responsibility. Her lips curl into a wicked grin. "Oh yeah, total puppy love. Not your fault." She sets the fresh red glass in front of me. "It could just be the elevated hormones. Unless you guys have already…" Her voice trails, same as her eyes which trail up and down my body.

"Maybe let's not talk about this," I suggest.

Sara's eyes not so subtly look down at my crotch. "Have you played with the piping recently?"

I pinch the bridge of my nose. "Lance explained it to me, so let's not."

She snorts. "Oh, right, and Lance is an expert."

"If you want to claim to be an expert in werewolf dick, be my guest," I shrug.

I expect a snarl, but Sara just rolls her eyes in return. "Just be careful you don't tear him apart. Adrenaline tends to make it harder to maintain a human form."

"I can transform without the moon?" I ask, though I've seen hints of what she's saying. Like my nails being sharper than they should be. First it was the shredded bedsheets and then there was last night when I accidentally pierced the skin on Lance's hip.

"Well, how the hell else did you get turned? We have to be at least partially transformed for any sort of venom to transfer. Though it's easier when the moon is near full. Near impossible during a new moon."

"You've mentioned venom before... Back at the safe house," I think aloud.

"Look, I'm not an expert. Maybe you can call it our germs instead, but if we bite someone while we're transformed, we transfer lycanthropy. That, or if anyone drinks our blood. So, stick to fucking witches and avoid the vamps, yeah?"

I roll my eyes and get up from the bar but grab the fireball cranberry and take a long swing. I need it after that comment.

"Where are you going?" Sara asks as I set down my half-finished drink.

"To find Lance." I turn to leave. "That's pretty obvious," I mutter under my breath.

Sara comes out from behind the bar and follows me. "And how are you going to manage that? Lost dog posters? Look, let me bring you back to the safe house and I'll go look for him."

I don't even stop to look at her. "No thanks. I'll handle it."

I step out into the parking lot of the One-Eyed Dog, Sara a few steps behind. "If you run off now, we won't be able to find you in time for the full moon," she informs me. "Taylor should be back in an hour or so, and then the three of us—"

Sara stops suddenly. I turn, not sure what I expect to find, but it's not Sara in a chokehold. Her feet dangle off the ground as the Blood Moon Pack member with long black hair covering his face holds her neck with his elbow.

I'm about to lunge at him when two sets of hands grab my arms and push me down to the ground, forcing me to my knees. It's not a bad move, but I have a better one. I ram my head back and to the side, hitting one of the men in the nose. Once my arm is free, I grab the uninjured man by the arm and toss him forward. Unfortunately, he's bigger than I expect, and I end up rolling forward with him. I have a split second to decide if I should try and get on top of the man and pin him or get back on my feet.

I lift my hips and roll off the asphalt, landing on my feet. I look back at Sara who is biting and clawing at the massive man's arm, but he appears unphased. Sara shouts at him, her teeth coated with his blood. "Let me fucking go, Malcom!" She starts kicking her legs wildly. If she's able to scream like that, he isn't putting pressure on her windpipe.

With Sara doing a lot more damage to her captor than he is to her, I decide to run.

Only for a fist with metal accessories to hit me square in the nose. I stumble back but manage to keep my footing. The wolf that bit me, Dominic— stands in front of me, looking pleased with himself. Before I can strike, the two other gang members appear and push me back down to my knees. My knees on the ground, Dominic punches me again, the cold metal details of his rings cutting my cheeks. He keeps punching me, and I can taste copper in my mouth. Sara continues to scream obscenities behind me.

Dominic pauses his assault to shout at Malcom. "Deal with your girlfriend, Mac!" Sara's screams become distant as she's dragged away. Dominic gets down on one knee, his face hovering above mine. "Cause I'm nice, I'll offer you the option to come quietly. Er, consciously."

I spit blood in his face, and Dominic practically falls backwards. "Fucking gross!" He wipes the spit and blood off his face with his hands then wipes them on his jeans. "Your stupid boyfriend pulled that move too," Dominic mutters, and I smirk, proud of Lance. "Well?" He snarls at the two men holding me down. "Do it already. What are you waiting for, an invitation? Idiots."

A cloth is placed over my mouth and nose. The obvious sweet smell makes me panic, and I immediately stop feeling the stinging pain in my face. I try to move my head but one of the men grabs my hair to keep me steady. I'm able to do very little as darkness begins to cloud my vision. I should have went looking for Lance earlier. What if they already have him? What if they've already hurt him like they said they would in that warehouse?

This is all my fault, and I find myself hoping Lance will someday forgive me for all of this, just before I pass out.

CHAPTER TWENTY-THREE

LANCE

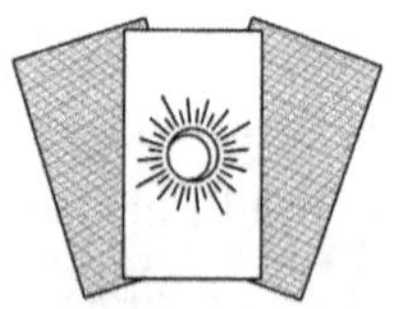

AN ANNOYING AND FAMILIAR CHIME URGES ME TO wake. I groan, my head feeling light as I blink sleep out of my eyes. I rub my eyes with my palms. Finally able to see, I pull my hands away and I recognize blue dust smudged across my hands. It reminds me of the time Jason and I dressed up as *Rocky Horror* characters for Halloween and I forgot not to touch my eyes. Except I know that's not highlighter making my hands all sparkly. "Stupid alchemy," I mutter.

The chime echoes again and I finally realize it's my cell phone. I pull it from my pocket and answer it without bothering to check the caller ID. "Hello?" I say, my voice groggy.

Daphne's voice comes through the line, sounding stressed. "Lance, you're not at the safe house. Did you forget the danger you're in?" Her voice makes my blood run cold. It's like I'm a teenager again and my Mom just found weed in my bedroom.

I shake my head, trying to knock some of the magical sleep away. "I'm sorry, I had to do something."

"Something Taylor or I couldn't help with?"

"No." I tell her in a firm voice. "No, Daphne, it was something *I* had to do. Something I should have done a long time ago."

There was a pause before Daphne replies. "Did you succeed?" A mix of anger and hope paints her voice. I know she wants what's best for me. It's the whole reason she's upset in the first place.

I wish I could tell her it was all worth it. That Minerva and I reconnected, that I'd finally faced a part of my past, that I'd made a difference. There's no point in lying. "No... n-nothing bad happened though." Damn my stutter.

But Daphne doesn't mention it. "Lance, things have gotten worse. Where are you?"

How could things have gotten worse? How long was I knocked out for? "What's happening?" I finally ask.

I can tell she's at the end of her immortal rope. "Just tell us where you are."

Even more questions pop into my head but I comply. "I'm in Highland Park... I think Palmer Park is close by—"

"Don't move! We'll come to you."

"Daph, I am in a random lot in a part of the city I don't know super well. Just meet me on Covington near the park entrance and we can get onto Woodward from there." The highway will get us wherever we need to go, even if it's just back to the safehouse to get chewed out by Daphne and Taylor.

"Fine. But stay on the line with me till we pick you up."

"Alright." It's a reasonable request. I start walking towards the park, the houses becoming more inhabited as I continue north. Daphne and I are both silent on the line. Somehow, I just know it's better to ask her in person what was going on.

I make it to the park promenade and in less than ten

minutes. A familiar white van pulls up, its tires screeching. The van door slides open, and I almost don't want to get in. Taylor's voice calls to me. "Hop in." He doesn't sound upset with me, which is reassuring.

I slide into the van, and the second I shut the door, Taylor has his foot on the gas. "Let me get my seatbelt on!" I complain, still uncomfortable with how fast this van can go. It looks like one of those church vans for old ladies, not a fucking heist vehicle. But with Taylor hunched over in the steering wheel and Daphne dressed in her 'daytime' garb, it certainly feels like we're trying to rob something.

Daphne looks back at me. A thick, square set of sunglasses covers her face. She has on a wide, white brimmed hat with a lace veil like a bride. Despite it still being early fall she wears a thick white turtleneck, and her hands are covered white dinner gloves. Vampires can only handle so much sunlight. At least Daphne found some way to make herself look couture with her own brand of tactical gear.

"Okay," I huff. "Now can we now talk about what is happening?"

A voice from behind chimes, "It's my fault." I jump and turn to see Sara crawl up front from the back of the van.

"Put your seatbelt on!" I scold her while she stands next to my seat. I guess if we crash, she'll just scrape herself off the pavement once she healed, werewolf and all that. I just don't really want to see it happen.

Sara ignores me. "Reagan was looking for you and I took him to the bar."

"Shit," I hiss. Sara said it was her fault, but if Reagan had left the safe house to look for me... "You had no way of finding me," I remind her.

Daphne calls from the front, "Then she should have

stayed with Reagan at the safe house until you came back." She turns around in her seat. Even with the glasses and lace blocking a good portion of her face I can't miss her deep-set frown. "Or until Taylor dragged you back. What were you thinking, Lance?"

"Listen," I raise my hands in exasperation. "It sounds like none of us had the brightest of ideas today. But no one is telling me what's going on."

Daphne finally explains, "Blood Moon has Reagan."

As soon as she says it, I feel like such an idiot for not piecing it together. Everyone is in the van *except* Reagan. I'd left him and he went looking for me. I fucking left him after everything we did last night. Being with Reagan gave me the courage to face a part of my past. But my courage was blind. I had gone in with no real plan of what to say to Minerva. Then I was disappointed I failed. I'm a fish who figured it was about time he started walking on land despite having no actual concept of lungs or legs. I'm not brave. I've never been brave. What made me think today was the day that all changed?

Reagan.

Reagan made me feel like I could be as brave and strong and comforting as he was. As if being with him made us similar. It feels like I'm about to cry. I should cry. But nothing comes. No tears or wails, not even a sniffle of sadness. I'm despondent.

Sara gets right up in my face, and I know she's speaking to me but all I catch is silence. At most, I hear a distant ringing, like hearing a bell on the shore while I'm lost out at sea. Taylor's voice from behind the wheel finally pulls me from my self-inflicted hypnosis. "LANCE!" He leans on the horn, and everyone groans as they cover their ears.

"Fuck— okay!" I shout, letting everyone know I'm

finally putting myself back together. But my voice falls to a whisper. "What are we going to do?" I don't even know who I'm asking. I don't know if it's a question for anyone in the car or just the universe itself.

Sara speaks up. "We're not completely lost. That's what I was *trying* to tell you. We know where Blood Moon is going for the full moon."

I bury my face in my hands. "I *forgot* about the full moon." I have and I haven't. I knew it was coming but I never made any sort of plan. That's Taylor's job sure, but I could have come up with a backup.

Even with my hands obscuring my vision, I can tell from the tone in Sara's voice she's rolling her eyes. "Okay, well, it's tomorrow night, so I hope you're not going to just cry about it till then."

I lift my head and look at her, not even sure what expression I'm portraying, but I can feel every muscle in my face straining. "Really uplifting words there, Sara."

I hear a groan from the back of the van and look at the back row of seats for the first time. It's a good thing I'm wearing my seatbelt because I almost jump out of my seat. The large scarred man from Blood Moon is laying on the seats wrapped in what looks like silver chains. Something pulled from Daphne's collection of antiques, no doubt.

"Why is he here!?"

"Don't wake sleeping beauty," Sara snaps just as loud as me.

The man continues to wake, soon realizing the situation he's in. The chains rattle as he flexes and writhes in the backseat. He mutters a few curses under his breath.

"Malcolm here is going to tell us where Blood Moon hangs out during the full moon." Sara looks back at her captive. "If he can *actually* find it."

Malcom's voice is groggy. "What the fuck am I doing?" He sit up best he can, and I finally feel like I can getting a good look at him. Back at the warehouse, all I could focus on were his scars. With his hair out of his face I see his scars, sure, but I also see he has a strong nose with a slight bend at the bottom and a heavy brow above steely gray eyes. I try to focus on the normal side of his face instead of opposing side, marred with what I think is a gnarly burn scar. I realize that's why he's always covering his face with his hair, and I feel bad for him. Feeling bad for a gang member isn't really reasonable, but he is also hogtied in the back of a van.

Sara looks over her shoulder at Malcolm. "You're going to use that hamburger head of yours to tell us where the pack is gathering for the full moon." There's a sweetness in her voice, like she's teasing him on the playground, calling him dumb without actually saying it. Poor guy. Hogtied and no doubt about to be lambasted by Sara for the rest of the drive.

"You don't have to insult him," I tell her. "We kinda need him on our side," I speak softly, not wanting him to hear.

"Please," Sara scoffs. "He likes it."

I'm about to object but I catch a smirk tug at Malcolm's lips. It disappears as quickly as it appeared, and I look at Sara to see if she caught the expression as well. If she did see it, she's disinterested.

"Settle in," Taylor announces. "It's a few hours until we get to the state forest."

CHAPTER TWENTY-FOUR

LANCE

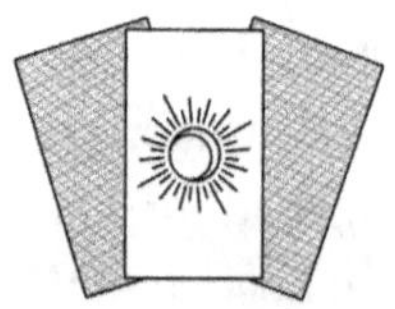

By the time we reach the cabin, it's already nightfall. A not-quite full moon reflects off the van's tinted windows. I stare at the reflection in awe. Right now, staring directly at the moon feels like staring up at a god. In most myths, seeing a god meant burning up, going mad, turning into a pillar of salt— whatever punishment that deity was feeling that particular day, I guess.

Sara drags Malcolm towards the cabin like he's a body bag, his arms and legs still wrapped in chains. Taylor takes over and just scoops Malcolm up and puts him over his shoulder. Daphne, meanwhile, joins me back at the van. "How are you feeling, dear?" She's taken her sunglasses and hat off so I can see the sympathy in her eyes.

"I feel nothing, actually." I return to my staring contest with the moon's reflection. "Numb is better than something right?"

"Not when it prevents you from acting." She might as well have just slapped me.

I whip my head in her direction. "How long have you been wanting to lay that one on me?"

Her head tilts and she gives me her signature angelic smile, fangs and all. "Does it matter? So long as you hear it now?" Daphne doesn't wait for a response, instead threading her arm through mine and leading me towards the cabin. Good thing too, because I didn't have a rebuttal.

Inside the cabin, Malcom is flat on his back on the couch, still chained up like one of those rubber corpses you see at a Halloween store. Sara leans over the back of the couch, looking down at him as if she's his warden. I shake my head. "Are we going to let him relieve himself or anything?"

Sara snorts. "For once, you've got a point." She walks away and I follow her into the cabin's kitchen. Taylor is cutting potatoes, an open can of tomatoes and a large pot next to him. "I'll take over," Sara tells him. "You go hold Malcolm's dick."

Taylor's face scrunches, clearly not happy with his new job. "He'd probably prefer you hold it." Sara smacks Taylor in the chest before pushing him aside and taking over the cutting board.

Taylor gives me a nod as he walks past me. I approach Sara. "Can I uh... Help?"

"Not sure how, but if you can find some rice, that might be good to add." She doesn't look up from her cutting. I start opening cabinets, desperate to find some way to be useful.

A NEW NIGHTMARE plagues me that night, one that reminds me of an Impressionist painting: vibrant, blotchy, and distorted. Every figure both man and beast. I see my brother, watching his nose, the same nose as mine, elongate and become black. The beak absorbs his lips. His light hair turns black and becomes light and airy like feather down. Daphne's Renaissance face appears before it turns gaunt. Her features shrink and ears become rabbit-like, but hairless, the skin almost translucent. Eventually she appears as a bat with wrinkled features and beady black eyes.

I watch my Father's jaw expand as scales start to cover his body. His pupils and nose become slits as a proud and terrifying dragon stands before me. The last thing I see before I wake is Reagan's dark brown hair, growing from every pore, his fingernails being replaced with claws, and those eyes that I love so desperately glowing without warmth. Then the beast, Reagan, lunges at me.

I bolt upright in the bunk bed, my forehead almost slamming against the slats of the bed above me. I start crying. I'm used to it, and I'll get over it, except I have a roommate. Sara's asleep in the bunk above me, like we're staying at a very depressing adult summer camp. I roll onto my stomach and sob into my pillow, muffling my wails and sniffles.

To my dismay, I hear Sara's voice. "Lance?" She asks as if confirming I'm awake. I just let out a whimper, not really wanting or being able to talk. I hear Sara let out a heavy sigh. "You know, it could be worse. You've got us. Lots of people have no one." She has no idea I'm acutely aware of the phenomenon of loneliness. But at least she's trying. My face still buried in my pillow, I eventually fall back asleep and suffer no further nightmares.

HIKING HAS NEVER BEEN my favorite activity if I'm being honest. Hiking towards a pack of werewolf bikers doesn't make the experience any better. I walk at the back of the group while Malcom leads, his hands still wrapped in chains. If I were in a better mood, I would make a joke about him being our search and rescue dog. I think it would have gotten a chuckle out of Sara at least.

"What sort of magic are you going to use?" Sara calls over her shoulder.

"Are... you talking to me?" I ask, sounding stupid even to myself. "I don't... I don't have any magic *planned*."

Sara glares at me, but I realize I deserve it. "We're going into a den of wolves on the full moon and you don't have any clue how you're going to protect yourself?" She scoffs. "Because I'm not doing it. I'm crowd control."

Taylor speaks up. "I'll be getting Reagan." He sounds so sure, as if this has already been discussed.

"You're going to rescue Reagan?" I ask

"He'll be feral, Lance," Taylor explains. "Someone will subdue him. We just have to make sure it's not Blood Moon Pack."

Sara adds, "And even if they do get him to submit to Dominic or another pack member, we can still pull him out."

Malcolm snorts loudly, less like a pig and more like a boar. "And torture the poor bastard? I mean, fuck 'em, but that's a pretty harsh sentence."

I feel my stomach flip. "What is he talking about?" I'm now trying harder to keep up with Sara and Taylor along the hike. I trip over a root embedded in the dirt but catch myself before I land flat on my face.

When I'm stable, I see Malcom looking back at me with a smug expression. "When a wolf submits to another wolf they'll be compelled to run with that wolf during the full moon. If a wolf can't run with their pack— with their *alpha* —they'll feel excruciating pain."

I've heard about wolf runs but not that extra detail. Wolves roam together in packs when the moon is full. Coming across a werewolf pack under a full moon is a death sentence, at least according to stories passed down from witch to witch. Everything I've ever heard was from witches, which is quite the caveat.

Sara cuts in, "Alphas are bullshit! And the pain fades with time so long as he doesn't keep running with you bone-heads." She looks back at me. "Don't listen to his scare tactics."

Taylor appears to be the only neutral part I can talk to right now. "If you don't get to Reagan first, what's going to happen?"

Taylor purses his plush lips. "If Reagan is overtaken by a member of Blood Moon, he will want to run with them, that's true. But only when he's fully transformed. When he's in his human form, he won't feel any pull towards whoever he submitted to. A wolf is more likely to submit to a person they care for, but it doesn't work the opposite way around."

Malcolm starts to grumble. "Running with us has its perks." Sara kicks him in the back of the shin, and he grunts but manages to stay upright.

"But Malcom *is* right," Taylor continues, ignoring Malcom's comment and Sara's act of violence. "If Reagan can't run with the wolf he submitted to, then he will be in pain. Self-inflicted pain."

My blood goes cold. The chill reaches my throat and my voice sounds like breaking ice. "He'll hurt himself?"

"He'll do anything in his power to reach the pack. So..." his voice trails.

"Does he have to submit to a wolf?" I ask, almost pleading for the answer I wanted to hear.

Sara and Malcom answer together: "Yes."

"No," Taylor follows with a rumbling, commanding voice. Everyone stops walking, Sara and Malcom both looking at Taylor with confusion. "It's rare but it happens."

"Wait..." I say. "Did you submit to Daphne?"

Taylor looks appalled. "Lance, I had my first transformation when I was thirteen. Daph isn't a cradle robber like *that*. My Father was the one to keep me in check. He's passed away now, but I've long since been a mature enough wolf to have no real master."

Sara jumps in, "Just like me."

"Well..." Taylor speculates. Malcolm chuckles and Sara tries to kick him in the shins again, but he manages to step back in time. "Right. Mature wolves, the both of you." He shakes his head before getting back on topic. "There have been wolves who have submitted to non-wolves. Heck, they've even submitted to regular humans. A good master, for lack of a better word, keeps a wolf grounded. Reminds them of their humanity, that they're more than a wolf."

"They're... wolf men..." I muse.

Taylor chuckles, "Exactly."

We return to hiking in silence. Regardless of if we succeeded or not, Reagan will forever have some sort of master in his life. Well, not forever, but a long time, especially if he continues to run with whoever he submits to. I stare at the back of Taylor's head, asking myself if I really wanted Reagan to be tied to him.

I have no reason to object to Reagan submitting to Taylor... But the idea made my face hot.

CHAPTER TWENTY-FIVE

REAGAN

I wake up to find my hands tied behind my back, sitting real deep in the depths of the woods. Blue sky barely peeks through the branches and foliage above. I struggle and realize my hands are wrapped in chains, but my feet are free. Not that I can risk just sprinting into the woods like this with nothing but hope of finding civilization. Really, the only thing I can do is walk around the tent city the Blood Moon has made for themselves. A couple dozen guys and a handful of women all sit around drinking, smoking, laughing, and cooking. Like a full moon tailgate party.

I sit on the edge of it all just observing. Dominic approaches me looking smug. He waves a beer in my face. "Thirsty?"

"Water might be nice," I frown. "You aren't really used to taking hostages are you?"

Dominic's cocky expression falls away to one of confusion. "What gave it away?"

"Uh, I've had no water, you don't actually have a place to hold me captive, and I've seen all your faces. I can keep going."

Dominic just laughs. "Doesn't matter. After tonight, you'll be one of us." He gestures back to the tent city. "All the beer and bitches you want."

"I'm not in high school," I point out. "I don't really care about those things."

"*Everyone* cares about getting tail. Just wait till you go into heat." He pops the tab on the can. "Then you'll be thankful we've got so many bitches."

"Are you saying bitches in a derogatory way or... in a female dog way?"

"What?" Dominic looks even more confused, or maybe just miffed that I'm not really buying his pitch. "What does it matter? The girls like it just as much as we do."

"Do they tell you that afterwards? After five whole minutes of bliss?"

Dominic pours the beer in my face, which, after a day and half of no access to water or a sink, actually feels sort of good. "Fuck you, pup," he spits through his teeth. "You'll get what's coming to you once the sun sets." He turns to leave, but not before lobbing the beer can at my face. I manage to dodge.

Alone again, I start to gnaw at my cheek so bad it bleeds. I don't know what to expect once the full moon arrives. I have my dreams and old movies I watched years ago... So, only the most reliable of sources. I curse myself for not at least trying to make friends at this fucked up event. These people are scum, but they know what it's like to be a werewolf. Sara used to be one of these punks, and she's alright as far as I'm concerned.

I people watch, wondering just how many of these folks want out. Or, conversely, how many of them would rather die than give up running with the pack. There's definitely a comradery in the air, and I would be lying if I said it doesn't bring me some strange comfort. The more I watch, the more I think back to basic training, how we all became so close after the worst days of our lives. Some people were happy to join the service while others were already looking back and realizing they'd been taken advantage of. What lies did Dominic tell these people to get them all together? A promise of security? Of family?

I sit, dreading the incoming twilight, but of course time moves way too fast when you want to take it slow. As the sky turns purple, people begin tossing aside their drinks and food leaving the tents behind. Dominic and the bald guy from the warehouse come over to me and pick me up by my arms. "Got something to show me?" I ask, pretending like I'm not scared as hell.

"We just want to give you the space you need," Dominic explains in a sticky sweet voice. "The first time is a big day for a pup like you."

"Pretty sure I'm older than you," I point out. Dominic can't be a day over thirty, and I suspect he's younger than that.

"In human years maybe, but you don't know shit about being a wolf."

We walk, but I make sure I can stare right into Dominic's dark eyes. "Sara told me you killed the last alpha."

His eyes get big and ghoulish, and a smile curls at his lips. "That's right. Old man was getting crotchety. Couldn't let him drag us all down."

"Sounds like you need to respect your elders."

"Sounds like you need to shut the fuck up."

I do, not because he told me to, but because talking to him feels like talking to a high school delinquent. I'd rather ruminate on how tonight is going to ruin my life than keep digging for Dominic's humanity.

Eventually we reach a clearing, and I'm horrified to find the sky a deep blue, not quite black but close enough that I know I'm running out of time. I'm tossed to the ground, landing on my knees, bent over so my face is deep in the dirt and weeds. I feel my hands being unwrapped from the chains but do nothing to celebrate my new mobility. This act of kindness is not for my benefit.

I look up and see there aren't nearly as many people with us now as there have been in the camp. As if he can read my mind, Dominic speaks up. "Don't worry, we'll join the rest of the pack once you're initiated." I watch him start to slip off his rings and worn leather jacket. Afraid to look at the sky, I lower my head back down at the ground. I doubt it matters. I probably don't even need to be outside for the transformation to start. It's a scary thought that the moon could affect me anywhere.

I feel a tingling in my toes and fingertips and immediately know what's about to happen. My heart races—faster and faster, until I'm scared it will explode. The tightness in my chest makes my veins pop, veins I didn't even know I had in my forehead and neck bulging beneath my skin. My skin becomes thicker and thicker with fur by the second. I gasp as my teeth vibrate. Not my gums or my mouth, but my **teeth**, the bones becoming larger and longer. My heartbeat is overshadowed by loud popping and cracking sounds, like firecrackers, coming from inside my body.

I don't scream or groan. I don't think I have it in me to make any sound.

There is something in the air. Pungent and rich smelling, not at all disgusting in its notes, yet it drives me up a wall. I remember back at the safe house, the rage that bubbled inside me. It was always just below the surface, and I was oblivious to it until something broke. Then Lance would appear and clean it all up, making the rage disappear. Now, there's nothing I can do about it: *kill, maim, destroy* —**kill, maim, destroy.** Over and over, the mantra rings in my head as my vision fades to black.

I see nothing. Experience nothing. Not even the pain of my body. All that remains is that voice of desire... To kill, to maim, to destroy everyone who did this to me.

CHAPTER TWENTY-SIX

LANCE

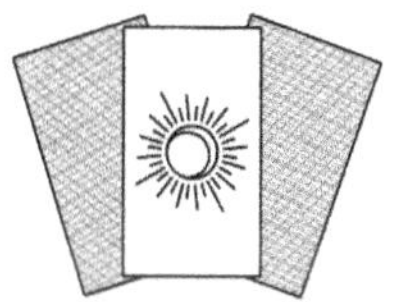

"The sun is setting," I croak, my heart leaping into my throat. Everyone looks back at me with a *no shit* expression, and I don't know if they're more annoyed with me or with the impending moon. "Are we almost there?"

"We're here," Malcolm announces. He nods ahead. "About ten yards away, there is a clearing. That's where we bring all our new recruits."

"Okay, then let's go." I march forward past Malcolm, only for Taylor to grab my shoulder and pull me back.

"You stay here where it's safe." He gives my shoulders a squeeze. "Please, Lance, if you get hurt, I can't promise I'll be able to do anything for Reagan."

Malcolm snorts. "A pissy witch in a wood full of wolves? Nowhere is safe for him."

"I'm not *pissy*," I hiss at him. "And last time I checked, I did pretty well dealing with your pack last week."

"Lance," Taylor leans down. I'm always aware that he's taller than me, but I do forget he's taller than the majority of people. That is until he gets down at eye level with me, standing the way he would when speaking to a child. "Please don't die on this rescue mission."

"Is that... your advice?"

"It's a plea," he explains. "I don't want you to die. Daphne doesn't want you to die. And most of all, *Reagan* doesn't want you to die."

"Okay," I huff. "But... what if I could help? I could be the one to subdue Reagan." I glance over and see Sara and Malcom looking at each other, neither one of them looking convinced. "Taylor, you said that anyone—"

"I should have never told you that."

"But it's true, isn't it?"

Taylor grumbles something under his breath before releasing my shoulders. "Do what you want." He began walking in a random direction.

"Where are you—" Sara bumps into my shoulder. "Excuse me." She turns, and I almost fall backwards. Her once green eyes are now a sickly yellow and glowing. Her canines have already grown past her bottom lip, threatening to puncture it. She glances at me just long enough to give me her signature glare before continuing on, deeper and deeper into the brush.

"The change is starting," Malcolm explains. "Those with the least control change the first." His tone is cocky, but as I look at him, I see the transformation begin to take hold of him as well. His back and shoulders hunch but he's still his normal, massive height. There's more thick black hair on his knuckles and face. I start to back away. Not consciously, just out of survival.

"Lance!" Taylor calls from somewhere in the brush, his voice gruff like I've never heard before. "Go. Hide."

I bolt, not caring about where I'm going. I'm not sure it even matters. If a werewolf wants to kill me, with their fast legs and heightened senses, then, well, that's that. If I had bothered to bring any sort of focus, I might be able to defend myself against a wolf. But I stupidly hadn't. I run until it hurts to breathe, and then I just let myself fall to the ground. The floor of the forest is covered in leaves, and I seriously consider covering myself in them and just laying here until morning. I probably should. Otherwise, I'll just get in the way. Lance the pissy, useless witch.

No, fuck that. Fuck that voice in my head telling me the worst things about myself. I've protected myself and Reagan from the Blood Moon Pack before. I made a focus out of nothing, and I can do it again. I remember Taylor's plea. I wish I had thought to tell him then that I want to live, *of course* I want to live, but I want to live a life I can be proud of.

I sit up, leaves in my hair. If I could just find the clearing... Everything around me looks pretty much the same, and it's hard to remember where I came from. All those fairytales of getting lost in the woods don't feel so fantastical now. I'm even looking for a big bad wolf. I shut my eyes and just listen, wondering if I can hear howls and padded footfalls of werewolves.

Nothing.

I consider my options. I can try and use a tree branch as a focus. I don't have any experience with using plant materials beyond mixing them in potions, which I'm not even very good at. I grab a pine tree branch, my palm becoming sticky with sap. "Sorry," I whisper to the tree as I snap the branch. There is a big difference between using plant materials for magic and using plant life for magic. Namely that plants can and will kill you, which I guess some plants can already do that without witch meddling.

I hold the branch out in front of me like a wand, trying

to channel the same energy that aided me back at the warehouse. I feel a snap of energy like a piece of thread reaching its limit. The end of the tree branch burst into flames. "Shit!" I drop the lit branch onto the dirt and stamp it out, making sure not a single ember is left behind. I thought maybe pine needles and pine bark would be different enough materials to work as two conductors. If only I'd thought of not using the damn branch as a focus.

With the embers now reduced to ash, I take a second to think about what magic I'm actually good at. Not summoning, or any type of elemental magic. None of the flashy things that might actually be of use in a fight. My Mother used to say that my magic, our magic, is cerebral. It goes by many names, but she always just called it the sight. The ability to see beyond our mortal bodies. I place my palms flat against the ground. The earth, which has been untouched, filled with unseen natural materials. Untapped minerals, animal bones, plant material...

I close my eyes and pull energy from the earth: from tree roots, from the animals decomposing amongst the mushrooms and leaves, precious untapped stones buried deep in the dense dirt. As soon as I feel the energy course through my body, I speak an incantation. I picture Reagan in my mind. Not just his appearance, but his aura that I've grown so fond of— that brings me comfort. I don't know if he'll be quite the same now that he's in wolf form, if he's too corrupted for me to reach. Except, I can't imagine Reagan's passions would be subdued by his lycanthropy that he would be any less confident and strong.

I close my eyes and let the magic return to the dirt with one purpose: *find Reagan.*

Then I see it, my eyes still shut, a clearing where a

handful of wolves tussle with each other like puppies. I can't hear anything, but I feel a pull in a certain direction. Opening my eyes, I follow the pull. Running, occasionally stopping to touch the dirt and make sure I'm still following the path towards the clearing. The invisible, proverbial line of breadcrumbs, is faint, no matter how far I run. But it's something.

The trees start to thin out and I hear a snarl following a dog's whimper. I run even faster and almost get knocked out by a flying werewolf. A large mass of fur careens towards me, forcing me to jump down into the brush. There's a loud snap as the wolf hits a tree that then collapses onto the forest floor. I looked at the wolf, its gray coat and healed gash along the belly alerting me that this can't be Reagan. I scramble, continuing to run.

I reach the clearing and I see him. Reagan—neither man nor beast. Everything about him is massive, from his head to his clawed hands. The fur on his body is the same chestnut brown as his normal hair and his blue eyes glow in the darkness. He stands on two feet, but his legs bent in an unnatural way, similar to wolf haunches. His lips curl up to bare his teeth, and drool drips from his maw.

I watch him swipe at another, smaller wolf who backs off before lunging at him again. Just then, a third wolf comes up from behind and bites Reagan on the shoulder. I scream before I get a better look at the attacking wolf. It has a gray and brown hide with dark, almost black, eyes that somehow still glow. Its teeth are deep in Reagan's hide, but it wraps its arms around his chest as if trying to hold him back. I have to reassess, figure out who is friend and who is foe. The grey wolf is probably Taylor, which means the smaller wolf should be from Blood Moon.

Another wolf—the smallest I've seen yet—runs circles around the two grappling wolves. The wolf jets forward and takes a swipe at Reagan before returning to its laps like the attack was just part of a relay course. Its coat is a light brown with familiar yellow eyes that illuminate the dark and make it easy to track the creature's movements. Sara. The wolf Reagan had been fighting prior to Taylor's ambush lets out a noise like a laugh. It has to be Mullet—based on the size and just that *sound* he makes, like a hyena.

Taylor still has a grip on Reagan, and with Sara assisting, I think things are going well. Famous last words. Mullet uses his back legs to bolt forward onto all fours, running like Sara in a terrifying mix of speed and strength. He barrels into Taylor and Reagan like bowling pins, knocking both wolves back to the ground with Mullet on top of the pile. Reagan unfortunately sandwiched between the two, all three wolves snap their jaws at each other.

Sara keeps running circles around them and I want to cry out for her to do something. Then a large wolf, black as midnight, stalks out of the tree line. He lets out a low growl before locking onto Sara and going after her. Sara is much faster, but I know that if the other wolf manages to snatch her, she won't be able to put up much of a fight.

Meanwhile, in the very literal dog pile, Taylor has reached forward and grabbed onto Mullet's neck like he's a novelty chicken. Reagan sees this as an opening and bites into Taylor's arm, the gray wolf letting out a bark of pain. Mullet catches on and turns his entire focus onto

Taylor, scratching at his arm until his fur is matted with blood. Taylor's barks turn into howls, pinned down by the two other wolves. Even if he's the largest of the three of them, two against one isn't great odds.

Reagan releases Taylor's arm from his maw and manages to wriggle his way out of the werewolf sandwich. Only, now he jumps back onto the pile, focusing his ire on Mullet, who squeals. The small wolf is slippery and breaks Reagan's grapple with ease. Instead of maintaining focus on Mullet, Reagan just continues his assault on Taylor. To my surprise Mullet just... watches. It's easy to forget there is a logical, human brain buried under all that fur. If he means to wait it out, let Reagan get out most of his energy fighting Taylor before swooping in so he can make Reagan submit, he's a lot smarter than I gave him credit for.

Meanwhile, I'm just standing here doing nothing, slack jawed like I'm watching a movie. Finally, I use my voice. "Reagan!" I shout across the clearing. Nothing changes, the violence continues. I start running towards the group without thinking. I'm a few yards away when I shout again, "Reagan!"

Finally, he sees me, his blue eyes boring into my soul like a hot nail. I stop running, standing out in the open. "Reagan please! Just... just..." Oh, fuck, what do I say now that I have his attention? *Good boy, nice boy, heel for daddy?*

Taylor swipes at Reagan's face and blood pours from Reagan's torn cheek like a waterfall. I think maybe my distraction is enough for Taylor to get the upper hand, but then something grabs me by my shirt collar and lifts me up off the ground. It's the gray wolf I barely dodged in the woods. To my surprise, he does nothing further but growl, his attention set on Reagan. Those glowing blue eyes are locked onto me. When Reagan bolts towards us, I wince. He's not as fast as Mullet or Sara, but the power in his stride is apparent and unnatural.

He pounces on the gray wolf, who drops me in the scuffle. I land, and when I look up, I find myself face to face with Reagan and the prone gray wolf. Reagan's teeth are buried in the neck of the other wolf, then he rears his head, back tearing out a mouthful of muscle and ligaments. The gray wolf makes a bubbling sound, his neck hardly even a part of his body anymore.

Reagan is still reveling in his kill when I lunge forward, wrapping my arms around Reagan's neck and burying my face in his chest. His coat smells of dirt and blood and just the faintest, familiar smell of Reagan. His sweat, musky and ripe, reminds me of when he let me sit on his back as he did push-ups. Warm blood starts to drip down my neck and back, but I just hold onto him tighter. I even begin to wrap my legs around his torso, holding onto him like a koala holding a tree in a forest fire.

Reagan growls, his chest rumbling, but he doesn't attempt to pull me off. "Reagan," I speak into his fur. "Reagan, let's go home together. Watch bad TV and have coffee with cinnamon..." The wolf let out a huff. I lift my head to find Reagan staring down at me. His gaze is as affectionate as LED headlights, and just as painful to look at. There's still something raw and bloody between his teeth, his ears pressed flat against his head. "Is that what you want?" I reached up to touch his nose. "To come home with me?" Reagan huffs again, his hot breath assaulting my palm. Finally, my hand makes contact with the wet of his nose and his ears perk up. I can feel his nose twitch underneath my hand as he smells me. "It's me, it's Lance. Let me take you home, Reagan."

His eyes blink, slow, as if considering my words. Then his eyelids close shut like he's fallen under a spell. But I'm incapable of casting any magic right now. Reagan's eyes shoot open, and he wraps his arm around me, pushing my body even closer to his. Reagan starts to run, not as fast as he was on all fours but fast enough. I grab into his fur and bury my face in his chest, not wanting to see or hear anymore fighting. The longer I hold onto him, the longer I'm close to him like this, the more accustomed I become to his wolfish scent.

CHAPTER TWENTY-SEVEN

REAGAN

I wake up feeling the sorest I've ever felt in my life. Which is saying something. Months of basic training, decades worth of strength training, going on bar crawls with my platoon buddies—none of it compares to the aches I feel right now. I groan as I open my eyes, groaning even louder I'm greeted with blinding sunlight. "Fucking hell."

Something stirs beside me. I glance down, not wanting to move my neck if I can help it, to find Lance covered in blood. I suddenly don't care about my body aches. "Lance." I pull him into my lap and touch all along his body trying to find the source of the blood. "Lance, wake up, please. Wake up, Lance!"

He grumbles, knitting his thick brows until his whole face scrunches. His eyes flutter open, bright and green as ever. "It's been a long night," he breathes before falling forward to rest his head on my shoulder. He yawns, clearly intending to use my shoulder as a pillow. "Let me sleep some more."

It takes me a second for me to remember what happened last night, only to realize I don't remember anything beyond being led away from the Blood Moon camp. I have questions, but instead, I just stroke Lance's blood-matted hair. "Just tell me you're alright..." I whisper.

He sounds like he's in the middle of a dream. "I'm with you, aren't I?"

My heart skips a beat and I accept that I'm in love with him.

Lancelot le Fay, the son of a terrible and terrifying witch that has been a thorn in my side since I joined the bureau. The *man* I love. There are so many implications to that statement setting into motion all the things Lance brought up back at the safe house. Future puzzles I'll have to solve on my own. But those can wait. Right now, I simply wrap my arms around him and rub his back while he sleeps against my sore body. I feel his breath puff against my neck, and it feels better than a sauna treatment. I wonder if witches can heal in their sleep or if it's just that nothing felt better than his skin pressed against mine.

I start to nod off myself when Lance stirs again, this time of his own volition. He pulls his head away from my shoulder, his eyes only halfway open. "Did I..." he yawns. "Did I fall asleep?"

"Twice." I grin as I watch him wake up.

A few more seconds of lethargic blinking and then Lance's eyes light up. "Reagan, do you... remember last night?"

"Uh, no," I admit. "I was hoping you could fill me in. Why are you covered in blood?"

Lance looks at me like I've just burst into flames. "Because you ripped out a werewolf's throat to save me? Do you not remember that?"

"N-no," I stutter, taken aback by his words. Lance looks up at me with those emerald eyes and I can't for the life of me read his expression. That is until I see tears like crystals well up around his eyes. Then they overflow, falling down his cheek. "Hey, don't cry," I tell him softly. Which only makes him start to bawl. I take his face in my hands and wipe his tears with my thumbs, swiping away blood and dirt as well.

Lance just blubbers, trying to speak but only little words coming out. "You... blood... wolves..."

"Right," I nod. "I think I'm starting to get the picture." I feel bad that he's so overwhelmed while I'm coping just fine.

"I... I thought—I didn't know how to help."

"Considering we're both here, I think you must have helped a lot." Lance starts crying more, and I have to chuckle, accepting that he just needs to cry out his feelings. "You're absolutely spent." I kiss his forehead before bringing his face to my chest. "I'm tired too... Much too tired to carry us out of here."

Lance sniffles, "You're naked, also..."

I somehow didn't realize I'm stark naked sitting in the dirt until that moment. "It's fine," I assure him. "Not like anyone is around to see us."

A voice breaks through the calm air. "FOUND THEM!"

I pull Lance to my chest, ready to shield him with my body. A twig snaps and I turn to see Sara standing a few yards away, her hair a tangled mess. She leans back on her heel and crosses her arms over her chest. "Didn't mean to walk in on the love fest."

I growl, the sound rumbling from a depth of myself I didn't know existed. I know Sara is a friend, but my gut tells me to scare her off so I can be alone with my mate. Then I rethink that thought and the word *mate* sticks out. Stupid dog brain. I stop growling and shake my head, which I immediately regret as it brings on a splitting headache. I wince and Lance reaches up to touch my temples. I hear Sara snort. "I didn't realize you were like that, Lance." She shoots us a thumbs up. "Taking werewolf dick like a champ."

Lance's head turns so fast it might as well be spinning on a turntable. "We did not have sex!" he shrieks, and I wince again. "Oh, sorry," he says softer before covering my ears with his hands.

Taylor appears, his arms marked with scratches, brown skin looking ashy, but he still looks the most put together out of all of us. Taylor looks at me, then at Lance, and says nothing. He pulls a satellite phone from his pocket. "Dear? We found them... Yes, Lance is alright. He doesn't look great, but I don't think he has any injuries. I'm also fine, thank you for asking... I'm sorry for being sassy, love, I'm just trying to break the tension."

Eventually Sara helps us up, and Taylor provides me with a pair of basketball shorts, an undershirt, and a beat-up pair of sneakers. It's not ideal hiking gear, but it's better traversing the woods in the nude. As I change, Lance speaks up. "Is Blood Moon still looking for us? Should we run?"

Sara shakes her head "Nah. They're probably too busy licking their wounds. Dominic especially. He's gonna have to explain to the pack what happened last night." I can hear the smile on Sara's face.

We start walking, Taylor telling us there's a road just a half mile away.

Normally a half mile is nothing, but it feels like someone is hammering glass into my calves with every step. "How are you two not ready to keel over?" I ask. Lance looks concerned and I reach over to rub his back, trying to assure him I'm okay. Which, I guess is a lie, but it's a lie with a good purpose.

"The initial transformation will do that," Taylor explains. "Leave you feeling especially weak and in pain. But it'll get better with time, like a lot of the changes you'll experience." Taylor stops walking to look back at me. "I apologize for not being around to talk to you about these things."

"I get it, we need to lay low. And Sara told me a few things," I inform him.

Taylor glanced down at Sara, who looked rather proud of herself. "I don't want to dismiss Sara's information... But things are different for men."

"Here we fucking go," Sara rolls her eyes and tilts her head back. "Go on, Taylor, tell him about the pheromones."

"Get your head out of the gutter," Taylor shakes his head. "It's not *just* about the heat."

I'm not sure I want to push for more information, both curious and a little concerned about going into heat like... Well, like a dog. But from the top of the hill we're standing on, I see a road below.

Just as we reach the road, a white van with dark-tinted windows pulls up. Sara slides the door open, and we all pile in, Taylor hopping into the passenger's seat.

"My, you all look awful," an airy, aristocratic voice coos. I look at the driver, a full-figured woman with a smile as big as the square pair of sunglasses that cover half her face. She's got on a big sunhat and white gloves that go past her elbows. "So sorry to meet like this. I was hoping it would be over tea of some sort. Perhaps a double date, but oh well."

Taylor clears this throat. "Reagan, this is my wife, Daphne."

"Oh..." I reply, not sure what else to add. Daphne

continues to smile, and I notice her canines are longer and pointier than they should be. She clearly knows who I am, enough to want to take me and I guess Lance on a double date. I feel like I've been out-spied, which isn't great, but I'll live. Right now, it's just nice to be able to sit down.

Lance sits beside me on the plush van bench, but I quickly pull him into my lap again. I bury my face in his neck and take a deep breath, searching for his sweet smell underneath the smell of the earth and dried blood that cakes his skin. I can feel everyone's eyes on me, on us, but no one says anything. Not that I would care a bit about what they have to say. All I can focus on is Lance in my lap... and what I want to do to him once we're alone.

CHAPTER TWENTY-EIGHT

LANCE

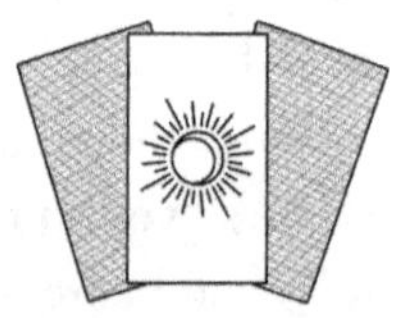

THE DRIVE BACK TO THE CABIN IS TOO SHORT. I WANT Reagan to hold me forever, regardless of the looks we're getting from everyone. I can't confirm that Daphne is snooping, but of the three, she's the sort to be the most enamored with blossoming...whatever this is. Once we get to the cabin, Taylor slides the door open and starts clapping like a camp counselor. "Alright, let's go, hit the showers."

Reagan grumbles and Taylor just grins. "Oh, you're gonna be even more grumpy when you see all the ice I bought just for you." Reagan buries his face deeper in my neck. He's barely moved the whole drive, only shifting his head to give me light kisses on my collarbone. "Come on," Taylor encourages. "You know it'll help with the soreness." He looks us up and down. "And maybe a few other things..."

I take Reagan's hand in mine. "We do both need a bath." As nice as it is being close to Reagan, the dirt and the blood covering both of us is pretty gross. I slide off his lap and pull his arm until he stands up. We go inside where Daphne is already taking off all her 'protective gear,' fluffing up her silky white-blonde hair. Taylor pops into the kitchen then comes back with two massive bags of ice which he brings to the bathroom.

Sara sits at the dining room table. "Just remember the *rest* of us also need to shower."

Reagan and I got to the bathroom where Taylor is filling the bathtub with ice and water "There's plenty of shampoo and shower gel," he explains. "Use as much as you need. We buy in bulk. Doesn't matter how long you've been a wolf, you gotta get clean afterwards. Dirt gets in places you don't even think about 'til it's there."

I grimace, and Reagan mutters, "Thanks for that."

Taylor leaves, and I start stripping the soiled clothes from my body, intentionally avoiding the mirror over the sink. I'd probably have a heart attack if I saw what I look like right now. But that doesn't matter to Reagan, who grabs my hips the second my pants hit the floor and pulls me back against his chest. "We could take a shower together," he suggests in a husky voice.

"Absolutely not." I tell him before holding his wrist and pulling them away from my hips. "I want to get clean. And I can see how tight your muscles are right now." I look over at the ice bath. "It can't be that bad."

"Have you ever done one?"

I haven't, but that's besides the point. "Don't be a baby."

Before he can object any further, I hop into the shower, turning the knob all the way to the hottest setting. I'm ready for a whole new layer of skin, more than happy to wash off last night and forget about it. A few moments later, I hear a shrill trill from Reagan as he gets into the bath. I almost regret getting into the shower so fast because I'm sure his face was priceless. Working my fingers through my hair with a good glob of shampoo, it doesn't feel like enough to wash all the grime out. Eventually I accept I'm as clean as I'm going to get and step out of the shower.

Reagan is sulking in the bath, his eyes fixed on the ceiling. I laugh and make my way over to him. Only to regret it when I see the water. "Oh, yuck." It's as dingy as I expected, but the ice bobbing around adds an extra ick, the worst punchbowl ever concocted.

"I'm trying not to think about it," Reagan is still looking up. His eyes flicker to me. "You clean up nice," he teases.

"Please don't flirt with me in front of the bog water."

Reagan snorts. "It's more like werewolf soup."

"Nasty," I scrunch my face in disgust.

Reagan reaches down into the opaque water and pulls the stopper before standing up. "I'm gonna wash off in the shower."

"Good. Please do." While Reagan works on getting properly clean, I brave the mirror. At first, I think there's still some dirt on my face, but as I pull at my skin, I accept that it's just dark circles under my eyes. Must be from all the stress and the bad night's sleep. I run my fingers through my hair and find a few flakes of blood still clinging to my roots and scalp. I shutter, remembering that none of it is my blood. Caught up in my grooming I don't realize Reagan is out of the shower.

He grabs my hips once again, pressing his dripping wet body against me. "I have you all to myself," he smiles against my ear. With one hand still holding my hip, his other hand begins to explore my body, caressing my stomach and chest.

"You do," I practically sing in a breathy voice. Reagan's hand trails up my neck. "And you have all of me." He wraps his hand around my neck, not squeezing but holding it firmly. In contrast, he kisses my shoulder lightly, then my cheek. I feel a shiver run down my spine all the way to the tip of my cock. I arch my back so my ass presses against his crotch. Reagan groans, his grip on my hip tightening. I feel his erection swell against the round of my ass.

"Maybe we should get back in the shower," he mutters in my ear.

"You can fuck me right here," I gasp. I forget all about moons and blood as his hand around my waist slides back and grabs one of my cheeks, spreading it. He grinds his hips against my ass and I whimper. I keep forgetting how big he is, how he's even bigger with the swell of his knot. "I don't know if you're going to fit..."

A primal noise bubbles at the back of Reagan's throat. "I'll make it fit," he says in a voice that both frightens and excites me. The tip of his index finger starts to massage my entrance. "You've done so well before, it'll fit."

There's a harsh banging on the door. "I know what you two are doing in there!" Taylor's voice calls through the door.

I get stiff, but Reagan remains cool. "I'm still in the bath!" He lies. "Lance is just freshening up." He gives me a wink in the bathroom mirror.

"I wasn't born yesterday!" Taylor yells. "Get out! No fucking in the cabin!"

"What?" I shout back before, sadly, taking Reagan's hands and pushing them away from me once again. I give him a sympathetic look and sigh before I grab a towel to wrap around my waist. It doesn't do a great job of hiding my half-mast. I open the bathroom door halfway, poking my head out. "What kind of rule is that?" I ask Taylor.

He huffs, "If any of us go into heat, it could trigger the rest of us. Which would be... awkward."

I appreciate him saying 'any of us' like it's everyone grabbing each other's asses at every available opportunity.

Still, I roll my eyes. "Oh nooo, you might have sex with your hot wife. What a tragedy."

I can hear Daphne giggling from the living room, followed by Sara shouting. "I'm here too, asshole! And I still want to take a shower. Preferably without slipping on jizz."

I shake my head, pretty much every horny thought in my brain disappearing now that the word jizz is floating around. "Okay, fine." I open the door and exit. "Bathroom is all yours."

Reagan is about to leave the bathroom as well, holding the towel at a strange angle that better hides his crotch. Taylor touches his shoulder. "Reagan, we need to talk. Man to... wolf-man."

"Okay..." Reagan glances at me, then back at Taylor. "Let's talk." They go to the back of the cabin while Sara takes over the bathroom. Daphne appears beside me and touches my arm. "We should also discuss some things..." She winks. "Wolf-lover to wolf-lover."

CHAPTER TWENTY-NINE

WE SETTLE INTO THE MASTER BEDROOM. TAYLOR GIVES me some clothes and I undress in front of him. It's not like he hasn't seen me naked. Taylor doesn't appear to care, though he does avert his eyes, looking in the closet where he's pulled the extra clothes from. "So... what all did Sara tell you?"

That conversation felt like forever ago when it's only been two days. "She explained that I would submit to you... And uh... Honestly, we mostly talked about Blood Moon."

Taylor nods. "Sara does know more about how they operate than I do. Poor girl."

"She'd hate that you said that."

"Oh, I know. That's why I never say it with her in the room."

Once I'm dressed, Taylor and I both sit on the edge of the king size bed. "I hate having this talk." He clears his throat, "Anyway, we'll start with the heat."

"Is this werewolf sex ed?"

Taylor ignores me and continues his lecture. "The frequency of heat differs from person to person, depending on things like age and how many other werewolves are around. It can also be affected, even triggered, by another werewolf going into heat. We can smell it on each other. The pheromones are like an aphrodisiac to us and our mates."

"Mates," I perk up. "Is that just the werewolf word for wife or boyfriend?"

Taylor shakes his head "It's much more than that. Mates are for life. When you find that special someone, that person you would burn the world for, you'll feel compelled to bite them during... uh, the act." Taylor rubs the back of his head. "Sorry. I've had this conversation with dozens of turned wolves and it never gets any less awkward."

I nod, blocking out the memory of Dad giving me the birds and the bees talk. Only the core information remains, and a faint memory of my dad calling women's downstairs *oysters and pearls*. In that regard, Taylor is doing a much better job. "Is Daphne your mate?" I ask, figuring that will lighten the subject.

"I know she is in my heart. Unfortunately, if I were to mark her as is tradition, it would kill her." So much for a smooth change of topic. "But that's only because she is a vampire. There is a possibility the mating bite wouldn't harm her any more than it normally does. The bite mark is permanent, you see. But I can't risk it. There is a much longer history of werewolf bites killing vampires and vice-versa than there is of vampires and werewolves mating."

"So, you two are an uncommon pairing?"

Taylor grins. I'm referencing their difference in... species, I guess, but there are obviously a few other things that make them stick out. "We like causing controversy wherever we go. But yes, we've never met another werewolf and vampire couple like us. There are whispers that in the past there have been bonds between werewolves and vampires, but it's hard to confirm anything." He shakes his head, "But I'm getting off topic."

"So long as you don't bite someone while you are transformed, you won't turn them. Biting your mate shouldn't turn them, but you need to be careful."

"Sara said adrenaline can cause a transformation."

Taylor hums, "Yes, being able to transform is now a part of your fight or flight, so adrenaline does cause us to change. You could accidentally turn Lance. It has happened, *does* happen, to wolves whose mates aren't lycan."

I freeze. I never thought about the possibility that I could turn someone, especially not Lance. I nibble at the inside of my cheek as I debate if I should tell Taylor my theory. He seems pretty protective of Lance, and I'm not sure how he'll take it, but I go for it. "I think Lance is my mate."

To my surprise, Taylor is unphased. "Could very well be. You did submit to him on the full moon."

He might as well have hit me with his van. "I did? I... I don't remember that."

"I've never met anyone who remembers their first transformation. But yes, you were completely feral until he stepped in. Then all you cared about was protecting him, effectively making him your master. And likely your mate." There's a pause. "Congrats." I must have made a face because he adds, "I'm being serious. Lance is a good man. Troubled, but you're very aware of his situation.

"Which reminds me." Taylor stands up and goes back into the closet, pulling out a bag with a lock on it like the ones that kept money at events. He dials in the code and pulls out a cell phone. My cell phone. "I had to take it from you after the incident. I wanted to smash it, but Daphne said that was overboard."

"It's my work phone so... not the worst idea honestly?" I take the phone from him, but it no longer feels like mine. The last time I held this, I was human. The timeline is just now starting to hit me. "Shit," I muttered. I press the edge of the phone against my forehead. "I am so fired."

A belly laugh erupts from Taylor. "What? You really think they're going to be upset you disobeyed orders and went AWOL?" He shakes his head, still looking amused before he lets out a scoff. "In all honesty Reagan, you guys were never going to stop the le Fay family. All that time you spent trying to cuff him could have been spent at a petting zoo for all the good it did. Or, I dunno, cleaning up some of the abandoned lots in the city? Just a thought." I know he's got a point, but he just keeps going. "And then what would have been your next assignment? Some McCarthy-era spying? It's best if you let that life go."

I don't know if I can leave it all behind. Unfortunately, the whole turning into a wolf once a month thing isn't going to work with my day job. I hand him back the phone. "Probably best if you destroy this."

Without a moment's hesitation, Taylor snaps the phone in half like dry pasta. He lets out a satisfied sigh. "You know, we could always use help."

I raise a brow. "We?"

"Daphne and I, we... Well, you've seen first-hand what we do. People get in trouble, we help. A safety net for supernaturals. It's sort of like being a public servant, just for a very specific population."

That doesn't sound all that bad, plus having an employer that understands my condition is a big plus. "How's the pay?"

"We'll look into the budget."

"Is there healthcare?"

"Seeing as I was born and raised in Canada, I can't in good faith *not* give you health insurance." I already like him more than my last boss.

WE SPEND a night in the cabin before driving down south back to the city. The rest was necessary, but also torture. Daphne and Taylor got their bed while the rest of us were in the bunks. Once in the night, I tried slipping into Lance's bunk just to lay next to him, but the tight fit wasn't going to work long term. When I gave up and left his bunk, I caught Sara glaring at me from her top bunk, which I refused to acknowledge.

In the van, Lance and I sit beside each other, even if I want to be even closer. Sara sits in the row of seats in front of us while Taylor drives and Daphne looks like she's on her way to Sunday church with her big lacy hat.

"So..." Lance speaks up about thirty minutes into the drive. "If Reagan submitted to me during the full moon, does that mean I have to come on runs with you guys?"

"Oh!" Daphne chimes. "You should! We can all come up to the cabin once a month, let you three run while Lance and I enjoy an evening in."

"Oh, sure," Sara complains, "Make me a fifth wheel." She crosses her arms and sinks further down in her seat. "Not to mention I'll probably vomit watching those two paw at each other the whole time." Lance kicks her seat. Sara and I both look at him surprised, though Sara's expression has much more malice. "Getting pretty bold now that you've got your dog on the leash, huh?"

"I will turn this van around—" Taylor threatens. "And Sara, you can mope in the woods while the four of us have a nice time." Taylor takes Daphne's gloved hand and kisses her knuckle. "Or you all can behave."

"He started it," Sara mutters.

"Payback. For the drive up here," Lance explains.

"What?" Sara groans. "I wasn't mean at all on the drive up. Was I, Daph?"

Daphne shrugs. "I don't recall anything out of the ordinary."

"See?" Sara stresses.

Daphne continues. "Now Sara, that doesn't mean you weren't rude. It just means you weren't any crasser than you normally are."

"I think she was playing nice because Malcolm was there," Lance suggests. The corners of his perfect pink lips curl. "She was giving him all this attention—"

Sara completely turns around in her seat. "You really want to start a fight, huh?"

"Alright, alright," I take Lance's chin in my hand and tilt his head towards me. "Behave please? So, we can get home." I lift my brows, reminding him what we could do once we're back at the safe house, or his apartment, or wherever we go. I don't care, I just need him alone.

"Can this car move faster? I think they're gonna start feeling each other up," Sara announces, and I'm tempted to kick her seat as well.

Taylor looks at us in the rearview mirror. "You three are really going to distract my driving on top of everything else this week? I do not need to be pulled over driving an unmarked white van." All three of us deflate a little. "Lance, Reagan, behave or separate. You too, Sara."

"Fiiiine," Lance whines and inches away from me.

Daphne lets out a dreamy sigh. "Reminds me of us," she says to Taylor.

His replies in a dry voice "The childish bickering?"

"No! Remember how we pawed at each other? When we finally admitted some things..."

"Dear..." I can hear the embarrassment in Taylor's voice.

"It was romantic," Daphne continues despite her husband. "We couldn't stop kissing, never mind the rest of it."

Sara has to comment, "Wasn't that like a billion years ago?"

"It was the '80s..." And with that, Daphne goes on a long, winding but interesting story about her and Taylor and the '80s. I listen, but my eyes are focused on Lance most of the time.

CHAPTER THIRTY

REAGAN

Finally, the van pulls up to Lance's familiar apartment building. "Do you think it's safe for us to settle here?" I ask. "Blood Moon does know where Lance lives."

Sara is the first to respond. "Yeah, and if anything happens to you two, they're the first people we'll harass. Honestly, as dumb as Dominic is, I don't think he's dumb, enough to bother you two anymore."

Daphne adds, "I've scheduled a friend to come by and ward the apartment. Sorry Lance, I wasn't sure how familiar you were with that sort of magic."

Lance shrugs. "I haven't drawn a ward in years, the most I could probably do is prevent bugs from entering the apartment."

"Not a bad skill," I tell him, and he gives me an amused smile.

Lance takes my hand then looks at everyone in the van. "Thank you all, for everything so far and everything that's to come." I nod, not sure what to add. I don't think there could be a better mentor than Taylor when it comes to navigating lycanthropy. And Sara may be obnoxious, but she's pretty loyal. Daphne clearly cares about Lance about as much as I do. All of them kept Lance safe, and for that, I'm forever grateful.

The van leaves, and I don't think I've caught a slower elevator in my life. My leg bounces the whole ride up to Lance's apartment. Once we finally get to his place, Lance rushes to the bedroom shutting the door behind him. I raise a brow before following him, but as soon as I turn the knob he shouts, "Wait!"

I shake my head in disbelief. "Haven't we waited enough? Come on..." I press my forehead against the bedroom door like a dog begging to be let inside. "Lance, honey, please. I want to feel you so bad."

"Just give me a few minutes!" He insists. "Grab some water bottles from the fridge!"

I don't know what that's about, but I listen, going to the kitchen and grabbing four water bottles, two for each of us. I walk back to the bedroom and knock at the door. "Okay, I have the waters, can I please come in now?" I don't want to sound desperate, but we're already well past that point. I want Lance so bad—even to just kiss him and hold him tight with the knowledge that he's all mine.

Lance opens the door, wearing nothing but a tight pair of briefs that leave little to the imagination. I can already see he's half-hard, the head of his cock outlined by the fabric. He hooks the neckline of my shirt with his finger and pulls me into the bedroom. That's when I see the bed has been outfitted with more pillows and blankets, forming an almost nest-like structure.

"Daphne said it was best to make the bed as comfortable as possible. That we might be here for a bit..." Lance's hands slip under my shirt, his palms rubbing my abdomen. It seems like Lance got his own talk about werewolf mating.

I clear my throat. "Well, let me set these down then." I slip past him and place the water bottles on the nightstand. Turning back to him I see his side profile and realize the briefs are open in the back, like assless chaps but without the chaps. I feel my own cock stir, looking at him, soaking in his lithe body.

Finally, I sit down on the edge of the bed. "Come here," I command. He joins me, straddling my hips and wrapping his arms around my neck. He kisses me desperately and I return his desperation while my hands reach back to grab his ass. I groan into his mouth as I play with his bare ass, appreciating how soft yet firm he is in my hands. Something begins to build inside me from my core. Something bigger than my erection or my racing heart.

Lance releases my lips and starts kissing my neck, not hesitating to drag his teeth along my flesh. Then he grabs a chunk of me between his teeth and bites down, surely leaving a mark. I groan in approval and push my hips into his. Lance keeps kissing and nibbling my neck and I decide he needs more room to work is magic. I grab my shirt by the collar and jerk my hand down, the fabric ripping halfway down my body. Lance doesn't need any further explanation, his lips finding my collarbone and then my sternum. He takes one of my pecs in his mouth and started teasing the nipple with his lips and tongue.

I grab a handful of his hair, not to pull him back but to keep him there. "You love my body, don't you?" He whimpers against my skin. "You worship me..." My other hand slips between the crack of his ass cheeks and teases his entrance with my fingers. Lance whimpers again and starts grinding his hips, his mouth still locked onto my nipple. Then I pull his head back by the hair so he's forced to look at me. I hungrily press my lips into his and his thrusts only get faster.

I pull out of the kiss, taking his bottom lip between my teeth. "Desperate..." I hiss at him. "You're so fucking desperate. Lay on the bed." Lance pouts as he dismounts my hips but does as he's told. Lying flat on his stomach, I get a great view of his ass in those cute briefs. I hook a finger through the elastic. "I do like this a lot." I snap the elastic against his pale skin and he yelps. I slip my hand down my pants and began to palm my erection. "You ever try lacy underwear?"

Lance lifts his head to glance back at me. "What color would you like?" His question makes my cock twitch.

"God, don't ask me about colors right now. I can't even think of any."

Lance chuckles and the sound makes me smile the same way a dinner bell makes a dog salivate. I've had enough teasing. I take my pants and briefs off in one swift motion, then grab the bottle of lube from the nightstand. I pour a generous amount into my hand, letting it warm up a few seconds before slathering it on my cock.

"Reagan," Lance whines. "Do you have to torture me?"

"Waiting is torture for me too," I remind him. I grab one of his ass cheeks while my other hand keeps my dick steady, lining it up with his entrance. I press the head of my cock against Lance, slipping inside with ease. The immediate warmth of his ass makes me shiver. I lean down so I can press my lips against his ear. "Tell me how badly you want it." I hiss in his ear, not yet pushing my hips forward.

"Reagan, all I could think about that drive back was how I missed your cock. About how much bigger you are since you've fucked me. A-about how we're going to get your knot to fit..." I hear the hesitation in his voice and kiss the conch of his ear.

"We don't have to do it all at once," I tell him. "You already feel amazing..." I can't deny us any longer, even if I could listen to Lance beg for hours. I press my hips forward, my length sinking inside Lance.

A sharp breath catches in my lover's throat before he releases it as a heavenly moan. "There's so much," he breathes just before my knot makes contact with his body. "You're so deep." Slowly, I start to pump my hips. Lance let out soft breaths and moans with each stroke, deep but slow, and I can feel his whole body relaxing.

"Here I thought you liked it rough," I tease. "But you're so at peace when I fuck you slowly." Lance just whimpers in response, another sound I could listen to for hours and hours. "Arch your back," I tell him, and he complies. With a new angle, I quicken my pace, Lance gasping every time I'm fully inside him.

"I'm gonna cum," he announces.

"Already? Fine. I'm going to keep fucking you like the toy you are." My admonishment is met with a low groan from Lance. "That's right, your ass, your mouth—they're mine to fuck how I please." I see Lance grip the sheets of the bed, his vocalizations sounding more and more like a song. I keep my pace, not wanting to disrupt Lance's orgasm. With a few more strokes, I feel his hips and torso shiver just before he lets out a satisfied sound.

With that taken care of, I begin to buck my hips and Lance cries out immediately. That warm, bubbling feeling in my abdomen continues to burn inside me until finally it overflows. I grab Lance's thick blond hair and his shoulder, using it as leverage as I fuck him rough. Animalistic grunts and groans fill the room as I fuck him without a single care beyond my own orgasm.

Lance repeats my name over and over. "Reagan, *Reagan...*" It's like a mantra, growing louder and louder with each thrust. As Lance's voice crescendos, I feel my own orgasm on the horizon. I stop, my cock still deep inside him. I let myself feel his tight ass around my girth for a few moments before I pull out completely. "D-don't stop," Lance pleas. "Why did you stop?"

I flip him over so he's on his back. There's a large wet spot in the center of his briefs. "Because I want to watch you take my knot," I tell him, as if it's obvious. Lance's eyes go wide for a second before he starts nodding enthusiastically. "That's it. My little cock slut who can't get enough." I peel off his briefs before grabbing the lube again and pour it right onto my knot, figuring it isn't possible to use too much lube.

Lance takes my length with ease. Then we get to the knot, and I tell him in a soft voice, "Relax." Lance takes a slow inhale as I grab his hips tight. On his exhale, I pull his body to me, while my hips jut forward. Half my knot slips inside Lance, who writhes on my cock. Keeping his hips still, I push the rest of my knot inside and feel it begin to swell. I've never felt anything like this before and the waves of pleasure make my vision blur. "Amazing," I breathe. "You're amazing."

I lean down to kiss him while I thrust my hips. Lance gasps against my lips, managing to speak past them. "R-right there—more, right there!"

I mutter against his parted lips. "Anything you want." Lance writhes underneath me like he's coming for a second time.

His eyes are glassy, and his mouth hangs open, his lips

wet with my saliva. "I love it, Reagan," he breathes. "I... I love..." He doesn't need to finish his sentence. I'm already so close, even before I knotted his insides.

I let out a low groan as I cum inside him, my hips jerking as ropes of cum fill him. "Fuck, take it, take it all." My knot swells, growing larger than I thought possible. But I'm completely spent.

I wrap Lance in a hug before turning us both on our sides so we can look at each other. "You're still inside me," Lance breathes before closing his eyes. "It feels so good—you're pressed up right against my prostate."

I chuckle, brushing some hair out of his face. "I think... we might be here for a while."

"Good," Lance tells me with complete certainty. He keeps his eyes closed as if he's shutting out everything but the feeling of my cock. Which is fine by me. Seeing him overwhelmed with pleasure is better than looking at any statue or painting in the world.

I give him light kisses along his collarbone, run my fingers through his hair, and whisper to him "You're so beautiful." I rinse and repeat the process until I see Lance is hard once again.

I reach down between his legs and begin stroking him. "R-Reagan!" he gasps with surprise, his eyes finally opening.

"What? Were you hoping I'd suck you off?" I tease. "Want to fuck my mouth again?"

"Reagan, I can't think about anything other than what you're doing right now," he admits.

"Then don't think." I tell him as I stroke him faster and he cries out. My knot is still too engorged for me to pull out. But the thought of him being absolutely full of my seed, the head of my cock pressed against his prostate, and now feeling the pleasure of my hand is more than enough for me to get off.

Lance grabs my shoulders, panting and writhing until finally a spurt of cum splatters both of our chests. Lance collapses into my chest, breathing heavily. Finally, my knot starts to return to its normal size, but I don't move to pull out just yet. Instead, I rub his back as he rests against my chest and kiss the top of his head. "You know I want nothing more than to make you feel good," I tell him.

"You make me feel so very good..." he hums. "I might... fall asleep on your dick."

I can't help but snort with laughter. "Maybe I did go a little overboard. Poor thing." Three back-to-back orgasms is a lot. I finally pull out of him, slowly, with a satisfying pop. Immediately cum starts to drip out of his ass, and I roll over to grab some tissues. Lance grumbles and pulls himself closer to my body. "You can rest," I tell him softly. "I'll be here when you wake up." He shut his eyes and his breathing becomes slow and dreamy.

I just watch him. I feel compelled. But what else would I bother to look at when he's right there, peaceful in the afterglow glow of gratification? I don't want to leave this bed or leave his side. As he sleeps, I whisper to him, "I love you, Lance." Maybe soon I'll have the courage to say it when he's awake.

CHAPTER THIRTY-ONE

LANCE

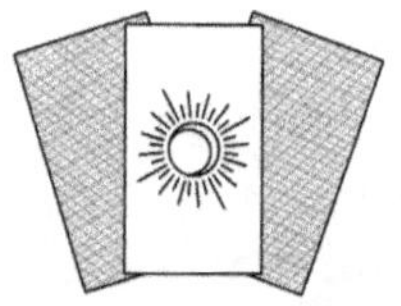

I've lost count how many times Reagan and I fucked, but I'm glad we had those water bottles ready. We just never stopped except to nap and hydrate. Reagan waited for me, growling my name when he pinned me down to fuck me again. Sometimes he was rough but other times, he would hold me as close as possible and grunt into my ear. It was hard to understand him, but I swear he said over and over: *I love you, I love you.* I don't know which I liked more, Reagan growling sweet nothings in my ear or calling me a slut for his knot. I guess they aren't mutually exclusive.

I wake up, and for once, I find Reagan peacefully asleep, his head resting on one of the pillows I'd placed on the edge of the bed. I roll onto his chest, the slow rise and fall of his breathing like resting on a boat. I trace the line of stubble along his cheeks, then trail my finger down his straight, long nose. He really is so handsome. And strong. And mine.

I kiss his chin before sliding down his body to his hips. I kiss along his happy trail while my fingers brushed along his length. Within moments, his cock stirs, clearly liking the attention. Reagan groans, his eyes peeking open. "Relax..." I whisper to him before I move down the length of his body. I reach the thick curls of his bush before taking the head of his cock between my lips.

"Lance..." I hear Reagan breathe. I slip my lips further down my shaft till the head of his cock is at the back of my throat. His cock is only half hard in my mouth, and there's still a bit of shaft before I hit his knot. But I want to remain comfortable as I lay there with his dick in my mouth.

Reagan blinks away some sleep before he sees what I'm doing. His deep blue eyes go from sleepy to excited, a grin spreading across his lips. "What a nice surprise," he reaches down to stroke my hair. "Better than breakfast in bed, that's for sure." I felt him twitch in my mouth and then a bit of precum on the back of my tongue. Reagan rolls his head back onto the pillow with a satisfied sigh. His fingers continue to play with my hair as I warm his cock.

Eventually I slide my mouth off his cock. I start lapping the head, his shaft becoming rigid, beads of precum rising from his slit. "Fuck, that's nice," he breathes. I keep licking the head before he sits up with a suggestion. "Why don't you ride me?"

"Oh," I blink. "I like that idea..." I go to grab the lube on the bedside table only to find it not there. "Shit." I start feeling around the sheets. Reagan helps by placing his hands behind his head and chuckling at my intense search. Finally, I find the bottle, showing it to him triumphantly. "No thanks to you, jerk."

I squeeze the bottle, happy there's still some left. I'm definitely going to have to buy a new one after this. Probably a couple more if this is how sex is going to be from now on. My fingers slick, I slip one inside me, then another.

Reagan watches eagerly. "Mmm, I could just watch you finger yourself."

"Not a chance. I like your dick more than my fingers." Reagan's grin grows wider—wider still when I get on my knees to straddle his hips. I situate myself above his cock then lower myself down onto him. Reagan and I moan together as more and more of his length disappears inside me, until I reach his knot. It's still a bit of a struggle to get it inside me without a good amount of lube and Reagan's strong hips, but I'm already addicted to the feeling of his knot spreading me open.

I lift and lower my thighs, Reagan watching in awe as I bounce on his dick. His hands grab my body greedily, squeezing my pecs, my hips, my thighs, anything and everything he can get his hands on. "You're so perfect," he says in a husky voice. His hand slides up from my bicep to my neck. "My perfect little witch." He squeezes, his fingers carefully placed around my neck. "Riding my cock..."

I rest back on my calves and start grinding my hips against his body, his knot pushing against my hole. Reagan's lips part as he moans and looks at me with such reverence while he chokes me out like a whore. Reagan, fucking me rough, the way I always said I wanted it. But it also feels amazing when he's in control, fucking me slowly and with passion. I still want him to spread my legs and call me dirty, terrible things while he fucks me. We'll have to experiment and find a happy medium.

I pause my grinding and reach down between Reagan's legs to give his knot a squeeze. He grunts and releases my neck so I can speak. "I want this," I tell him, and he chuckles.

"You're going to have to be more specific." He trails his thumb along my jaw.

"I want your knot inside me," I tell him just before his thumb finds my bottom lip. I tilt my head so I can pop his thumb in my mouth, creating extra suction by pressing my tongue against it. Reagan's other hand grabs my hip with such strength I think his thumb must leave behind a bruise on the dip of my hip.

"That's what I want to hear," he tells me before lifting his hips and pushing me down onto his knot. I gasp and Reagan pushes my tongue down with his thumb, opening my mouth wide. "Mmm, fuck. I want to taste you." He sits up and starts to kiss me. His thumb, wet with my spit, still presses down on my bottom lip. It feels so romantic, meanwhile he's stretching my ass like no one else can. I moan into his mouth as I move my hips, feeling his knot swell inside me while his length massages my prostate. Reagan kisses me harder, and I ride his knot harder in return. He growls loud enough that his whole body vibrates.

His lips suddenly leave mine and he goes for my shoulder. He bites down. Hard. Harder than he ever has before. I whimper at first, then cry out in pain. It's a good pain, warm and radiating like a good spank on the ass, but it's still painful. Then I feel a swell of emotions, my pupil's dilating. "Yes!" I cry out, not even sure why I'm so emphatic. I just keep saying it over and over as his teeth dig deeper into my flesh. *Yes, yes yes.*

So enthralled with the bite, I don't realize how close I am until Reagan grabs my cock and rubs the precum along the slit. At the same time Reagan releases my shoulder and whispers in my ear.

"You. Are. *Mine.*"

It's enough to push me over the edge, and ribbons of cum cover his hand. I hear a familiar groan as Reagan fills me up as well, filling me with his hot seed that seems to be never-ending. I catch my breath, Reagan's swelled knot keeping me locked onto his lap. Reagan's head rests on my shoulder as he catches his breath. His hand caresses my cheek. "Are you alright?"

I just nod, not yet ready to speak and ruin the afterglow. After a few moments, Reagan lifts his head and I see blood at the corner of his lips. I think maybe he's bitten his lip too hard, but then I feel a twinge of pain on my shoulder. I try to get a good look but can't quite see the spot where my neck and shoulders meet. "Reagan?" He doesn't look at me. "Reagan when you bit me did you... break the skin?" Reagan continues to look away from me, like a dog caught in the act of stealing food from the table. I lift his chin, so he'll look at me. "I'm not upset... Daphne explained all of this to me."

I don't think he hears me, because he just blurts out, "Lance, I want you to be my mate." I blink, only for Reagan to hit me with another confession "I'm in love with you." So, when he said it over and over in my ear, he meant it. "I'm more in love than I've ever been in my life."

I could float off his dick, I'm so happy. My face must still be processing everything because Reagan furrows his brows. "I should have talked to you before mating you... biting you... whatever it is."

"Marking me?" I offer with a small smile. "Maybe we should have talked about it, but since when have we planned any part of our relationship?"

Reagan groans and presses his cheek against my neck. "I guess when I say it out loud, being in love with a man I met less than a month ago is... Wow, it's really weird to say."

"You can just stick to saying you love me," I offer, then kiss the crown of his head. "Because I love you too." I hold his face in my hands. "How could I not? You've saved me..."

"Lance," Reagan chuckles, pulling me closer to him even though we're about as close as we can possibly be, our bodies still locked together. "You're the one who saved me from a pack of biker werewolves... twice." I feel him smile against my neck. "But please, tell me again how lovable I am."

CHAPTER THIRTY-TWO

LANCE

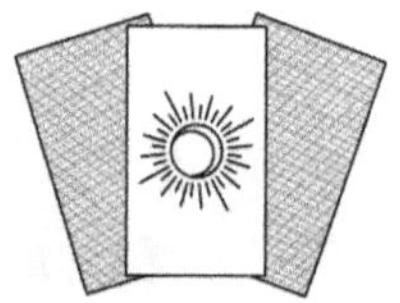

We cuddle until Reagan's knot deflates to its normal size, then we cuddle some more. Reagan runs his finger along my new bite mark, which has healed extremely quickly, as if I'm a werewolf as well. I wish I could mark him some way. His eyes light up every time he glances at the mark, and it makes me feel all the more special.

We shower—together of course. But we're both good about not doing anything more than kissing and petting which is inevitable since we help each other rub soap all along our bodies, Reagan being extra gentle with the bruises on my neck and hips.

We're toweling off after the shower when Reagan asks outright, "Am I too rough?"

"I'm not complaining," I tell him. Though I'll have to mention later how much I like slow sex too. Which is quite the revelation.

I grab the first comfortable thing I can find. A pair of light blue linen drawstring pants and a matching blue tank top. Reagan has a lot more trouble. He grabs a t-shirt and tries to put it on, the bottom of the shirt hanging just above his belly button and the fabric struggling to contain his shoulders. He tries to reach for something else and the shirt rips along his back muscles. "Shit, sorry," he apologizes. "Was this expensive?"

"No," I lie. It cost more than most people would pay for a t-shirt, but he doesn't need to know that. I start looking for the one piece of clothing I'm almost sure will fit him. A long and loose black button up tunic with a hem that reaches the top of my knees.

I offer it to Reagan, and he looks at it, confused. "Is this a dress?"

"And if it is?"

"Well, if it fits..." He takes the tunic and holds it up to his body. On him, it's just a normal shirt. I find him an old pair of sweatpants that don't go past his ankles.

"We can go shopping tomorrow, at least for the basics," I tell him.

"Yeah, not that I don't want to play dress up but..." He pushed back some of my clothes, a floral quilt jacket catching his eye. "I mean, I'm sure you'll make me look good no matter what. I'm just not used to men's fashion."

"We both have a lot to get used to," I tell him, taking his hand. "I swore I'd never live with roommates again after I got this apartment. But I guess for you, I'll make an exception," I fake an over-the-top eye roll and he laughs.

We go into the living room where Reagan offers to make us some food. The offer alone makes my stomach audibly growl, at which point Reagan steps into the kitchen. I follow him then spot my deck of tarot cards still waiting on the counter for my return.

My spread from the night I was kidnapped still lies on the counter: The Hanged Man, The Moon, The Knight of Swords, The World, Four of Cups, and Strength. Looking at them now, my reading wasn't half bad. Nice to know I hadn't completely lost my touch. Still, one card bothered me... The Moon, inverted. When I did the reading the first time, I just thought it was telling me that I was blinded by fear. Which wasn't inaccurate, but it feels like this Moon wants more from me.

I run a little test, shuffling all the cards back into the deck. Reagan notices me and looks over his shoulder while standing in front of the stove. "Do you want to play cards?" I show him the back of the neck and he nods, "Ah, right." He returns to cooking what looks like basic pasta, which is probably one of the few things that haven't gone bad while I've been away. I dread opening the fridge.

Once I feel the deck is sufficiently shuffled, I set it down and draw a single card: The Moon, inverted.

"Fine," I huff under my breath. "Be that way." I return the card to the deck. Reagan is shaking his head over at the stove, but I catch him smiling to himself. I wait for Reagan to plate the food before I take his hand, trying to lead him back into the living room. "Can we talk? About me?" Reagan looks confused so I just keep talking, pushing through with the momentum I've already built up. "I know you want to know about my Father. What his deal is."

"I don't care about that anymore," Reagan interjects. "Really, Lance, I don't."

I give his hand a squeeze. "Good, because you being obsessed with my dad would be super weird. But I still think I should tell you why I left."

Reagan blinks, then takes my hand. "Only if you want to tell me."

I nod before placing my other hand atop his. "My Father is... eccentric."

Reagan snorts, "That's a nice way of putting it."

"No interrupting, please," I tell him. If he distracts me, I will use it as an opportunity to never talk about this again. Reagan nods in agreement.

"So, yes. If you haven't noticed, Arthur le Fay is an eccentric guy. Even for a witch. He loves collecting old artifacts he believes were owned by witches. But his number one obsession is discovering immortality. I don't know why. It seems fruitless to me. I mean, I've talked to Daphne, and she says being trapped in time in a curse. I certainly wouldn't want to live forever. Plus, if one could become immortal through magical means, you'd think witches would have figured it out by now. But my Father thinks..." I swallow. "He thinks he can become immortal with blood magic." My stomach churns just saying it aloud.

"Lance." Reagan stops, remembering the no interrupting rule.

"That girl..." I strain my brain to remember her name. I should remember her name, as painful as it is to do so. "Logan. She was a latent witch. Her powers didn't appear 'til she was older. No coven, which made her our mark for... the ritual. Reagan, I killed her. I stabbed her in her heart because my Father told me to." I look down, not feeling worthy enough to look at him directly. "I've... never said that out loud."

Reagan pulls me into a hug. I grab the dark fabric of his tunic, clinging to it like a life raft. To my surprise, I don't start bawling like I thought I would. Reagan pulls out of the hug and holds my face in his hands. "I knew...that he made you do terrible things. I just knew." He shakes his head, "Things you would never do on your own."

I nod. Reagan knows Father's ties. It's not a stretch to think the Father figure with deep connections to scummy humans might have his kids do something unsavory. Despite everything, a soft smile pulls at Reagan's lips. "I'm glad you trust me enough to tell me."

"I'm glad... that I could tell you." Finally, the tears come, and it's a relief. Reagan smiles, his cheeks ample and smile lines forming around his eyes. I reach up and run my fingers through his dark mane, touching him just because I can. Reagan catches my falling tears with his fingers.

The buzzer to my apartment rings and I start rubbing my eyes and tears with my palms. "Do you want me to get it?" Reagan offers. I just shake my head and he gives me a kiss on the forehead before I get up and go see who it is.

I walk as quickly as I can to the intercom, which wasn't very fast considering I've been fucking Reagan for the past few hours. I push the button. "Hello?"

Jason's familiar voice blares through the intercom. "JERK! I have been coming to your apartment for days now! Your door guy said you came home a few days ago but you never responded! I was so close to calling the cops, but I didn't want to—"

I cut him off best I can over the intercom. "I have a guy here," I inform Jason.

"Okay, okay. Well then I forgive you." Over the intercom, it's hard to gauge his level of sarcasm, but he seems to accept it for now. I'm not sure how to explain to my very human friend what all has transpired, but the excuse that I've been too busy hooking up with some guy seems to fly. "Now can I come up?"

I let out a heavy sigh. "Sure." I ring him in.

"Love you, biiiitch!" Jason sings.

"Love you too. Bitch." I released the button on the intercom.

Reagan approaches me, looking concerned. "A friend of yours?" Reagan asks, clearly a bit confused by the dynamic.

"Yeah, Jason. He knows you, you don't know him. Okay, well he saw you at the club when you were dressed really slutty and I thought your name was Adam."

Reagan looks down at the black shirt and sweatpants combo. "Am I not dressed slutty now? Do the gray sweatpants do nothing?"

There's a knock at the door. Jason must have sprinted up the stairs or fate smiled upon him with a fast elevator. I open the door and Jason beams. "Ohmygod, you are alive. I thought your evil twin had replaced you."

"Don't even joke," my nose crinkles, the sweet smell of Junior's alchemy flooding back. "I've seen that asshole more this month than I have in the last decade."

"What? Why? Spill." Jason steps into my apartment but only makes it a few steps before Reagan catches his eye. "Hello," Jason says, a little taken aback. "Wow, you're still here?" Jason looks over his shoulder back at me and whispers. "He's still here?"

"Sorry, I don't think we've met." Reagan steps forward to meet Jason. "I'm Reagan, Lance's boyfriend."

He's called me mate and told me he loves me, but something about the title of *Lance's boyfriend* makes my cheeks light up like a fire siren.

"*Really?* That's a first. You must be pretty special if you got this tomcat to settle down."

Reagan looks at me with a knowing, cheeky smile. "I hope I'm that special."

EPILOGUE

Lance - One Month Later

"How are you still packing?" Reagan asks, leaning against the doorway of our bedroom. "It's a three-day trip. In the woods. With bugs." He already has on the dark brown leather jacket with detailed branches along the shoulders. Gucci, of course. I couldn't spare a dime when it came to dressing him up.

"Maybe I want to look nice for the bugs," I announce defiantly as I hold two different sweaters, trying to decide which to take up to the cabin. One is lighter than the other and I'm worried I'd get cold. Especially on the night of the full moon when it'll just be Daphne and me in the cabin.

"I'm sure they'll find you very sexy. The mosquitoes especially." Reagan's phone buzzes and he turns away from me to take the call. "Hey, yeah, we'll be down in a minute. Lance is still packing... Yeah, still," Reagan chuckles.

When the dust settled, Reagan started doing work for Taylor and Daphne. Helping them with their 'guests,' teaching them self-defense, showing them how to cover their tracks and remain anonymous. We weren't the only ones with big bad supernaturals breathing down our necks. Reagan seems to like the work. He always comes home with a smile and a kiss, but he refuses to tell me about his day. Client confidentiality.

I shove the heavier sweater into my bag and zip it up. "Okay, I'm ready."

"We're on our way down," Reagan says over the phone before hanging up. I meet him in the doorway with my bag slung over my shoulder. Reagan takes my hand and leads me out of the apartment, grabbing his backpack off the kitchen counter as we walk.

"Did you even pack your toothbrush?"

"Honey," he says, exasperated. "I know how to pack a bag."

"Hm, fine. But you're not borrowing my toothbrush once we get there."

Reagan shakes his head. "Fine, but you can't complain when my breath smells bad." We get in the elevator. "Was my breath bad last time? After the transformation?"

"I don't know," I tell him, "I wasn't really focused on that at the time."

"But we were kinda on top of each other, so you would have noticed if it was bad."

"I think I had blood in my mouth that wasn't mine," I remind him.

"Right..." his voice trails. "Forget I asked."

We leave the elevator and my apartment complex, walking to the side street where the van is parked. Reagan slides open the van door, only to be ambushed. A yellow dog leaps out and into Reagan's arms. He somehow manages to catch the creature. I jump back and made a rather embarrassing noise. Sara's voice calls from inside the van. "Lemon, down!" The dog is too busy lavishing Reagan with kisses to listen. "Lemon, heel!"

"Alright, alright," Reagan sets the dog down on the ground and it begins twirling in circles, chasing its tail. The dog is one of those bully breed type dogs with a wrinkly face and a thick body.

Sara appears in the van door. "Who's your new friend, Sara?" I asked with a cheeky smile.

"Lemon. She's a rescue." There's actually a bit of pride in Sara's voice, a hint of joy. Then her familiar glare returns. "Why, you got a problem? You know pitties are super sweet. They used to be called nurse dogs."

"I just think it's funny you brought a dog to a couple's retreat."

Daphne's voice calls from the front seat. "Lance, let's not start a fight before we've even hit the road. Lemon is a wonderful companion."

I look down at the dog who's settled, a glob of drool dripping from her light pink tongue. "She is cute," Reagan admits, giving the dog a scratch behind the ears. "What shelter? Maybe we could..."

"Reagan, I am still getting used to having one dog in my house." I cut in, and Sara lets out a laugh.

Reagan concedes, "Fine, fine."

Sara claps for Lemon to get back in the van and we follow. Reagan takes my bag and puts it in the very back seat while I settle. Sara sits in the row of seats in front of us, Lemon standing at attention next to her, and she shuts the van door. As soon as the sunlight disappears behind the tinted glass, I see Daphne reach to touch Taylor's thigh. Even from my seat I can see them looking at each other and smiling. It occurs to me that this is basically a family vacation. The sort I never had growing up...

Reagan joins me, and as soon as he's buckled in, we're off. Daphne immediately starts asking about Lemon. She seems pretty interested in adopting pets for a woman who adopted supernaturals all the time. I only half listen, my mind somewhere else. I feel Reagan grab my thigh and give it a squeeze. "What's up?" he says softly, so only I can hear.

"I don't know... Just all of us here. It's like a family..." Reagan smiles wide, not quite getting at what I'm hinting at. "It's so different from my family."

Reagan's face falls, and he purses his lips. "I know you're worried about Minerva."

Worried is an understatement. Junior has confirmed that something wicked, devised by my Father, is heading Minerva's way. I stopped by to warn her properly this time, but somehow, she's gone, completely moved out of the duplex that had been her home all her life. She left no forwarding address and the neighbors weren't any help either. She's gone, as if she used her magic to teleport herself and her things to another plane. She might very well have. And she's probably safer doing that than accepting my help.

Reagan cups my cheek. In time, I'd told him everything about my family, including Minerva. "Hey," he says in a tone that makes it clear he sees me getting caught up in my thoughts. "We'll find her. Even if she doesn't want our help."

I shake my head. "I'm not sure hunting down my sister is going to make things better between us."

Reagan shrugs. "We won't know until we try. We have to at least try." I like how he says *we*.

I take his hand in mine, lifting it off my cheek just enough to kiss his palm before pressing it again to my face.

Daphne makes an excited noise. "Oh! I almost forgot." I

hear some rustling from the front seat before Daphne's gloved hand reaches back holding a little box. Sara takes it and passes it back to me, Lemon lifting her head to sniff the box with interest. "I made an absolutely marvelous find. It was in an old box of jewelry I purchased... Goodness, back in the '40s?"

I open the box and am left speechless. Inside is a ring with a large flat blue stone embedded in a thick, art deco style band. Reagan looks over my shoulder and lets out a low whistle. I lift the ring out of the box to examine it. "Is it..."

"Real silver! Sorry, Reagan," Daphne adds. "But what's really stunning is the ammolite."

"That's what it is." I thought I recognized the stone. "My Mother had a necklace with ammolite." I line the ring up with my fingers trying to decide which one it'll fit best.

"So..." Sara starts saying as she absentmindedly pets Lemon. "You're less useless now with that ring?"

"Did you just call my boyfriend useless when your dog is flooding the van with drool?" Reagan scorns.

"Hey!" Sara covered Lemon's ears as if to shield her from Reagan's comments. "She's a guard dog!"

"If elevator music was a dog, it would be Lemon. There are no thoughts behind those eyes." Reagan leans forward and started scratching Lemon's head. "No," he says in a baby voice. "You're not the smartest. But you're cute. Yes, you're cute." Lemon's butt wiggles back and forth and I reconsider us getting a dog.

I slip the ring onto my thumb, finding the band fits most comfortably there. As I examine the stone in the faint light, I see it shift from blue to vibrant green. "How long have you been holding onto this?" I ask Daph, having a sneaking suspicion she's wanted me to have this for a while.

"Well, I wanted to give it to you when we met but dear Taylor thought it might be a bit forward."

Taylor adds, "I just thought Lance might find it a bit... presumptive if we gave him a focus so early on."

"I think now is the perfect time for me to have this." I assure both of them. I slip my ringed hand into Reagan's, aware that this moment of happiness might someday be dwarfed by my nightmares once again. But I also know this happy moment won't be our last, and that... That's my everything.

PLAYLIST FOR TEETH AND TAROT

First I'm Sorry - Haley Heynderickx
Games I Play - Katie Gregson-Macleod
Mellow - Elton John
Yellow - Kevin Abstract
The Wolf - SAIMES
What's the Trick? - Jack White
Candles - Daughter
Love and Anger - Kate Bush
Baby Boy - Kevin Abstract
Moon, I Already Know - Mount Eerie
Hounds of Love - Kate Bush

ACKNOWLEDGMENTS

It's difficult to acknowledge everyone who has helped me throughout this journey of getting Lance and Reagan's story in the hands of readers but I will try my best.

Thank you to my copyeditor Brynn and to my sensitivity reader Kelsea. You both encouraged me and helped me make this book better than it was before you read it.

A special thank you to Boop, the first person to read my manuscript and fellow werewolf enjoyer. To Helen, whose google drive comments made me chuckle.

Thank you to The Haven, a group of enabling and thirsty individuals who have made me smile for over a year now.

To everyone who I've met since starting my self-publishing journey. The support and encouragement of the community makes it easy to love writing.

Finally to my partner who has watched me work and listened to me stress for months, but always supported me—despite having no idea what's going on in my manuscript. I love you Bear.

ABOUT THE AUTHOR

Arin was born and raised along the American east coast and has called the city, the shore, and the country their home. They've come a long way from writing anime fanfiction in their bedroom and even have a BA in creative writing. When they're not writing Arin enjoys playing tabletop games, drinking coffee, and collecting bits and bobbles. They currently live in Stephen King's backyard with their partner, cat, and lizard.

Teeth and Tarot is their first novel.